AF650505

Alexander McCall Smith is the author of over eighty books on a wide array of subjects, including the award-winning The No.1 Ladies' Detective Agency series. He is also the author of the Isabel Dalhousie novels and the world's longest-running serial novel, 44 Scotland Street. His books have been translated into forty-six languages. Alexander McCall Smith is Professor Emeritus of Medical Law at the University of Edinburgh and holds honorary doctorates from thirteen universities.

By Alexander McCall Smith

The No. 1 Ladies' Detective Agency Series

The No. 1 Ladies' Detective Agency
Tears of the Giraffe
Morality for Beautiful Girls
The Kalahari Typing School for Men
The Full Cupboard of Life
In the Company of Cheerful Ladies
Blue Shoes and Happiness
The Good Husband of Zebra Drive
The Miracle at Speedy Motors
Tea Time for the Traditionally Built
The Double Comfort Safari Club
The Saturday Big Tent Wedding Party
The Limpopo Academy of Private Detection
The Minor Adjustment Beauty Salon
The Handsome Man's De Luxe Café
The Woman Who Walked in Sunshine
Precious and Grace
The House of Unexpected Sisters
The Colours of All the Cattle

The Isabel Dalhousie Novels

The Sunday Philosophy Club
Friends, Lovers, Chocolate
The Right Attitude to Rain
The Careful Use of Compliments
The Comfort of Saturdays
The Lost Art of Gratitude
The Charming Quirks of Others
The Forgotten Affairs of Youth
The Uncommon Appeal of Clouds
The Novel Habits of Happiness
A Distant View of Everything
The Quiet Side of Passion

The 44 Scotland Street Series

44 Scotland Street
Espresso Tales
Love Over Scotland
The World According to Bertie
The Unbearable Lightness of Scones
The Importance of Being Seven
Bertie Plays the Blues
Sunshine on Scotland Street
Bertie's Guide to Life and Mothers
The Revolving Door of Life
The Bertie Project
A Time of Love and Tartan

The Corduroy Mansions Series

Corduroy Mansions
The Dog Who Came in from the Cold
A Conspiracy of Friends

The von Igelfeld Entertainments

The 2½ Pillars of Wisdom
Unusual Uses for Olive Oil

La's Orchestra Saves the World
The Forever Girl
My Italian Bulldozer

A Distant View of Everything

ALEXANDER
McCALL SMITH

ABACUS

ABACUS

First published in Great Britain in 2017 by Little, Brown
This paperback edition published in 2018 by Abacus

1 3 5 7 9 10 8 6 4 2

Copyright © Alexander McCall Smith 2017

The moral right of the author has been asserted.

All characters and events in this publication, other than those clearly in the public domain, are fictitious and any resemblance to real persons, living or dead, is purely coincidental.

Quotations from the poems of W. H. Auden copyright © the Beneficiaries of the Estate of W. H. Auden, reproduced by kind permission of the Estate.

All rights reserved.
No part of this publication may be reproduced, stored in a retrieval system, or transmitted, in any form or by any means, without the prior permission in writing of the publisher, nor be otherwise circulated in any form of binding or cover other than that in which it is published and without a similar condition including this condition being imposed on the subsequent purchaser.

A CIP catalogue record for this book
is available from the British Library.

ISBN: 978-0-349-14269-2

Typeset in Bembo by M Rules
Printed and bound in Great Britain by
Clays Ltd, St Ives plc

Papers used by Abacus are from well-managed forests
and other responsible sources.

MIX
Paper from
responsible sources
FSC® C104740
FSC www.fsc.org

Abacus
An imprint of
Little, Brown Book Group
Carmelite House
50 Victoria Embankment
London EC4Y 0DZ

An Hachette UK Company
www.hachette.co.uk

www.littlebrown.co.uk

This book is for Dave and Jenny Mant

and

Erwin and Diane Rodrigues

1

'Adlestrop,' said Isabel Dalhousie.

Jamie thought for a moment. They were sitting in their kitchen, on one of those indecisive days that was summer, but not quite yet; a day when the heating might as well be off as on, but when prudence – and superstition – required it still to be kept going. If you lived in Scotland and you turned off your heating too early, then the weather gods – stern, Nordic, and unforgiving – could send a body of cold air down from the Arctic, and remind you that they, not you, were in control.

Jamie at least had taken off his sweater – as an act of faith, thought Isabel – while she had kept hers on. One of the newspapers, glimpsed in the local newsagent's shop, had featured the headline *Weathermen say summer will be scorching!* but Isabel remembered that this particular newspaper said much the same thing every year, out of concern for its readers, she decided, who otherwise were deprived of good news, and who were desperate for any meteorological crumb of comfort.

'Yes, I remember it,' said Jamie, looking at her from over

the table. 'Although I've never been there, of course. It all depends on what one means by *remember.*' He paused. 'Not that I want to sound too much like you, Isabel.'

She smiled; the allusion had not been lost on her. They were playing Free Association, a game they sometimes resorted to when conversation failed, when there was no newspaper or magazine to browse, or when there was simply nothing else to think about. Each would come up with a name of a person or a place and then the other would describe the thoughts that the word triggered. They had not invented it, of course: Isabel was careful to credit Freud for that, even if there were plenty of other practitioners, including Proust, who, she felt, only had to glance at something before he would be off into several pages of triggered memories.

Her reference was to the railway station at which Edward Thomas's train had stopped one day in 1914. Adlestrop – seeing the name on the platform sign had prompted the famous poem: the steam hissed; somebody cleared his throat; no one came or left on the bare platform. *Yes, I remember Adlestrop* was the first line, and this had been what triggered Jamie's response. She was proud of him: few people bothered to remember poetry any more, but Jamie did and could reel off screeds of it. 'It somehow sticks in my mind,' he once said. 'I just remember it. All sorts of poetry.'

'Things you learned at school?'

He nodded. 'Especially those. We were encouraged to commit poems to memory. Shakespeare's sonnets, Wordsworth, Byron. The lot. Remember *Hiawatha*? Longfellow's still there.' He smiled at her. 'Or some of it. *On the shores of Gitche Gumee/Of the shining Big-Sea-Water/Stood . . .*'

'Nokomis,' supplied Isabel. 'My mother loved that poem and read it all to me – all how many stanzas? It goes on forever, doesn't it? Still, Nokomis ... Now then ... *Stood Nokomis, the old woman/Pointing with her finger westward ...*' She paused as the words, with their insistent, repetitive rhythm came back to her. She had not thought about Nokomis for a long time. Then she continued, 'Nokomis sent him off to avenge her father, didn't she?'

'She did,' said Jamie. 'It was somewhat vindictive of her, don't you feel?'

'Oh, I think you're being a bit unfair. Nokomis was right to encourage him to deal with Megissogwon who was, after all, *Tall of stature/Broad of shoulder/Dark and terrible in aspect/ Clad from head to foot in wampum* ... My goodness, why did I remember that?'

Jamie laughed. 'What exactly is wampum? I was never quite sure what the word meant.'

'Shell beads,' said Isabel. 'They were used as money, as well as being worn. You might describe Wall Street brokers as clad in wampum. I suspect they probably are.'

But now it was his turn. Leaning back, looking up at the ceiling, he said, 'Glyndebourne.'

Isabel's reply was immediate. It was a rule of Free Association that if you did not reply within ten seconds you lost your turn and the other player had another go. It was a further rule – invented by Jamie – that if you hesitated twice in a row you had to get up and make tea.

'Wagner,' she replied.

He looked at her. 'Glyndebourne doesn't make me think of Wagner,' he said. 'It makes me think of Britten.'

She shook her head. 'That's not the point of this game, Jamie. You say the first thing that comes into *your* head, not into somebody else's. And another rule is that you can't argue with the other player's association. If I say *Wagner*, it's because I thought of Wagner, and your saying *Britten* counts as a hesitation. If you do that again, you have to make us both tea.'

He pretended to sulk. 'Your go, then.'

'Tea,' she said.

'Mist,' came the reply.

She looked at him enquiringly. 'Why mist?'

'Now *you're* arguing.'

She defended herself. 'No, I'm not. I'm just interested in why you said mist. I'm not saying you *can't* think of mist, I was just wondering why.'

'Because that's what I see. I thought of a tea estate somewhere up in the hills, in Assam, maybe. And I saw women in saris picking tea leaves.'

'Fair enough.' But she was back in Glyndebourne. 'I thought of Wagner,' she said, 'but not any old Wagner. I thought of *Die Meistersinger von Nürnberg*.'

'Ah.' He looked at her cautiously. He had almost taken a job at Glyndebourne – a long time ago, before they married. That road not taken could have been the end of their relationship, and they both skirted around the subject.

'Don't worry,' she said. 'It was not an unhappy memory.'

And then, years later, they had eventually made it to Glyndebourne together, leaving Charlie in the care of the housekeeper, Grace, who had moved into the house for the weekend. Charlie loved Grace, and she loved him in return, although something in her background – something that Isabel could not fathom – made her adopt a brisk, and slightly distant, manner with children. 'You have to be firm,' she said. 'If you aren't, then they'll take advantage. They watch us, you know. They look for the slightest excuse to avoid bedtime.'

They had flown down to Gatwick and then gone to a pub in the Sussex Downs that had rooms at the back for opera-goers and enthusiasts of real ale. The two groups, sitting in the pub, could not have more easily identifiable had they sported large labels. The beer enthusiasts were bearded and loud; the opera-goers, elegantly dressed and feeling out of place, spoke more quietly than they would do later amongst their own in the opera house bar.

It was Isabel's first visit to Glyndebourne. She had been invited before, once when she was living in Cambridge and again after she had returned to Edinburgh, but had been unable to make it on either occasion. The second of these invitations had come from her niece, Cat, who had been given two tickets by one of her customers, and had offered to take Isabel with her. When Isabel had been unable to go, Cat had gone with a friend, and had complained about the opera, Tippett's *The Knot Garden*, which she had not enjoyed.

Even Cat, who was musically hard to please, would have luxuriated in *The Meistersinger*, a rich and spectacular production. Isabel sat transfixed and had to be prodded by Jamie to return to reality at the interval, when they went off to have dinner in one of the opera house's restaurants. And at the end, when they went out into the summer night, the sky still light enough for them to read the programme notes, Isabel did not want the evening to end. But Glyndebourne's spell was slow to fade, and it was still upon them when they returned to the room they had booked in the pub, and closed the door and lay together on the lumpy double bed, still in their evening clothes, holding hands like two students newly in love, staring up at the ceiling with its uneven ancient beams of darkened oak. And she thought: *how extraordinarily fortunate I am to be here, with him, when my life might have been so different if he had not come into it.* She looked at him, and loosened his black bow-tie – a gesture that struck her, even as she performed it, as one of ownership. It was a curious feeling – one of . . . what? she wondered. Sexual anticipation? The feeling that you have when you realise that you will be sleeping that evening with the person you most want to sleep with in this world.

The game of Free Association might have continued had it not been for the sudden eruption of sound from a small monitor perched on the kitchen dresser.

'Magnus,' said Jamie.

'Bottles,' said Isabel. 'Endless nappies. Sleepless nights.'

Jamie laughed. 'I had stopped playing Free Association,' he said, pointing to the monitor.

'I know,' said Isabel, smiling. 'But I couldn't resist the associations.'

Magnus was their second child, who had arrived three months earlier, and who had just signalled that he had woken and was in need of attention. His nap had overlapped with Charlie's; Charlie, although still sleeping, would shortly wake up too and make his presence felt.

'Do you remember what it was like?' said Jamie, as he rose to his feet.

'What what was like?'

'When we only had Charlie.'

Isabel rolled her eyes. 'Life was so absurdly simple then.'

'Not that I'd change anything,' said Jamie hurriedly. 'I love them both to bits.'

She knew that he did. He loved his two boys to bits and she loved them that way too. She also loved Jamie to bits, and he had assured her that he loved her to bits. And if an inventory of affection were being made, she thought of so many things she could add to it: their house in Edinburgh, with its shady garden and elusive resident, Brother Fox; their city, with its fragile, spiky beauty, its mists and its skies and its romantic history; and her country, too, Scotland, with all its curious quirks and its capacity to break the heart again and again.

'I'll go and get him up,' said Jamie. 'I'll change him if he needs it.'

'I'll entertain Charlie when he wakes,' said Isabel.

'How do people who have four or five children cope?' asked Jamie.

'Or six?'

'Six!'

'The older ones look after their younger siblings,' said Isabel. 'Look at old photographs. Fifty, sixty years ago. Look at pictures showing children in the street – the young ones are holding hands with their older brothers and sisters who are clearly baby-sitting. An eight-year-old would look after a one-year-old, and a six-year-old would look after a four-year-old.'

'Everybody looked after everybody else, I suppose.'

'They did,' agreed Isabel. 'And did so without complaint.'

The monitor gave a further squawk. 'Yet they didn't even have monitors,' said Jamie.

Magnus's arrival on the stage had been two weeks early, brought about, Jamie half seriously suggested, by Isabel having listened to a foot-tapping piece of music from the Penguin Cafe Orchestra. She had closed her eyes as she listened and then opened them suddenly, wide-eyed at the stab of pain.

Her breath had been taken away from her and it was a few moments before she could speak. 'She's coming,' she said. They had been calling the baby 'she' although they had asked not to be told what sex it was. Yet they were convinced; it would be a daughter this time. They knew they should not make any assumptions, but somehow they felt certain.

Jamie had looked puzzled. 'But it's two weeks . . . '

She did not let him finish. 'I need to phone the midwife. I need to let them know.'

He realised that she was serious. 'I'll take you to the Infirmary,' he said hurriedly. 'Grace can look after Charlie. I'll phone her right now.'

Isabel held up a hand. 'Hold on,' she said. 'They'll tell me to wait. We'll have hours.'

But she did not have much time. Things happened quickly and she was in the labour ward within three hours, Magnus appearing twenty minutes later.

'A boy,' said the obstetrician, passing the glistening infant to a waiting nurse.

Jamie gasped. They had been so sure.

'A little boy,' muttered Isabel.

The nursing staff fussed around the baby before handing him to Isabel, loosely wrapped in an off-white cotton blanket. Swaddling clothes, thought Isabel. But this is loose, and is not proper swaddling.

Jamie cried, wiping at his tears with the back of his hand. They were tears that came with the cathartic welling up of more than one emotion: relief, sheer joy, love. These had all been his companions at the bedside, where he had sat through Isabel's short labour; now they found release. A young nurse in training, attending her first birth, was similarly afflicted, struggling to force back her own tears, but finding the battle too much. A senior nurse, standing at her side, whispered something in her ear, and touched her briefly on the shoulder.

'Are you sure he's a boy?' asked Isabel.

The obstetrician peeled off his gloves. 'I've never been wrong on that one,' he said.

The trainee nurse giggled.

'You need to get some sleep,' said the senior nurse. She looked at Jamie. 'Father too.'

'We thought it was going to be a girl,' said Jamie.

'Well, there you are,' said the nurse. 'You were going to get one or the other, weren't you?'

Isabel held the baby, her cheek pressed lightly against his tiny forehead. She saw that the baby's blanket had letters printed on it, and they suddenly registered. RIP: what a tactless thing to put on a swaddling blanket, but then she noticed that the letters actually said, RIE. The Royal Infirmary of Edinburgh. That was considerably better. The eye could so easily deceive – as when, a few months ago, she had misread a newspaper headline *Pope hopes* as *Pope elopes*, and had, for a moment, been both shocked and surprised. Of course now that a pope had broken with long historical practice and retired, it was always possible that a radical successor might feel that the time was ripe to elope.

Through the euphoria of the morphine they had given her right at the end, she felt a small niggle of disappointment. She had so wanted a girl, but she knew that she must not allow herself to think about it. She had a healthy, breathing baby and that was all that mattered. Perhaps it had been a mistake to remain ignorant of the baby's sex; the sonographers had found out when they performed the ultrasound scans but at her request had deliberately not shown her the screen. Perhaps they should have asked, because that would have prevented their building up hopes. She had wanted a girl because there were things a mother could do with a girl. They would be friends, as mothers and daughters so often are, and would share their world with each other. This was a boy, and it would be like Charlie all over again; not that she regretted anything about him, but the demands of a boy were different.

Jamie held her hand. 'Well done,' he whispered.

She squeezed his hand. 'Twice as many things for you to do now that he's a boy,' she said drowsily, not knowing exactly what she meant, or why she said it.

2

In and out again as quickly as possible was the philosophy of the maternity unit at the Royal Infirmary – a policy approved of by accountants as much as by medical opinion. The accountants would have preferred it if nobody were in hospital at all, empty beds being less of a drain on the state's resources than those occupied by patients, while doctors for their part understood that recovery was always quicker on one's own two feet. Isabel, as a second-time mother in good health, was judged to require only one night in hospital before being allowed home. That suited her – at least in some respects, as she found the atmosphere of the post-natal ward less than peaceful. Babies were no respecters of normal hours when it came to choosing their time of arrival, and the delivery suite, just down the corridor, was a noisy place. Deprived of sleep, she felt utterly exhausted; even more so than she had felt after the birth of Charlie, when she had endured a much longer and more difficult labour. She was a bit weepy, too, and Jamie, alerted at childbirth classes to the possibility of post-natal depression, exchanged an anxious word with one of the doctors.

The response was reassuring. 'It's utterly normal to feel a little low after a birth,' said the doctor. 'But we'll watch her – I'm sure she'll be all right.'

Jamie brought Charlie to the hospital to meet his new brother. Charlie, who was now almost four and every bit as articulate and aware as a child a year or two older, had been encouraged to talk about the arrival of a sibling, but had said very little about it. During the pregnancy, even while eyeing Isabel's increasing girth he had been tight-lipped.

'You're going to have a brand new sister or brother,' Jamie had said cheerfully. 'Lucky boy!'

Charlie, showing no sign of emotion, had changed the subject. 'I want to play football,' he said.

This provided Jamie with an opportunity. 'Just think,' he said brightly. 'When the new baby comes, you'll be able to play football together. Think of how much fun you'll have.'

There was no response.

'And other games too,' enthused Jamie. 'Hide and seek. Pirates!'

Pirates were a current interest at the time, but even the prospect of games of pirates evinced little response.

Now, making their way into the maternity unit, Jamie clutching a bunch of flowers in one hand and leading Charlie with the other, the crucial first meeting was about to take place.

'I don't like hospitals,' said Charlie, looking about him. 'I want to go home.'

'But we must see Mummy,' insisted Jamie. 'She's looking forward to seeing you.'

'I want to go home.'

Jamie's tone became firmer. 'After we've seen Mummy. And your new brother.'

Charlie shook his head. 'I haven't got a brother,' he said. 'No brother.'

'Yes, you have,' said Jamie. 'You're very lucky. You've got a brother now and he's called Magnus. Isn't that a nice name? Magnus.'

'A smelly name,' said Charlie.

Jamie gave an inward groan. He had been warned that this might not be easy. And when they reached the maternity ward, the extent of the problem became apparent. Isabel opened her arms to Charlie and embraced him warmly, but the small boy remained stiff and rigid, his arms firmly down by his sides.

'Kiss for Mummy,' said Jamie, catching Isabel's eye.

'Want to go,' said Charlie.

'But you're going to say hello to Magnus,' said Jamie, with forced breeziness. 'There he is. Look. That's Magnus right there.' He pointed to the small crib beside the bed in which the wrapped bundle of Magnus lay.

Charlie averted his eyes.

'Say hello to Magnus,' said Isabel gently. 'I think he would love that. I've told him that you were coming to see him. He was very pleased.'

Charlie saw through this. He closed his eyes. 'Don't need a baby,' he muttered.

Isabel glanced anxiously at Jamie before turning to Charlie. She stroked the small boy's cheek gently, only to have her hand brushed away. 'But, darling, we're very lucky to have a baby. Especially such a nice baby as Magnus. Your brother, you see. Your own, very special brother.'

'Don't want this baby,' said Charlie. 'He can stay here.'

'But we can't leave poor little Magnus in the hospital,' appealed Isabel. 'He's so looking forward to coming home.'

'It's not his home,' said Charlie resolutely. 'He lives in the hospital.'

Jamie whispered to Isabel. 'I think we should perhaps move on. He'll come round.'

Isabel sighed. 'I don't feel I can face this right now.'

Jamie sought to reassure her. 'I'll work at it,' he said. 'I don't think it's at all abnormal. After all, whose nose wouldn't be out of joint in such circumstances?'

Charlie was now investigating the lifting mechanism underneath Isabel's bed and they were able to speak more freely.

'I couldn't bear it if he became hostile,' said Isabel.

'He won't be. He's just warning us not to forget that he's the kingpin. When he realises that Magnus is no threat to him, he'll be fine.'

The problem, thought Isabel, was that Magnus really did constitute a threat from Charlie's perspective. 'Well, let's hope . . . ' She sighed again. 'I've heard some awful stories of children who've gone into a huff for years when a new sibling arrives.'

'That won't happen,' said Jamie. 'We'll make him feel special.'

'Bribery,' said Isabel.

'If you must call it that,' said Jamie. 'I call it the judicious use of collateral benefits.'

'Ask them to take the baby away,' came a little voice from under the bed. The tone was plaintive; the request heartfelt.

Jamie took a deep breath. This had become an issue of appeasement. For a moment he hesitated, but then decided. 'Certainly not,' he said.

Charlie was silent.

'You see,' whispered Jamie. 'Psychology up to a point – and then a firm hand.'

'I hope you're right,' said Isabel. She looked at the flowers that Jamie had brought and then, quite inexplicably – at least she could see no reason for it – she began to cry.

Jamie bent forward to put his arms about her. He felt the tears on her cheek. 'My darling . . . '

'I feel so helpless. Tired and helpless.'

He stayed where he was, awkwardly embracing her. 'It'll be different when you're back home. We'll have Grace there to help. And me too, of course. Everything will be fine.'

But Isabel was thinking of other things; the world, viewed from a hospital bed, can seem a daunting place. 'There's the *Review*,' she said, between sobs. 'I'm all over the place with the next issue.'

The *Review* was the *Review of Applied Ethics*, the journal that Isabel not only owned but edited from the study of her house in Edinburgh. It was not a full-time job, as the *Review* only appeared quarterly, but like anything that involved a deadline it was a taskmaster that was always there in the background. No sooner had an issue been consigned to the printer than the next one would have to be planned, put together, and copy-edited. And then there were the articles for the following issue and the issue after that – these had to be solicited or selected from the uninvited submissions, the latter category being a rag-bag that included a good measure of rants and obsessions, often amounting to defamatory diatribes directed at other philosophers. An argumentative tribe, Jamie had labelled philosophers, and the unsolicited papers tended to confirm this judgement.

'Get somebody to help,' said Jamie. 'What about the editorial board? What's the point of having an editorial board if you can't ask them to take some of the burden off your shoulders?'

Isabel shook her head. 'They're useless,' she said.

Jamie pursed his lips. He had never heard Isabel describe her board in this way; indeed, she had often said how helpful its members were. He thought about them: there was that professor in Aberdeen whom he had met and who had struck him as being so level-headed; and that woman in Dublin, in Trinity College, who had gone out of her way to help Isabel when there had been that row with the professor from Cork who had accused her of insensitive editing because she had proposed a cut on the length of his piece on . . . what was it again? Self-delusion and moral reasoning, or something of that nature. These people were not useless by any stretch of the imagination, even if some of the board members were far-flung. Modern electronics made Singapore and New York neighbours to Edinburgh, and surely a bit of virtual help could be invoked for the next issue – at least until Isabel was back on her feet. He looked at her. Could she not see that?

She reached for a tissue from her bedside table. 'I'll be all right,' she said. 'I just feel that things are on top of me.'

'Quite natural,' Jamie said soothingly.

From beneath the bed there came a winding sound. Charlie had found the handle that altered the angle of the bed, and was turning it energetically.

'Don't do that, Charlie,' said Jamie. 'You don't want Mummy to fall out of bed, do you?'

'I do,' came a voice from below.

Jamie sighed. 'Patience,' he muttered.

But the effect on Isabel was quite different. For the first time on this visit, Jamie saw her smile.

'There's a professor in Bloomington,' Isabel suddenly said. 'His address is written on a pad on my desk – you'll find it easily. Could you send him an email telling him that I've almost finished editing his paper and that we'll use it in the next issue? Could you do that?'

Jamie felt that a corner was being turned. 'Of course.' And then he added, 'What's it about? His paper?'

'Friendship,' said Isabel. 'A well-written essay on friendship.'

'I hope I'll get the chance to read it.'

'Of course you will.' She had pulled herself up in her bed, partly to counteract the alterations that Charlie had achieved. And Charlie himself had appeared from down below and was peering over the edge of the crib.

'His eyes are closed,' said Charlie.

Jamie and Isabel exchanged glances. 'That's because he's sleeping,' said Isabel. 'Babies sleep a lot.'

'Can I make him some popcorn?' asked Charlie.

Isabel smiled. 'Yes, of course. We'll make him popcorn together. Would you like that? It may be a little while before he can eat it, but we can certainly make it.'

'And a hamburger?' asked Charlie.

'Yes,' said Isabel. 'We could make a hamburger for Magnus . . . but, will you be able to eat it for him?'

Charlie nodded.

'Psychology,' whispered Jamie.

'*Psicologia omnia vincit*,' said Isabel. 'If Latin has such a word as *psicologia*.'

'I'm sure it does,' said Jamie. 'Or something like that. And if it doesn't, it should.' He paused, looking at her fondly. *My wife*, he thought. *My coiner of words. My wonderful Isabel.* 'I think you're beginning to feel better.'

'Possibly,' said Isabel.

'Let's take Magnus home,' said Charlie. 'Now.'

*

Grace was busy in the kitchen when Jamie and Charlie returned from the hospital. Although Jamie was a keen cook, Grace had insisted on preparing meals for them while Isabel was in hospital. Jamie had tried to dissuade her, as he found Grace's cooking too heavy, but she had brushed aside his objections. 'You have so much else to do,' she said. 'This is no time for you to be attempting to cook.'

Jamie might have taken offence at her unfortunate choice of words – deliberate as it was, rather than accidental. But he always handled Grace carefully, as she was quick to take offence and see any criticism, even the gentlest, as a direct slight.

'I enjoy being in the kitchen,' he had once said. 'I know some men don't, but I do.'

'Yes, it's a nice place to sit,' said Grace.

'No,' said Jamie. 'That's not exactly what I meant. I like cooking.'

Grace continued with what she was doing, but smiled wryly. 'You're right about a lot of men not liking to be anywhere near the kitchen.'

'*Some* men,' said Jamie mildly. 'Men can be excellent cooks, you know. Look at all those chefs on television.'

Grace sniffed. 'Television doesn't show what really goes on,' she said. 'You see the pots and pans on the cooker and you see people stirring things, but everybody knows that most of the dishes are already cooked.' She paused, and looked at Jamie defiantly. 'By women. Did you know that? By women who are employed by the television studios to cook in the background.'

Jamie stared at her incredulously. 'Where on earth did you hear that?'

Grace tapped the side of her nose. 'Everybody knows it,' she said. 'I'm surprised you didn't.'

He was finding it difficult to contain his irritation. Sometimes he felt there was an open season on men, many of whom seemed passive in the face of even the unfairest attack. Well, he would not let this sort of thing pass; tact was all very well, but there came a point where one had to defend oneself. 'I don't like to disagree with you,' he said in measured tones, 'but I think you might be a little bit out of date on this. Just a little bit. The days when men couldn't cook are over. Boys are taught how to cook at school. And girls learn woodwork. It's all changed.'

'Hah!' said Grace. 'Some things never change.'

'I disagree,' said Jamie. 'The world is not the same place it was twenty years ago. Sexism is a thing of the past.'

He knew, even as he spoke, that this was not true. There was less sexism, perhaps, but it had not disappeared entirely. And there were plenty of societies where the lot of women was still appalling; half the world, it seemed, was prepared to countenance their subjugation. And the other half was frightened to talk about it.

Grace just looked at him and shook her head, but by unspoken consent neither pursued the issue any further. From Jamie's point of view, he realised that nothing he could say would shift Grace from her position; she was convinced that men were inferior cooks and that he, Jamie, may be able to make potatoes Dauphinoise but could not do much else. He would have to leave the discussion there; when Isabel returned the next day, rationality would once again prevail. So now, as he brought Charlie into the kitchen on his return from the Infirmary, he accepted that the lumpy Irish stew that Grace was cooking was going to be their dinner and he could do nothing about it. He knew that Charlie referred to Grace's Irish stew as 'Irish mud', although he hoped that he would not use the term in her presence.

Grace quizzed Charlie on his new brother. 'You must be very excited about Magnus,' she said. 'A brand new brother! What a fortunate boy you are!'

Charlie busied himself with one of his toy cars that he had found under the table. The toy, a model of an old Citroën police car, with miniature metal doors that could be opened and shut, had come to rest against the table leg after some forgotten car chase. A few inches away, lying abandoned on its side, was a battered red Mercedes that had been the getaway car of some tiny desperadoes. The small-scale drama of flight and pursuit had ended in victory for the law, and indeed on the faces of the diminutive metal figures in the front of the police car broad smiles had been painted, reflecting this fact. In the world of these models, theirs was a permanent triumph.

Grace waited for an answer, but none came.

'Answer Grace,' said Jamie. 'She's talking to you, Charlie. Answer her, please.'

'I was wondering what you thought of your new baby brother,' said Grace gaily.

Charlie made a strange, throat-clearing sound.

'You liked him, didn't you, Charlie?' volunteered Jamie.

'No,' said Charlie.

Jamie caught Grace's eye. 'The tune seems to have changed,' he said. 'Earlier on, I thought we were making progress.'

Grace put a finger to her lips. 'Later,' she said. 'It's time for the afternoon nap.'

With Charlie upstairs and asleep, the conversation in the kitchen was able to resume. The casserole of Irish mud was now ready, and had been safely stored in the fridge along with several small dishes of accompanying vegetables.

'You can heat it up for Charlie at six,' Grace told Jamie. 'And then you can have yours later. Eight o'clock maybe.'

Jamie looked out of the window. He felt as if he were being spoken to as if he were not much older than Charlie. It was no business of Grace's when he had his dinner; if he wanted to eat at nine, he would do so, and now, in the face of Grace's bossiness he decided that was what he would do.

'No,' he said. 'Nine o'clock.'

Grace seemed puzzled. 'Nine's too late. You'll be awfully hungry.'

Jamie drew in his breath. It was quite foreign to his nature to be sharp with anybody, but this really was too much. 'I'll decide when I want to have dinner,' he muttered.

Grace glanced at him quickly, and then looked away. He realised that he had hurt her feelings and he immediately apologised. Grace could be difficult, but there was something that Isabel had said that always stuck in his mind. *Remember what you have and the other person doesn't.* It was simple – almost too simple – advice and yet, like all such homely advice, it expressed a profound truth. When he had pressed her for an explanation, she had said, 'Many of our dealings with others are unequal. We have an advantage because we are the customer or the client, or the one with the money, or the one who's paying somebody else. Or we may have somebody in our lives and the other person may not have anybody. Or we may be taller than them, or stronger, or older and more worldly-wise, or whatever it is. There are all these things that need to be borne in mind.' And then she had added, with a laugh, 'Not that I'm lecturing you.'

But she was right, and now, after his assertion of his right to choose when he had dinner – not an unreasonable thing for him to do – he felt that he should make some ameliorative remark.

'No,' he said. 'I'm sorry; you're right. Nine is very late. Perhaps eight-thirty.'

The compromise was enough.

'That's more sensible,' she said. 'And I hope you enjoy it. There'll be enough for tomorrow too, so Isabel needn't worry about cooking the moment she gets back.'

Jamie thought: *but I'll be here.* He said nothing, though, and they returned to the subject of Charlie.

'He was very stand-offish in the hospital,' said Jamie. 'At least to begin with. He refused to acknowledge that he had a brother. Then suddenly—'

'They're as changeable as the weather at that age,' interjected Grace. 'One moment it's this, and then the next it's that.'

'After being pretty awful, he suddenly perked up and said that we should bring Magnus home right away. Prior to that he'd even suggested leaving him in the hospital.'

Grace shook her head. 'Jealousy,' she said.

'Of course.'

'It's everywhere,' Grace went on. 'And it's not just children – adults are every bit as bad.'

'Some of them, maybe,' said Jamie. 'But most of us grow out of it, surely . . . '

Grace disagreed. 'Lots don't. And do you know, it can carry on – even on the other side.'

Grace was an enthusiastic spiritualist. Every week she attended a spiritualist meeting where a medium would contact what she called the *other side*, usually with messages of one sort or another for some of those present. She took it entirely seriously, and was also a regular borrower of spiritualist literature from the psychic library in the city's West End.

Jamie was intrigued by this twist. He had great difficulty keeping a straight face when Grace expounded on spiritualist matters, but this was a fresh dimension of the matter. Did the grudges and battles of . . . *this side* – if that was what one called it – run over onto the *other side*? It was a depressing thought, as it implied the existence of arguments and feuds lasting for all eternity, with petty disputes stretching out over the centuries, waged from whatever trenches people could dig for themselves in such firmament as the *other side* afforded.

'Oh yes,' Grace continued. 'We had an example of this the other week. It was a visiting medium – a man from Inverness, actually, who has always been rather good. He had somebody coming through from the other side who said that she still resented the fact that her sister had been more successful than she had.'

Jamie sought clarification. 'More successful on this side?' he asked. 'Or on the other side?'

Grace frowned. 'No, this side. Once you're on the other side, you don't have to be successful at anything.'

'Because there's nothing to do?'

Grace was quick to dispel the heresy. 'Oh, there's plenty to do on the other side,' she said.

Jamie found himself wondering whether there were offices, perhaps, or even factories. Did one have to work on the other side, or was there a full social welfare system? He decided not to ask.

'The point is,' said Grace, 'that jealousy persists. It doesn't go away.'

Jamie contemplated this. 'So we're in it for the long haul with Charlie?'

'Maybe,' said Grace. 'People can dig in. And children do that as much as anybody else. But you never know. My cousin's daughter ignored her little sister for the first ten months and then suddenly saw the possibilities. That changed everything. She started to dress her up in all sorts of outfits – ballet tutus and the like. She treated her like a doll, and even told her friends that she ran on batteries.'

Jamie smiled. 'We assume so much, don't we? We assume that our children are going to be reasonable. We assume they're going to see things as we see them. And then suddenly we discover that they can look at things quite differently.'

'Yes,' said Grace. 'And maybe we're bound to be disappointed because we want our children to see things in the same way as we do, and they may not.'

Jamie made a gesture of resignation.

'But,' said Grace, brightening, 'I don't think it'll last.' She looked at her watch. 'I'll be off then,' she said. 'You'll be all right, I hope.'

Jamie assured her that he would. 'Thanks for the Irish m . . . ' He stopped himself in time. 'Irish stew.'

He saw her to the front door. Closing it behind her, he turned back into the hall, stopped, and stared up at the ceiling. Grace's tactless words came back to him: *This is no time for you to be attempting to cook.* He smarted at the thought. *I can cook – I can cook just as well, if not better, than she can. My potatoes Dauphinoise . . .* He stopped himself, aware of how ridiculous it was to remind oneself of one's potatoes Dauphinoise. He might have been feeling slighted, but then women had put up with this sort of condescension from men forever, and it was only very recently that anything had been done to stop it. So if men now experienced something of that themselves, should they be too surprised?

Something that Isabel had said came back to him. She had remarked, he seemed to recall, about how in this life we were allocated people by chance. These were the people we knew or came across, the people who might be in our lives for no particular reason. In a sense they were allocated, rather than deliberately chosen, a concomitant of what philosophers called moral luck. Grace came with the house – so to speak. She had looked after Isabel's father and had simply stayed on. She could be opinionated, and that could be trying, but she had never let them down, not once, and . . . Jamie paused. He had never really thought about it, but it was probably the case that Grace loved them – him, Isabel, Charlie. He had never thought of it that way, because we tend not to use the word love when talking about how we feel about our friends and acquaintances – and how they might feel about us. We talk about affection or fondness, but rarely love. But it could be love – and of course in this case it *was* love, and to use a lesser word was to diminish the thing that was there. Now it came to him that the fact of this love was in no sense a burden – rather, it was a privilege.

He made his way back into the kitchen. As he did so, he thought, *I'm beginning to think like Isabel.* And then, as if in confirmation of this unexpected self-assessment, he said to himself: *we become the people we live with. Imperceptibly at first, but with a certain inevitability, we become the other.* He smiled as he imagined the composite Jamie/Isabel, who would play the bassoon, read philosophy, interfere in other people's affairs rather too much, drive a green Swedish car, and make legendary potatoes Dauphinoise.

3

'We need to remind ourselves,' Isabel said, 'of our latitude.'

They were lying in bed, and Jamie, who had just woken up, was unprepared for conversation.

'Why?' he asked drowsily.

'Plenty of people don't know their latitude.'

Jamie rubbed the sleep out of his eyes. Isabel was like this in the morning; he took a few minutes to come to, but she was the opposite, being at her most alert in the first few hours of the day.

'I'm sure you know exactly where you are,' Isabel continued.

He came up with a bemused guess. 'Fifty-something degrees, I suppose.'

'Not bad. But if you were lost, that wouldn't be good enough to be rescued.'

Jamie stared up at the ceiling above their bed. The light fitting, a Victorian rise and fall, threw a blurred shadow across the expanse of white. 'I know we're not sixty-something, because that's the Arctic Circle.'

'Fifty-six,' she said. 'Edinburgh is at fifty-six degrees, which is pretty far north. We're on the same latitude as Moscow and Copenhagen. But . . . '

'Yes?'

'But Stockholm and Helsinki are to the north of us. And St Petersburg too.'

'Oh, I see.' What could he say, he wondered, to this early-morning geographical onslaught? Perhaps 'Oh' was as good a response as any.

It was a few months after Isabel's return from hospital, and they were just getting to the point of enjoying a night's sleep once more. Magnus had cried briefly at eleven the previous evening, and then again at one, but on both occasions after a brief feed he had dropped off to sleep quickly enough. Now, just after six, they had both been woken up in response to an early beam of sunlight rather than a child's crying. The shutters in their bedroom, slightly twisted by age, succeeded in keeping out the light, but not all of it. In the winter that did not matter too much, but in the Scottish summer, when the sky was light at four in the morning, and even before, it made a difference. It was this that had prompted the early – perhaps slightly too early – discussion of relative latitude.

Jamie was wide awake now. 'What about New York?' he asked.

'Low forties,' said Isabel. 'At least, I think it is. The United States is more southerly than you'd expect. New Orleans must be – and as for Key West . . . '

'Deep south. South of south.'

'Yes,' said Isabel. She was thinking of Mobile, where her mother – her 'sainted American mother', as she called her – had spent her childhood. That was a place of shady streets; of moss that hung from the boughs of trees, as if draped there for adornment by some enthusiastic exterior decorator; of sultry, velvet evenings. Things moved slowly in Mobile, as they did, traditionally, throughout the South. And why should they not? If you walked quickly, then all you did was to reach your destination early; nothing had been gained. And if you spoke quickly, you got more words out, but were those words any better for that?

She sat up in bed, preparing herself to get up and check on Magnus. 'Latitude and attitude.'

'Oh?'

'Have you ever thought about it? About how latitude determines attitude? There are northerly attitudes and there are southerly attitudes.' She paused. 'Southern places are meant to be . . . '

'Friendly and laid back?'

'Yes,' she said, adding, 'And corrupt too, I suppose.'

Jamie raised an eyebrow. 'Is there more corruption in the south than the north?'

Isabel thought for a moment. 'Some would say there is.'

'So what makes Naples more corrupt than, say, Amsterdam?' Jamie paused. 'I assume Naples *is* more corrupt than Amsterdam.'

'I think it is,' said Isabel. She spoke with authority, but asked herself whether she really knew. Or was it something so obvious that concrete evidence was simply not required – such as a statement that it was warmer in summer than in winter or that dogs were more loyal than cats? Everybody – even, perhaps, the Neapolitans themselves – would surely agree that corruption thrived in the Italian south; of course it did, what with the Mafia and the Camorra. Did the writ of any of these criminal gangs run that far north? And what would a Dutch Camorra boss look like? Tall and ruddy-faced, big-boned as the Dutch so often are, but ruthless when it came to rackets in tulips and cheese . . .

'So?'

Isabel was still thinking of the Dutch Camorra. 'So?' she echoed.

Jamie was interested. 'And where does religion come into it? Are Protestant countries inherently less corrupt?'

Isabel was not sure it was that simple. 'No,' she said. 'I don't think it's that simple. The issue, I suppose, is whether a culture stresses telling the truth. That's the real point. It's not religion.' She paused, thinking through the implications of what she was saying almost as she said it. She was not unsympathetic to religious belief – we needed the spiritual, she felt – but a tradition of obfuscation and dependence on ritual did not encourage individual soul-searching. Christianity had unfortunately taken wrong turnings, she felt, at various points in its history. For a time, at least, a lovely message of love and redemption had become one of threats, fear and institutional self-preservation – almost to the extent of being swallowed up by all of these.

'It's perfectly possible to accept the tenets of a religion and still be honest,' she continued. 'It depends on whether the religion is compatible with honesty. Some aren't.'

'Why?'

'Because they ask you to believe in things that are patently impossible. And that's the same as asking people to believe in lies, to say that lies don't matter.'

Jamie wondered whether all religions might not have a lie at their very heart – some article of faith that simply beggared belief.

Isabel hesitated. Was a belief in God that central, impossible kernel? She did not want to say yes, because that left so little.

And she felt that there *was* something there – some force, some principle, that lay beyond our understanding but that we sensed and that, crucially, we needed. The identity one gave to that did not matter too much, although the clutter with which we surrounded it did. Some of that clutter was downright poisonous, insisting that there was only one way of recognising the divine, that all other views of it were simply wrong.

Jamie thought of something. 'Russia?' he asked suddenly. 'Very northern. Yet very corrupt. All those oligarchs.'

'Nothing to do with religion,' said Isabel. 'Everything to do with the destruction of civil society under the Communists. Everything to do with a regime of lies and fear that held sway there for . . . what? Seventy years. So the poor Russians, that great, much put-upon people, came to the end of the twentieth century with the moral fabric of their society in complete tatters. Hence the gangsters and the spivs who infest the place today.'

'Is it that bad?'

'Yes – and worse.'

'I see.'

'Yes,' said Isabel. She looked at her watch. It was only six-fifteen and they had already discussed religion, politics and at least some twentieth-century history. 'I must get ready to feed Magnus,' she said. 'He'll be waking up any moment.'

'Grub first, then ethics,' said Jamie. 'Who said that again?'

'Bertolt Brecht,' said Isabel. 'Although I suspect that he rather regretted it. Anybody who coins an aphorism tends to regret it – because it gets quoted back at him *ad infinitum* and is inevitably misunderstood.'

'But surely to have said something memorable must be very satisfying.'

'Possibly.' Isabel slipped out of bed and took her dressing

gown off its hook. 'Groucho Marx never withdrew his wonderful remark about membership of clubs.'

'About not wanting to be a member of any club that would admit people like him?'

Isabel nodded. 'Yes. Nor did Winston Churchill revise what he said about beaches ... Imagine if he said, "I never actually meant beaches; I meant to say that we'd fight on the bit above, you know, the bit where they park cars, not the actual beach ..."'

Jamie was amused. He loved Churchill's growl; so few people really knew how to growl. 'Can you imagine one of our politicians today making a speech like Churchill's? People would fall about laughing.'

Isabel thought he was right. 'Auden, of course, had a bit of difficulty with "We must love one another or die". People, including no less a person than Lyndon Johnson, have loved quoting that line, but Auden hated it. He said that it was self-congratulatory and insincere.'

'I don't think it sounds that way,' said Jamie.

'Well, he did. He tried to change it to "We must love one another and die". He failed because people really liked the original.'

'Of course people could see the truth of both versions.'

Isabel would concede that, but it was not the point; if the poet himself thought it insincere, he must know; after all, he was the one who wrote it in the first place. 'So he suppressed the whole poem,' she said. 'But people refused to let it go.'

'Hasn't the author the right to call something in, so to speak?'

Isabel looked dubious. 'No. It's like giving somebody a present. You can't take it back. If you present the world with your poem, then that's it. It's no longer yours.' She remembered

Virgil. 'We almost didn't have the *Aeneid*, you know. Virgil wanted it burned – and tried to set fire to it himself, but failed.'

'Just as well.' Jamie was slightly abashed. 'You know, I haven't ever read it. Is that an embarrassing admission?'

'Shocking,' said Isabel, buttoning the dressing gown. 'Neither have I.'

'Should we read it to one another?' asked Jamie.

Isabel considered this. 'At bedtime?'

'Yes.'

'A very good idea.' She thought the suggestion romantic; to read the *Aeneid* to one another in bed, by candlelight even . . . 'In Latin?'

'Not if we want to understand it,' said Jamie.

The day began. Magnus awoke, and announced the fact gustily. This brought Charlie into their bedroom, his now somewhat threadbare soft fox dragging behind him. 'There's a noise coming from somewhere,' he said.

Jamie and Isabel glanced at one another, hardly able to contain themselves. The denial of the obvious can involve heroic efforts, and Charlie was proving himself a master.

'Could be from your brother,' said Jamie at last.

But Charlie was far too young for irony.

Isabel had not stopped helping Cat in her delicatessen altogether, but her sessions there had been curtailed in the later days of her pregnancy. Cat, Isabel's niece, owned the delicatessen – with some financial help from Cat's own father – and Isabel liked working there from time to time. Standing behind the counter in the final month had been painful, and she had eventually told Cat that much as she enjoyed it, she would have to stop.

Cat understood, of course, although losing Isabel's help placed extra strain on both her and Eddie, her young assistant.

'We'll manage somehow,' she reassured Isabel. 'My friend, Katy, has offered to do some sessions and Eddie doesn't mind doing overtime.' She paused; not sure whether to ask the question she really wanted answered. 'Do you think you'll come back once the baby's settled? I don't want to press you, of course.'

Isabel saw no reason why she could not, even if her hours would have to be limited. 'Grace will be helping me – and Jamie will be around a lot. He's pretty hands-on.'

Cat was relieved. 'Of course he is,' she said. 'But two small children could drive anybody to drink.' There was a brief pause. 'Not that your children would do that to anybody, of course.'

Isabel smiled. 'We'll see. One shouldn't tempt providence.'

Now, on the morning of their discussion about latitude – and Virgil, and, it seemed, so much else – Isabel went back to the delicatessen for the first time, leaving Jamie to take Charlie to the nursery round the corner and Grace to fuss officiously round Magnus. Her decision to spend a few hours working with Cat was not entirely inspired by a desire to help – although that was part of it; it seemed an attractive alternative to sitting down to the editorial duties that awaited her at her desk. She knew, of course, that she would have to do that sooner or later, but she felt the need for just a few more days away from the demands of the *Review*. No doubt the emails were mounting up – she had not even dared to open her mailbox – and she could see, from the pile of envelopes in her study, neatly stacked there by Jamie, that paper correspondence was keeping pace with the electronic flow. She would carry out a blitz on these in due course, but not just yet; surely having a child – going through all that – was excuse enough for a brief break from one's desk . . .

Eddie, Cat's young assistant, was surprised to see her.

'She didn't tell me,' he said, nodding his head in the direction of Cat's office at the rear of the shop. He always referred to his employer as *she*; not in any disrespectful sense, but in a tone that almost, but not quite, capitalised the pronoun.

'I expect she forgot,' said Isabel. 'And I didn't give her much notice. I phoned her last night to tell her.'

Eddie wiped his hands on his apron. 'Where's your new baby?' he asked.

Isabel explained that Grace was in charge. 'It's good to get out now and then,' she continued. 'Babies tie you down a bit. Bear that in mind, Eddie, before you have any yourself.'

When Eddie blushed furiously, Isabel quickly said, 'I'm sure you'd be a wonderful father, Eddie.' She rubbed her hands together in a businesslike way. 'Still, here I am. What needs to be done?'

Cat emerged from her office to thank Isabel for coming in. 'I have to go to see one of our suppliers,' she said. 'It'll probably take all morning. Are you all right with that?'

Isabel knew that from Grace's point of view, the longer Isabel stayed out the better. She enjoyed her time with the children; it made her feel needed.

'Take as long as you need,' said Isabel. 'Eddie and I will cope.'

They set to work. There was a brief spike in activity immediately after the delicatessen opened in the morning, but this was always followed by a quiet period during which routine tasks could be tackled. Today there was stock-taking to be done in between attending to customers. The dried-food section – a region of porcini mushrooms, of flageolet beans and seaweed – needed to be checked, as did the refrigerated display, where sell-by dates could so easily creep up on one unless one was vigilant. Isabel started this, while Eddie busied himself with slicing parma ham for their filled lunchtime rolls.

At ten o'clock Eddie made them both a cup of coffee, which they drank together, standing behind the counter.

Eddie looked at Isabel admiringly. 'Is having a baby . . . ' He looked for the right words. 'Is having a baby really sore?'

'Yes,' said Isabel. 'It is.'

Eddie absorbed the information. 'I'm glad that women have them . . . not men.' He paused, becoming momentarily confused. 'Of course I knew that men can't.'

'No,' said Isabel. 'I'd noticed that too.'

'Because if men could have babies, then they'd . . . '

'Be a bit more careful?' suggested Isabel.

Eddie looked down at the floor. 'Do you think Cat will ever have a baby?'

Isabel smiled. It was easy to forget just how young Eddie was. Very early twenties?

'Most women would like to have a baby,' she said. 'Not all of them, but probably most of them. It's just something that women feel – a mothering instinct, I suppose.'

'But Cat's never said anything about wanting a baby.'

Isabel smiled again. 'Have you talked to her about it?'

He shook his head. 'Never. But when babies come in here, she doesn't go all soppy like some women do. You know how they coo and tickle the baby under the chin and so on? She doesn't do that. She just stands there and you can see her thinking, *Another baby.* That's all she thinks.'

Although Isabel might not have expressed it the same way, she knew what Eddie meant; she had seen Cat's body language in the presence of babies.

She chose her words carefully. She was aware that Eddie spoke openly, with a certain disingenuousness, and Cat could take offence if their conversation were reported back to her. At the same time, Eddie needed to understand. 'It might be that Cat wants to have a baby,' she said. 'Deep down she may want it, but the fact that she doesn't have one makes her a bit ... how should we put it?'

'Anti-baby?'

'No, she's not anti-baby. Maybe she's just a bit uncomfortable when she's with babies. She might react that way because she's trying to control her feelings. People are like that, you know.'

Eddie looked thoughtful. 'We had a teacher at school who was like that. He was called Mr Macgregor. He always wore the same suit every day – a sort of grey-blue suit made of that stuff that won't snag – you know, that heavy cloth.'

'Thorn-proof tweed?'

'Yes, thorn-proof. And he wore this tie, you see – a blue tie with thin red stripes going across it. People said it was something to do with the army. He'd been in the army, they said, before he became a teacher. He always stood very straight. And his shoes ... you should have seen his shoes. They were polished so much you could see your face in them. I'm not exaggerating. You really could.'

'I can just see him,' said Isabel.

'He was pretty stiff,' said Eddie. 'He never smiled, or only just a little bit – like this.' Eddie stretched his lips into a straight line. 'And when he talked, he kept his lips together. He talked through them. I don't know how the words got out, but they did. It made them sound a bit ... a bit tight.'

'Poor man,' said Isabel. 'Were you unkind to him?'

Eddie looked surprised. 'Me?'

'No, not you in particular. The students in general.'

Eddie shook his head. 'Some were, maybe. Not everybody. They gave him a nickname. He was called the Captain. But nobody dared to be rude to him to his face.' He finished his coffee and put the mug down on the counter. 'But then ... '

Isabel waited. She had a perfect mental picture of Mr Macgregor in his thorn-proof tweed suit and his military tie.

'But then he retired,' Eddie said. 'And he came round to every classroom to say goodbye. He stood there and started to say something about how much he had enjoyed working in the school and then ... ' Eddie looked at her intently. 'Then he started to cry. In front of everybody. He started to cry.'

Isabel stared at Eddie. She saw that the memory had caused him pain.

'Poor man.'

'I never thought of him as having feelings,' said Eddie. 'None of us did.'

'You don't at that age. Adults are just these remote beings. They don't have any of the feelings that teenagers have.'

Eddie smiled ruefully. 'When we were teenagers we thought we were the only ones who felt – or knew – anything.'

Isabel looked at her watch. 'We should get the rolls made for lunch,' she said. 'You know how Cat likes to have everything ready by twelve.'

They busied themselves with the rolls. Isabel sliced tomatoes and prepared lettuce leaves; Eddie peeled boiled eggs.

'Well, well!' said a voice. 'What a hive of industry!'

Isabel looked up sharply. She had not seen the front door open and Beatrice Shandon come in from the street. Now she stood before her, on the other side of the counter; Bea, as they called her, a friend from schooldays – the girl Isabel and her classmates had unanimously decided would be the first one to get married. The prophecy had been correct, as the predictions of those with whom we are brought up so often are: Bea had married at nineteen, while still studying at Aberdeen University. Her husband, who was the same age, was a fisherman on one of the boats that went out into the North Sea from Fraserburgh – a hard, cold job, full of danger. Her parents had been appalled, and in their desperation had resorted to asking Beatrice's schoolfriends if they could persuade her of the folly of her actions. If she wouldn't heed parental advice, then perhaps she would listen to her peers.

Isabel remembered the conversation. 'She doesn't know her own mind,' said her mother. 'And that boy won't know his either.'

'It's nothing to do with his being a fisherman,' added her father, the proprietor of two hotels. 'It's a perfectly honourable job.'

'Nothing to do with that,' chimed in her mother. 'Except he'll be away for long periods of time – weeks, perhaps – and, well, they'll not have much in common, I expect.' She looked at Isabel for support. 'What on earth will they talk about?'

Isabel had suggested they could be in love, which had brought forth a dismissive snort from Mrs Shandon. 'My dear, love is a very fragile plant; we all know that. Its blossom is often brief.'

'Very brief,' agreed Mr Shandon.

Mrs Shandon glanced at him. 'We *know* this isn't going to last. So all we want to do is protect our daughter. And you wouldn't want your friend to make a bad mistake, would you?'

'No.'

'Well there you are. Maybe you can tell her that. Maybe you can get her to see that she's in for a big disappointment once . . . ' She looked away. '. . . once the physical side of things wears off.'

Isabel had felt obliged to talk to Bea. 'Your parents don't think it's a great idea,' she said, as casually as she could.

'What do they know?' challenged Bea.

'I suppose they're worried you might change your mind.'

Bea brushed this aside. 'The real reason why they're against this is that Davey is a fisherman. They can't stand the fact that he left school at sixteen, you know. They think he smells of fish.'

Does he? wondered Isabel. It would not be surprising if he did, and to find oneself faced with a son-in-law who reeked of fish might be a bit of a shock if you owned two hotels in Edinburgh . . .

'He makes me feel good,' said Bea. She looked intently at Isabel. 'You know what I'm saying.'

Isabel thought she did, but found it hard to report this to the parents.

'She's in love with him,' she said simply.

'At least you tried,' said Mrs Shandon. 'And we're grateful for that.'

That was Bea's first husband, and he lasted for barely five months, much to the relief of her parents. They at least had the good grace to express regret on the divorce, but Bea did not believe them, and nor did anyone else.

Almost immediately, Bea met a young Englishman who was studying rural economy. They were together until he graduated and went off to work in a small property business in Suffolk, ending the relationship when he left Aberdeen. Bea did not mind. She had met an army officer, who lasted for three months, and a helicopter pilot, whom she saw for a slightly longer period. Then she returned to Edinburgh and took a job in a public relations firm in the city. There she married the junior partner in the business, rapidly became pregnant with the first of her four children, and never looked back.

'I've always needed somebody,' she had once confided to Isabel. 'From the age of seventeen, I have always had a man. I couldn't conceive of a situation where there was no man – I just couldn't.'

'You've been lucky,' said Isabel. She thought of the army officer and the helicopter pilot, both of whom had been handsome to the point of being considered dashing. The PR man by comparison was dull and unadventurous, but that in no sense made him undesirable. A dull man, Isabel thought, was exactly what she needed. She tried to remember Bea's husband's name. It was something old-fashioned; something redolent of ill-fitting cardigans and domesticity. It came to her in time. Arnold . . . 'You have Arnold.' She thought: *it's your destiny. Men are your destiny. We sensed that all those years ago.*

'We've been so happy,' said Bea. 'Right from the moment I set foot in that office, I knew that he was the one. From the very first day.'

Isabel imagined the scene, with Bea entering the office on her first day, surveying the scene for men, and immediately finding one. Sometimes she wondered whether men fully realised the peril they were in. A man might innocently enter the room unaware of the eyes that were upon him, of the calculations being made. *Good husband material?* Of course women entering a room might be the subject of exactly the same sort of assessment by men – it worked both ways. Men and women, it seemed to Isabel, were just as bad as one another.

'I've never felt tempted to look at another man,' said Bea. 'Not once. And Arnold has always averted his eyes from other women.'

He always averted his eyes from other women. It was, thought Isabel, a striking expression. Again her imagination got to work and she saw Arnold at a party, a hand over his eyes to ensure that he did not accidentally set eyes on another woman, rather in the way that someone trying to give up alcohol will look anywhere other than at the tray of drinks.

Isabel rarely saw Bea, as they moved in rather different circles. Isabel disliked cocktail parties and large gatherings where strangers shouted at one another over a background of hubbub. By contrast, Bea was always keen to attend such gallery openings and fund-raising dinners as were on offer. *Scottish Field*, the magazine that recorded such occasions in pages of photographs at the end of each issue, duly noted her presence at this or that charity ball – with Arnold, of course, alongside her, obediently wearing his formal kilt and smiling obligingly at the photographer. Isabel found that such people could be superficial, only concerned with being seen in public, secretly desperately anxious that their popularity might be on the wane. But not Bea: she believed in the good causes behind such events and was at her happiest meeting other people who enjoyed having their photographs taken. Arnold, though, was another matter: Isabel suspected that he was there under duress, dragged along like a consort obliged to accompany his wife, all the while averting his eyes in his much-vaunted loyalty.

She did not have a great deal in common with Bea, their friendship being in the category that Isabel described as 'historic'. Relationships entered into at high school were a classic example of historic friendships, as might be any of those made in circumstances where people were brought together because they were all in the same boat – metaphorically, of course. Mind you, thought Isabel, there must be friendships brought about by being in the same, non-metaphorical lifeboat after one's cruise liner goes down …

Yet although they did not share many interests, on the occasions when they did meet, Bea always treated Isabel as an intimate, quickly taking the conversation beyond the limits prescribed by mere acquaintanceship.

'How do you *feel* about things? Do tell!' was a favourite opening gambit of hers – as if inviting a frank outpouring of pent-up doubts and misgivings. This would have been irritating – and intrusive – had Isabel not realised that Bea meant well, and that she was ready to disclose her own inmost thoughts.

Isabel knew more about Bea's activities than Bea knew of hers. There were, of course, the events recorded for all to see in the social pages, but there were other things too. She knew that Bea was a good golfer, and frequently won the ladies' cup at the golf club of which she and Arnold were members. That had been reported to Isabel by another old schoolfriend who had struggled for years to improve her game, but without success. And there was another talent, one that was more unusual and perhaps not admitted to with the same readiness: Bea was a matchmaker – enthusiastic, calculating and incorrigible.

Not everybody encouraged her. 'You could get it wrong,' said one of her friends. 'Don't you think it could be a bit risky?'

'Why? What's risky about bringing people together?'

'What if the man's unsuitable … even disastrous?'

Bea was sceptical. 'That's highly unlikely. And anyway: what do you mean by disastrous?'

The friend shrugged. 'He could harm her.' There were plenty of men like that; men who preyed on women.

Bea made light of this. 'This is Edinburgh, not . . . ' She waved a hand in the direction of the world at large.

'I mean it,' said the friend. 'I really do. Do you *really* know half the people you bring together?'

'Yes,' said Bea. 'I do.'

'All about them?'

'Enough to know whether they might get on with somebody else.' She looked defiantly at her friend. Matchmaking was a helpful pastime. People liked to be brought together, she told herself, and some people, herself included, enjoyed doing just that. And why not? What was there to be ashamed of in bringing lonely people together?

'Are you sure?'

Bea said nothing. The conversation was at an end, as far as she was concerned.

4

Bea gestured towards one of the tables. 'I need to sit down. Could we talk?'

Isabel glanced at her watch and then looked at Eddie. He nodded. 'Things won't pick up for another twenty minutes,' he said. 'I'll cope.'

They went to the table while Eddie, having volunteered to make Bea a cup of coffee, busied himself with the controls of the espresso machine.

'A nice boy,' said Bea appreciatively, looking over towards the counter.

'Yes, he is,' said Isabel. 'My niece owns this place, you see. Eddie helps her – as do I.'

'I'd heard that,' said Bea. 'And I thought that I might come and surprise you here one day. But living on the other side of town, as we do, means that I hardly ever venture across Princes Street.'

'The great divide,' said Isabel.

Bea looked at her blankly.

'Australia,' explained Isabel, waving a hand vaguely. 'There's a great divide, you see – an actual physical feature . . . ' She trailed off. 'I'm sorry. I sometimes go off at a tangent.'

Bea shot her a slightly reproachful glance. 'Actually, this isn't really a casual drop-in. I wanted to see you. I phoned your house and your cleaning lady told me you'd be here.'

Isabel smiled at the description of Grace, who would not have taken kindly to being described as a cleaning lady. 'Strictly speaking, she's a housekeeper,' she said.

Bea laughed. 'These distinctions,' she said dismissively.

Isabel thought: *yes, you may laugh at these distinctions, but they can mean a great deal to some.* The small scraps of status, the petty trappings of office, helped people through their lives. She looked enquiringly at Bea. 'Anyway, you wanted to see me?'

'Yes. It's something—' She broke off as a frown crossed her brow.

Isabel waited.

'It's something rather sensitive,' Bea continued. 'I've made a terrible mistake.'

An array of possibilities raced through Isabel's mind. Bea had got rid of Arnold. She had started an affair with the window cleaner; Isabel knew somebody who had done just that. The woman had watched him as he cleaned her windows, had made him a cup of coffee and then, as reported to Isabel by another friend, 'They had ended up in one another's arms – even before she had paid the bill!' Isabel had listened to this breathless account and had said simply, 'It's important to pay one's bills immediately; I'm not sure if I approve. If one's going to start a passionate affair with a window cleaner, pay him first.'

She smiled at the thought, but Bea was frowning. 'I said: I made—'

'Of course, sorry. You said you made a mistake. I was

thinking of somebody else who made a bit of a mistake. Or it might not have been, for all I know. Perhaps she found what she was looking for . . . '

'Who?' asked Bea.

'Oh, somebody I know vaguely.' She made a dismissive gesture to indicate the reverie was over before continuing, 'Most mistakes can be rectified, of course.' But even as she uttered the anodyne, she reminded herself that there were some to which it did not apply: there were plenty of mistakes that simply could not be put right.

'I hope so,' said Bea. 'Particularly in this case.' She paused, her expression wistful. 'Although frankly I have no idea how to go about it.'

'Perhaps you should tell me,' suggested Isabel. 'If you want to, of course.'

'That's why I'm here,' said Bea quickly. 'You have a reputation for helping people. You know that, don't you?'

Isabel looked embarrassed. 'No more than others,' she muttered.

Bea shook her head. 'There's no need to be modest. You're known for it. You've helped any number of people. And you do it rather well.'

Isabel squirmed inwardly. There was something about Bea's manner that irritated her – a disingenuousness, perhaps – and this made it difficult for her to accept the compliment. She did not want her *interventions*, as she called them, to be the subject of praise. Yes, she might help people from time to time, but she did not like to dwell on it. She decided to move the conversation on. 'Why don't you tell me about what happened?'

Eddie was approaching their table. He placed a cup of coffee on the table in front of Bea, who looked up and thanked him. She waited until he had started to walk off before she continued.

'About a month ago,' she said, 'I held a dinner party. I like doing that, I'll admit.'

'So many people have given up on dinner parties,' remarked Isabel. 'They're too busy, or they just don't care. And, to tell you the truth, I'm one of the offenders.'

Bea smiled. 'You have your hands full. You have a young child.'

'Two,' corrected Isabel. 'Two boys now.'

'It's such a busy stage of your life,' said Bea. 'My youngest is in his late teens already. I started much earlier than you.'

Isabel almost responded, *We knew you would*, but did not. Instead, she said, 'I don't really have an excuse for not entertaining. My husband . . . '

Bea nodded. 'I've heard about him. I gather you have a very . . . delicious husband. I'd love to meet him some day.'

'I'm happy enough with him,' said Isabel evenly. 'But I was going to say: my husband's a very good cook. So, with two of us to shoulder the burden, we could entertain a bit more than we do.'

'It's not compulsory,' said Bea.

'You were telling me about a dinner party.'

Bea seemed to gather her thoughts before she spoke. 'Yes, a dinner party. You may know – or, put it this way, quite a few people seem to know – that I like to introduce people socially.'

Isabel said that she knew that. It was, she said, a thoughtful thing to do.

Bea acknowledged the compliment. 'Thank you. You see, I don't think that a dinner party should just consist of friends who know one another. What's the use of that?'

Isabel was not sure whether an answer was expected of her.

'So I make a point,' Bea continued, 'of inviting people who I think might like to meet one another.'

'Nothing wrong in that,' said Isabel. 'Hosts and hostesses have been doing that forever.'

Bea looked relieved. 'I'm glad you think that. However, I suppose there's always a risk that you might bring together two people who aren't right for one another. Somebody pointed this out to me in the past and I'm afraid I was rather dismissive. Perhaps I should have listened.'

There was real regret in Bea's voice now, and Isabel felt a sudden sympathy for her. 'I'm sure you weren't to know,' she said.

'I didn't.'

'Well, unawareness of something is a perfectly good excuse, you know.'

Bea looked at her intently. 'Do you really think so?'

'Yes, I do. Not knowing about something means that you can't be blamed for it.' She paused, her philosopher's training bringing up a niggling doubt in her mind. In certain circumstances one might be responsible for a state of unawareness, and this prior responsibility could mean that the consequences of unawareness could be laid at one's door. She looked at Bea; now was not the time to split philosophical hairs.

Isabel continued, 'But, listen, why not tell me what happened? I assume you made a bad match and now you're worried about it. Not that I think you need to be—'

Bea cut her short. 'But I *do* need to worry,' she said. 'This is a nightmare – a complete nightmare.'

Her voice rose as she spoke, prompting Isabel to try to calm her down.

'Listen, Bea, just tell me what happened,' she said.

Bea took a deep breath. 'All right, but, oh . . . '

'Just tell me. I'm not going to be sitting in judgement over you. Just tell me what happened at this dinner party of yours.'

Bea took a sip of her coffee. 'Do you know a woman called Constance Macdonald? She's usually called Connie.'

Isabel thought for a moment. There had been any number of Macdonalds in her life, including a Candida Macdonald and even a Clarinda Macdonald – 'Nothing to do with Robert Burns's girlfriend, I assure you,' she had said – but no Constance. She shook her head. 'I don't think so.'

'I didn't think you would. Somehow I thought she's not your type.'

'Oh. Why's that?'

Bea shrugged. 'She's a bit . . . how shall I put it? A bit loud. You know what I mean?'

'I'm not sure. Loud in the sense of . . . loud? She speaks at the top of her voice? Drowns everybody else out?'

Bea laughed. 'Oh no, not that sort of loud. Her tastes are loud. Yours are . . . well, yours aren't.'

Isabel looked away. Bea was . . . she struggled to find the right word, and then it came to her: intrusive. Bea intruded on people – as much through talking about them to their face, as she was doing now, as through her matchmaking.

'You make me sound muted,' said Isabel.

Bea looked surprised. 'But you are, Isabel. You're very muted.'

Isabel flushed. Was she being described as muted because she *thought*? 'I don't really think of myself that way. I have opinions, same as anybody else, and I do express them, you know.'

Bea waved a hand airily. 'Oh, one can have opinions and still be muted.'

Isabel struggled to contain herself. 'I didn't think we were going to start talking about me,' she began. 'I imagined—'

Bea interrupted her. 'Of course. We can talk about you later – if you like.'

'This Connie Macdonald,' Isabel persisted. 'This *loud* Macdonald – you invited her to dinner?'

Bea considered this. 'Invited her? Well, in a sense . . . But no, not actually invited.'

Isabel wondered what she meant. 'You asked her?'

'Yes, I asked her, but only after she had fished for an invitation. Some people do that, you know – you can tell when they're fishing for you to invite them. They don't come straight out with it; rather, they say something like "Perhaps we should have dinner one of these days", and then don't actually propose that you should come to dinner with them and it's clear that they mean they should come to you. You must get that a lot.'

Isabel looked blank. 'I'm not sure if we do. Jamie and I have people round occasionally, but not all that often. And I don't think I get many hints.'

Bea was incredulous. 'But somebody like you – somebody with that house of yours, and everything, and being well known too. You must. There must be people who want to have dinner with you – who want to be able to say "We were at dinner at Isabel Dalhousie's".'

Isabel sighed. She had not intended to, but the sigh escaped. 'I'm not well known. I don't know where you got that idea from.' She paused. 'You're the one who's well known. I see your picture in *Scottish Field*. Often. And you were in the *Evening News* the other day. You were at that premiere.'

Bea was obviously pleased that Isabel had spotted the picture. 'Oh, that. It was a bit tedious, I must admit, but it raised over twenty thousand for Waverley Care. You might know about their work. They look after people with HIV.'

'Yes, I know about them. But you were saying . . . '

'About Connie Macdonald?'

'Yes.'

Bea returned to the subject. 'What happened was that she made it quite plain that she had heard that I helped people meet one another. She then more or less invited herself – not that she used those words exactly. She said something like "I wouldn't mind meeting somebody" and then she said something about how she'd heard that I'd been behind Ivor and Jenny's marriage and didn't everybody think that was a great success, and so on. It all added up to a self-invitation.'

Isabel smiled. 'There are some hints that just have to be taken.'

'Yes,' said Bea. 'And I did. I rather liked her and although there are far more women than men looking for someone, I did have a spare man in mind.'

Isabel stopped her. 'Are there really more women than men?'

Suddenly Bea became animated. 'On the lookout? Oh yes – definitely. Beyond any doubt. Hundreds more.' She paused, looking intently at Isabel. 'Let me tell you something: if you're a man and you're wanting to meet somebody, then you are absolutely guaranteed to find somebody. Guaranteed. The only reason you won't is if you're utterly impossible – which few men are.'

Isabel asked Bea what she meant by 'utterly impossible'. She wondered whether she herself had met any man who could be described as utterly impossible – Christopher Dove? Professor Lettuce?

Bea addressed the question with the gravity she clearly felt it deserved. 'Utterly impossible men? There has to be something really seriously wrong. I'm not talking about appearance or anything like that. No, that's not an issue. I knew this man, Isabel, who looked like a pig. I'm not exaggerating – he really looked exactly like a pig. He had small porcine eyes and his skin – I'm not making this up – was exactly like a pig's. And the remarkable thing was that his voice was very nasal, with the result that it sounded like a series of oinks and squeaks. But he was speaking English, and you could work out what he was trying to say if you listened hard. It went a bit like this: "I think oink oink that there's oink squeak a possibility that oink . . . " And so on. All delivered in this very nasal way.' She laughed. 'Honestly, Isabel, it was almost impossible to keep a straight face.'

'Poor man.'

'Poor man, yes. But I didn't think he cared at all – because he knew that he'd always have somebody to look after him – to be the pig-keeper, so to speak – because he was a man and there were always, always women who would take on a spare man, even if he was completely porcine. His wife died, you see, and he was by himself for exactly four months when this really rather attractive person from Fife – she had a house in St Andrews, I think – met him and took him off to Fife with her, and that was it. So even he had no difficulty. Whereas . . . '

Isabel smiled. 'Whereas women who are looking for a man . . . '

Bea shook her head sadly. 'They have to join the queue. They find out that for each spare man there are ten or twelve, maybe more, contenders. Widows, divorcees – there are hundreds of them milling about, all desperate to get one of the handful of spare men available.'

Isabel suspected that all this was true. And yet were the demographics that skewed? Was nature making some sort of mistake – or was the mistake ours? 'Why?' she asked.

'Why?' repeated Bea. 'I suppose it must be because men die earlier. They're less robust, in a way. So that has an effect. And then more and more men seem not to be interested. It's easier for them than it was in the past. It's more of an option. So that reduces numbers even further. Or they decide that they don't need marriage because there's less social pressure to be married.' She shook her head. 'And that's a mistake, I can tell you. Letting up on social pressure is a serious mistake. Remove social pressure and nobody will do anything about anything. It becomes a question of what suits *me*. Me, me, me . . . that's all that matters to a lot of people these days.'

Isabel sensed that the discussion of social policy – and demographics – was taking them away from Connie Macdonald. She steered Bea gently back.

'All right,' said Bea. 'I'm sorry to go on about it, but it's a subject I'm really interested in. But it'll keep. Now, Connie. So I issued her with an invitation to dinner. It was going to be Friday – I had been thinking of Saturday, but something cropped up and I changed it to Friday. That's a good night for a dinner party – not as good as Saturday, but not too bad. Eight people. The ideal number, in my view. You probably know some of the guests.'

Isabel inclined her head. Edinburgh was not a large city: half a million people was small by the standards of the sprawling monsters that many cities had become, and this meant that it was still possible to go to a social occasion, even one outside one's normal circle, and encounter familiar faces. And there were other forms of recognition, too: like that which came from simply having seen somebody in the street or in a shop. You might never have spoken to a person, one might have no idea who they were, but they might still be known in a way, rather as one comes to know familiar surroundings. That morning, walking back from Bruntsfield, she had walked past a woman she knew on that basis; they each said good morning, and smiled, but neither knew who the other was. That was the intimacy of the small place – an intimacy that was normal and unsurprising in a village, where there could be no anonymity, but that seemed remarkable in a city.

'Tom and Kitty Michaelson?'

Isabel thought for a moment. 'I don't think so.'

'I thought you might have met them,' said Bea. 'They live in Regent Terrace – you know, overlooking Arthur's Seat. They have a painted ceiling.'

Isabel smiled. It was a strange way to talk of anybody – to refer to them by a feature of their house. *This is So-and-so – he has a magnificent bathroom . . .*

'But they do,' said Bea. 'Those Georgian houses are quite exceptional – even by the standards of the New Town.'

'Yes, I know they are,' said Isabel. Perhaps it was not all that odd for a ceiling – particularly a painted one – to carry social weight. After all, people who happened to own large houses often expected their social position to be dictated by floor space. Or was the floor space merely a sign of something that had always had a powerful effect: money?

'Their ceiling was in a bad way when they bought the house,' Bea went on. 'But they spent a lot on it and had it restored. They had to get somebody up from London to do it. He was an Italian. They have all those painted ceilings over there, of course – I suppose they're used to it.'

Yes, thought Isabel. The Pope had a painted ceiling that needed restoration. Perhaps somebody had said to him – at a dinner party – 'I have just the person to restore that Sistine Chapel ceiling of yours. I'll give you his number.'

Bea looked pained. 'Did I say something funny?'

Isabel shook her head. 'I'm so sorry. No, you didn't. I have a tendency, I'm afraid, to think at a bit of a tangent. I think of things at odd times. I know it's very rude of me, but it just seems to happen.'

This reassured Bea. 'I rabbit on a bit too, from time to time. I have a niece who keeps telling me that I talk too much, but she herself – you should hear her on her phone. She's rarely off it – talking to her friends. Gossiping away.'

'I was thinking of the Pope,' said Isabel. 'It was your mention of Italian painted ceilings. That made me think of the Pope, and of how he might get advice at a dinner party.'

And then she thought: imagine if somebody like Bea – a Roman version of her – invited the Pope to dinner in order to matchmake. And somebody would whisper to the hostess: 'But you can't, you just can't! He's the Pope. For heaven's sake – he's not available. No, it makes no difference that you think the two of them would get on – it's just not going to work.'

'You're smiling again.'

'Dinner parties,' said Isabel apologetically. 'The thought of dinner parties leads to all sorts of conjectures. But, look, tell me about these Mitchellsons . . . '

'Michaelsons. He's an architect, but I don't think he's ever actually built anything. He designs projects that are never made – cathedrals, and so on. No, I'm not making that up – he worked for years on a cathedral that never got built. Somebody somewhere or other wanted to build a cathedral, and they asked him. Apparently he's the only person in the country who can design a cathedral.'

Isabel remembered Christchurch Cathedral: the New Zealand Christchurch. Who had built that? And out of cardboard, after the earthquake? That architect who used cardboard because it was cheap and simple and could help people affected by disasters.

As long as you coated the cardboard with something waterproof, then it would do the job handsomely.

'Have you heard of the cardboard cathedral?' she asked.

Bea did not seem to be interested. 'No. I've not. And I don't think he wanted to use cardboard.'

'There's a Japanese architect,' said Isabel. 'He does such good work. He builds paper structures to help people after natural disasters – earthquakes and so on.'

'Oh well . . . You asked about them. That's who they are – or at least that's who he is. I don't really know very much about her. She's something to do with, oh, something or other. I forget exactly what. She goes all over the place doing something for whatever it is.'

'I see.' Isabel paused. She had an incomplete picture: an architect who had designed an unbuilt cathedral; a painted ceiling restored by an Italian; a woman who busied herself with some undescribed work on behalf of unknown people. 'And who else? You said there were eight people altogether.'

'Well, there were Arnold and I, of course, and Tom and Kitty – we've just been speaking about them – and then there were two people who were not a couple. I don't like to make it too obvious, and so I usually have people who may know one another but who aren't a couple. So I had my friend Frances, whose husband works a lot in Frankfurt and who's often by herself as a result. I had her and then I had another friend called Rob who lives by himself and likes coming to my dinner parties to make up numbers. He's very good with people. He's a good listener – and that's a great gift.'

Isabel agreed. 'A rare gift, too.'

'I've seen Rob sitting there smiling while the most terrific bores go on about something. And he makes them feel that he's really interested – which I think he probably is. You could talk to Rob about drains, or average times taken to get through the Panama Canal, or some such subject, and he would take it all in and say *how interesting* every so often – and mean it. I don't matchmake for him, by the way.'

Isabel found herself thinking: just how long *did* it take to get through the Panama Canal? She might ask Jamie, perhaps: it was the sort of thing he might know. As a boy he had devoured the *Guinness Book of Records*, he once told her, and could still come up with information on the world's tallest man or the largest steak pie ever made, even if his facts were now a bit out of date.

She prompted Bea. 'And then there was Connie and . . . '

She waited. Bea pursed her lips; she looked distinctly uncomfortable. 'A doctor,' she said. 'A surgeon, to be precise.'

'What sort?'

'Plastic. Facial reconstruction – that sort of thing.'

That information, Isabel thought, was neutral. The fact that Bea's final guest was a plastic surgeon told her nothing about him – other than, perhaps, that he was skilled, and intelligent, and capable of looking after himself in the difficult world of surgery. Yet that, she now decided, was not nothing – in fact, it was rather a lot.

'He's called Tony MacUspaig.'

Isabel expressed surprise at the name. 'MacUspaig?'

'It's a very rare Scottish name,' said Bea. 'He told me about it when I first met him. He said it was generally believed to have died out at the beginning of the twentieth century, but he was living proof that it hadn't. It's Hebridean, apparently – from one of the islands. I think he said Harris.'

'So he's the last of the MacUspaigs?' She stumbled over the pronunciation.

'I think so.'

'And he really is the last of a line of . . . of MacUspaigs?'

Bea smiled. 'So it would seem.' Her smile faded. 'Though I'm not sure now whether I should believe anything he said to me.'

'You're going to have to tell me more,' said Isabel.

She sat back as Bea spoke, trying to concentrate on what she was being told, but finding that her mind kept drifting back to the name. MacUspaig. What would it be like to be called MacUspaig? Every time you gave your name you would have to spell it for people. People would look blank; would look confused; or smile, perhaps, because it was so odd. One could become defensive about one's name, as people did who had those fine old English surnames, Winterbottom and Sidebottom. They saw nothing funny about their names – and why should they? Bottom meant field in old English, and there was nothing ridiculous about being called Winterfield or Sidefield. And yet there were people who went through life feeling ashamed, or awkward, about their names. To be burdened by a disgraced name must at times be unbearable, and yet some people did just that, rather than change their names: Adolf Hitler's sister was required to become Miss Wolf, but at least one member of the Himmler family stuck to the family name as part of an identity that she felt could not be changed, whatever the degree of shame and embarrassment. Svetlana Stalin, daughter of the monster, felt that being a Stalin entitled her to special treatment, as must the offspring of many dictators. Many of them, of course, are damaged right from the beginning: tyrants, Isabel reflected, generally made bad parents. But she put these thoughts out of her mind, as Bea was expressing the view that Tony MacUspaig was, on balance, a psychopath.

'So there you have it,' said Bea. 'I've introduced a woman to a psychopath.' She paused. 'And she likes him.'

5

Jamie cooked dinner that evening. Isabel kept him company in the kitchen, seated at their scrubbed pine table, sipping at a glass of the New Zealand white wine she favoured, watching Jamie chopping onions. She valued this time spent alone with him in the kitchen; like most parents of young children, they cherished such periods of peace.

'It seems so quiet,' she said. 'I keep thinking one of them is going to start crying.'

'If anybody's going to start crying,' said Jamie, 'it'll be me – with these onions.'

'There's a poem about onions,' she said. 'It's about how memory is like an onion – it makes you cry.'

Jamie did not turn round. 'Surely that's about memory, not about onions,' he said. 'There can't be many poems about onions.'

'Some, I suspect. There are poems about just about everything.'

Jamie paused at his task. Using the sleeve of his shirt, he wiped at his eyes. 'How do film stars cry?' he asked. 'Do directors wave onions about?'

'No,' said Isabel. 'I think they have to do it naturally. Some of them train themselves to think about things that really make them sad, and that does the trick.' But then she remembered something. 'There was a famous child actor, I seem to recall, who cried very convincingly on screen because the director had told him he was going to shoot his dog.'

'So, real tears?'

'Very real in that case,' agreed Isabel. 'But not what a director would do these days, I think.'

Jamie finished off the chopping of onions. 'The moral progress you talk about?'

'I suppose so. We're more sensitive to bullying.'

Jamie scraped the onions off the board and into a pan. 'Risotto,' he said. 'I know I'm always cooking risotto, but why not?'

'With mushrooms?' asked Isabel.

'Porcini. And Madeira.'

She thought: *how many women can sit in the kitchen and watch their perfect husband cooking risotto?* And for a brief moment she felt fear – fear that this was all too fragile, that it could not last. That was the problem with things that were exactly as you wished them to be; that was the problem if you found yourself in Eden – there was a snake in the garden.

Jamie turned to her and smiled. There she saw the shape of his lips; his mouth was wide, with its splendid cupid's bow. She lowered her eyes, as to gaze on physical beauty sometimes felt like defiling it. She would not look at him. She would not tempt providence to snatch him from her.

'Do you know the difference between a psychopath and a sociopath?' she suddenly asked.

Jamie was adding an extra knob of butter to the pan.

'Psychopaths always cook with butter,' he said. 'Sociopaths use oil.'

'Be serious.'

He laughed. 'All right: I haven't a clue. They're both to be avoided, I suppose. Apart from that, take your pick.'

'I had to look it up today,' said Isabel. 'Lots of people use the words interchangeably, and psychiatrists don't use them at all. They talk about personality disorders.'

Jamie adjusted the heat on the stove. 'Lots of those,' he said. 'There's a conductor I know, for starters. And Richard Wagner.'

Isabel sipped at her wine. 'One distinction is the way they're made. Sociopaths are made by their experience – by a bad upbringing.'

'And psychopaths are born that way?'

'So the psychologists say.'

Jamie hummed a snatch of tune.

'What's that?' asked Isabel.

'Something from Gilbert and Sullivan,' he said. '*Iolanthe*. It goes: *That every boy and every gal/ That's born into the world alive/ Is either a little Liberal/Or else a little Conservative*.'

Isabel smiled. 'One doesn't associate Gilbert and Sullivan with psychopathy. Except for . . . '

'Except for?'

'*The Mikado*,' she said.

Jamie stirred the onions. The sizzle, and smell, reached Isabel.

'Have you thought of how psychiatric insight changes opera?' she said.

'Or antibiotics,' Jamie suggested. '*La Bohème* would not be quite so tragic if antibiotics had existed at the time. Mimì would have made a good recovery. *Your tiny hand is no longer frozen* . . .' He looked over his shoulder at Isabel. 'Of course modern medicine would improve the outlook for sopranos – at least as far as opera is concerned. They have a terrible mortality rate, sopranos. They're always dying on stage – and they take a long time to do it. Tenors are much luckier.'

'Their mortality rate is lower?'

Jamie nodded. 'Distinctly.'

Isabel warmed to the theme. 'Of course a lot of people are stabbed in operas, aren't they?'

Jamie agreed. 'Yes, it happens. But never in the lungs. You need lungs to sing your final aria, and so they're usually stabbed elsewhere.'

He took the pan off the heat and turned to face Isabel. 'How did we get on to this?'

'I mentioned psychopaths.'

Jamie wiped his hands on his apron. 'Why?'

Isabel hesitated. Jamie was looking at her in a way that told her he already suspected. It was a look that mixed disapproval and disappointment.

'You're getting involved in something?' he said.

She did not answer for a moment. Her life was her life, she said to herself, and she did not have to account to anybody for what she did – not even to her husband. But then, even as that thought came to her, she doubted it. The point about being married was that you shared your life with another, and this meant that there could never be complete freedom. There were responsibilities that came with marriage – as indeed with any relationship with another – and these could limit your choices. If Jamie suddenly announced he was going to take up skydiving, she would have something to say about that. She would leave him in no doubt about her feelings: she would not like it.

For a moment she imagined the scene. 'This is something I have to do,' he would say. 'I've always wanted to . . . '

'Jump out of a plane?'

'It's more than that. I'd be proving to myself . . . '

'You don't need to prove anything.'

'But haven't you seen those pictures. People holding hands while they float . . . '

'Fall. You don't float when you jump out of a plane.'

There must have been any number of such conversations, she thought, between skydivers and their husbands and wives, girlfriends and boyfriends. Or did those who remained on the ground put on a brave face and say they did not mind – which surely could not be true. The families of skydivers must have moments of acute anxiety, she decided – whatever they said to the contrary. What was it like, she wondered, to watch a person whom you loved emerge from the door of a plane, a tiny black speck in the sky, and then wait until the life-saving canopy unfurled – if it did, because there were times when it did not, and those down below would see that happen before their eyes?

'Isabel,' Jamie repeated. 'Are you getting involved in something?'

She shook her head. 'Not quite.'

'What does "not quite" mean?'

She sighed. 'All right. I've been asked . . . ' She did not finish.

'Oh, Isabel, that's the way it always starts, isn't it? Somebody comes along and asks you something – and how many times do you say no? How many times do you say: "No, I can't do this because I have a job" – and you do have a job, you know. "I can't do it because I have two young children, and a husband, and a home, and so on."' He shook his head.

She looked up. They never really argued with one another; this sort of exchange was as close as they came. 'I haven't agreed to anything yet.'

Suddenly he broke into a smile. 'You haven't agreed? But you will, won't you, and yes, I know, it's none of my business. It's just the way you are, isn't it?'

He took a step forward and bent down to kiss her lightly on the cheek. 'It's all right,' he whispered. 'You have to do what you have to do. But . . . ' He hesitated. 'Be careful of getting involved with psychopaths. Or at least tell me who the psychopaths are, so that I can rescue you.'

She reached up and put her arms about his neck. 'You would, wouldn't you? You'd always rescue me.'

'Of course. I'll fight your battles for you.'

'And I'll fight yours.'

He laughed. 'We're a sort of NATO, aren't we? A private NATO.' He stroked her hair. 'That could be a song, you know. "Our Private NATO". Rather like "My Funny Valentine".' He hummed a few bars, and played with the words. '*Are your missiles far too tall/Are your troops a little small . . .* '

He returned to the pan. 'You're going to have to tell me now.'

She was relieved that the moment had been defused, and now she told him what Bea had revealed about Tony MacUspaig.

At first she gave him the background on Bea's matchmaking reputation.

'Somebody tried to matchmake for me once,' he said. 'It didn't work.'

Isabel expressed relief. 'I have reason to be thankful for that,' she said.

'Yes, me too. Had it worked, I would have been with

somebody else, rather than you.' He stirred the risotto. 'And I wouldn't be standing here cooking dinner for you, and you . . .'

'I wouldn't be sitting here with a glass of wine and telling you about . . .'

'Yes, carry on.'

'She held one of her dinner parties because she wanted to help a woman called Connie Macdonald, who had more or less invited herself to dinner because—'

'She wanted a man?'

'Yes. She wanted a man. She'd heard about Bea's reputation for doing that sort of thing and so she placed herself in her hands. And so Bea invited a man called Tony MacUspaig. She'd met him, apparently, at one of those Scottish Opera drinks parties.

'So she invited the two of them, and lo and behold the chemistry seemed to be right. Connie telephoned her a couple of days later to thank her for the dinner and mentioned, more or less as an aside, that she had heard from Tony MacUspaig and that he had invited her to some do or other. Naturally Bea was pleased. Another success, she concluded.

'She thought no more about it, she told me, until a few weeks later she bumped into one of the other people who had been at the dinner party that started it all off. This was a friend of hers, a man called Rob McLaren who's apparently a very good listener. He's a regular at her parties because of this. People like good listeners.'

Jamie interrupted her. 'I'm listening.'

'Good. Rob told her how much he'd enjoyed the evening, and then said, "Interesting guests." She said that the tone of his voice suggested that there was something he wanted to tell her, and so she asked him whether he'd met them all before.

He said he had, apart from the doctor – and that, of course, was Tony MacUspaig. Then apparently he went quiet for a few moments, and Bea knew that this meant he had major reservations.

'She knew him well enough to say, "Come on, Rob, spit it out." And this brought a bit of humming and hawing and comments about not wanting to pass on tittle-tattle. But then he got to the point and said, "I'm afraid he might not be what you think him to be."

'She asked him what he meant by that, and apparently this led to more humming and hawing before he eventually said, "I hear he doesn't treat women very well."

'She pressed him to spell it out. She asked him if he was a womaniser.'

'They're everywhere,' said Jamie. 'There's a brass player I know who—'

'Hold on,' said Isabel. 'Let me finish. And anyway, don't brass players have a reputation?'

'For drinking beer,' replied Jamie. 'They're always off to the pub after rehearsals – they're famous for it. But they chat up women a lot too, I think.'

Isabel shrugged. 'I suppose men and women have always been involved in that sort of dance round one another. After all, isn't that what dance is all about? Isn't that what it represents?'

'Perhaps,' said Jamie. 'But let's not get distracted.'

'But it was you who distracted me,' Isabel pointed out.

'Sorry – you carry on.'

'It came out eventually. It was a special form of womanising: highly motivated. And not by the usual thing.'

'Not sex?'

'No, it seems not. Rob eventually said that Tony MacUspaig

went for wealthy women. He got hold of their money somehow or other and then that was it – he was off. That's what he wanted to warn Bea about.'

Isabel sat back in her chair. She had finished her glass of wine and the risotto would not be ready yet for another thirty minutes or so. If she had another glass of wine – and she allowed herself two if she felt she had an excuse – the evening would cease to be productive. There were letters on her desk, and an irritating manuscript submitted to the *Review* by a demanding professor of philosophy was awaiting her attention. The professor's argument, she felt, was impractical and too extreme, and this view was shared by at least two members of her editorial board. But another two were strongly in favour of the paper and were pushing for its acceptance for publication. She could reject the paper if she wished – after all, she owned the *Review* and could do what she liked. But she had always been reluctant to use her position in that way. That would be petulant; that would be high-handed.

Thinking about the issue made her feel uncomfortable. 'Ridiculous Dutchman,' she muttered, as she fingered the stem of her wine glass.

Jamie laid aside his spoon. 'What was that?' he asked. 'Did you just mutter "Ridiculous Dutchman"?'

Isabel pursed her lips. 'Did I? I suppose I did.'

Jamie laughed. 'Why? Why did you mutter "Ridiculous Dutchman"?'

'Because he is,' said Isabel. 'He submitted a paper – this Dutch professor with an amusing name. Van der Pompe. And he goes on and on about rivers being allowed to follow their natural course and the wrongness of intervening in the world's topology. He doesn't approve of hospitals, either. They limit natural mortality, he says. Can you believe it?'

'So no medical treatments?'

'None,' replied Isabel. 'No antibiotics, of course, and even no aspirin.'

'Strange,' said Jamie. And then added, 'Ridiculous Dutchman.'

Isabel looked at him sharply. 'Well, he is. He *is* ridiculous. He's a sort of uber-Green, and uber-anythings are ridiculous. Uber-socialists, uber-free marketeers, uber-nationalists – they're all the same. He argues against the building of bridges. He says that bridges interfere with the natural limitations that the world imposes on us. If there were no bridges we would not move about so much and ultimately there would be fewer of us. Our economies would be smaller, you see, and that would mean a lower population.'

'And reducing the population – seriously reducing it – would be a good thing?' asked Jamie.

'That's what he says.' She paused. She remembered hearing new and virulent diseases being described as the only hope for mankind. 'Although people who want smaller populations usually aren't thinking of sacrificing themselves.'

Jamie put the lid on his risotto and placed the pan in the oven. 'Twenty minutes,' he pronounced.

'Of course he's right in a way,' said Isabel. 'There *are* too many of us. If the world's population were smaller there would be fewer crises – fewer arguments over—'

Jamie interrupted her. 'Over everything. Water. Minerals. Food.'

'Exactly. But is the solution to stop building things? He hates roads. He even disagrees with changing the shape of existing fields. He doesn't like ploughing very much. Bizarre.' She paused. 'He irritates me, you know. He's written five times about his paper – five times! He's so sanctimonious about it, more or less suggesting that the only reason why we wouldn't be publishing it is because we don't care about ecological issues, as if somehow the *Review of Applied Ethics*, and its editor in particular, were responsible for the silting up of the Nile, rising sea levels, and the retreat of glaciers.' It was hard not to be sanctimonious when one was so sure of one's ground. Few people, she thought, managed to be convinced they were right and yet not appear preachy and slightly disapproving of those who had yet to see the light.

Jamie crossed the room to sit next to her at the table. 'Perhaps he's got a point,' he said. 'If nothing else works, if we can't control population growth the usual way, then perhaps we'll have to look at solutions like that. Shrinking our economies. Leaving things in the ground. Stopping all this rushing around. Stopping all this going forth and multiplying.'

'Even if that means everybody becoming poorer?' She asked the question, although she had always been sure of the answer. We had to become poorer – or at least the rich part of the world had to, and that included China now – because the world could not sustain our depredations. The Chinese, with all their factories, were running out of breathable air; that was how serious it was for them.

He did not answer, but flicked at her glass with a fingernail. The crystal rang sharply. 'You could have another glass of wine,' he said.

She asked him what excuse she had.

'Oh, everything,' he said nonchalantly. 'Life. Van der Pompe. The *Review*. This ghastly MacUspaig. Psychopaths in general. People asking you to do things you don't really have to do . . . '

'Or I could celebrate,' she countered.

'Yes, you could celebrate. And I could join you.'

'But celebrate what?'

'Being here,' said Jamie.

'If that's grounds for celebration . . . '

He looked crestfallen, and she realised that her answer sounded world-weary and jaded, which had not been her intention. Isabel had no time for the cynical approach to life; cynicism, she said, was like hydrochloric acid – corrosive.

She started to apologise, but he cut her short.

'It's a tremendous privilege to be alive,' he said.

'Oh, I know that . . . '

'When you consider that the universe is full of inert matter – billions and billions of dead stars, and in the face of all those incalculable odds against life, we happen to have it, just for a tiny flash of time. It's against all the odds.'

She looked down at the floor and thought: *against all the odds, I have you* . . . He was right: how could anybody not appreciate the immense privilege of life? Unless, of course, life for them was painful, which it was for so many; putting things in context did not really help the immediacy and reality of suffering, and there was so much of that – oceans and oceans of it. Looking up would certainly put human pretensions in their place: those pictures of those distant galaxies did that for her. How could one worry about money or what somebody had said to you, or about being late for some appointment, or about encroaching wrinkles or expanding waistlines or any of the other things that people worried about when you and your world were so tiny and insignificant? But of course humbling as such a perspective was, when you looked down again you saw your feet and the solid earth on which they stood, and there were real clocks ticking, and real tears to be shed over petty things. We were stuck: we were stuck with our ordinary world and its petty concerns. Ultimately any meaning we could find for our existence was stubbornly located right there and demanded that we take it seriously. And what did that mean? The answer that came to her was as unexpected as it was immediate: that she had to be kind to Professor van der Pompe.

He rose to his feet and fetched another glass. The bottle of wine was on the table.

'*Slàinte.*' It was the Gaelic toast. Jamie used it with a smile. 'The full extent of my Gaelic, I'm afraid.'

She replied in kind. '*Slàinte.*' And then added, 'At least you admit it. Unlike some of those ardent enthusiasts for Gaelic road signs.'

He looked at her. 'Poor van der Pompe,' he said. 'You're going to end up publishing his paper, you know.'

She sighed. 'I know. And I shall. He'd be very unhappy if I didn't.'

'Do you really think he's ridiculous?'

She shook her head. 'I shouldn't have called him that. I'm feeling a bit tired – a bit frayed at the edges.'

He shot her a sympathetic look. 'Who doesn't feel like that from time to time? And anyway, you can still refer to him as a Dutchman. There's nothing pejorative in that, is there?'

'No. I would take being called Dutch as a compliment. Everybody likes the Dutch.'

Jamie smiled. 'Well, that's settled, isn't it?'

'But I still have a bad feeling about this MacUspaig.'

Jamie grimaced. 'Ridiculous . . . ' he said.

They both laughed.

'I'm going to have to do something about it,' said Isabel. She spoke with resignation, as one who is obliged to follow the promptings of a heart over which she has no control.

'Let's not dwell on it,' said Jamie. 'Let's talk about something else.'

'Such as?'

He made a gesture as if to show that he was choosing a topic at random. 'About how much I love you.'

'Oh.'

'Yes. But then you know that, don't you?'

'I suppose I do. And it makes me feel a whole lot less ... well, less like the way I was feeling before you told me how much you loved me ... If you see what I mean.'

He did. He took her hands in his. He stood up, pulling her up with him. He put his arms about her. The mystery of otherness, she thought: the feeling of the physical existence of another person; a miracle.

'Careful of my glass,' she said.

6

Isabel had already decided what to do by the time she dropped Charlie off at nursery school the following morning. Her time was at her own disposal as Grace had offered to look after Magnus all day, without even being asked, and she had partially accepted the offer: she would take over at lunchtime, if Grace could cover until then. Magnus still slept a large part of the day, and looking after him was by no means onerous.

The child's arrival had fired the housekeeper with new enthusiasm for her job, and she had come up with all sorts of reasons why Isabel should leave it to her to look after Magnus, on whom she so clearly doted. There were times when Isabel found herself resenting this – as often as not fairly strongly – but then she reminded herself that Grace was childless. That led to other reflections, the effect of which was to blunt any resentment: Grace did not have money – even if Isabel paid her generously – while she herself had more than enough; Grace lived in a rented flat while she and Jamie had living space to spare. There were many other ways in which Isabel's position was so much more fortunate than her housekeeper's, and the cumulative effect of these was that Grace was forgiven: she could be as demanding or as sniffy as she liked – she was forgiven.

Isabel had made a telephone call the previous evening – a rather late one, at ten o'clock, which was on the cusp of when it was acceptable to call people at night. Bea, she thought, was likely still to be awake, as she had not struck her as the sort to retire to bed early with a book and a milky drink. And she had been right: Bea answered on the second ring.

'Rob McLaren,' said Isabel. 'Have I got the name right? The man who told you about Tony Mac . . . ' She stumbled over the unusual name.

'MacUspaig,' prompted Bea.

'I want to speak to him.'

There was a momentary silence at the other end of the line. Then Bea said, 'Are you sure?'

'About speaking to him? Yes, I think I need to.'

'No,' said Bea. 'I meant are you sure you want to get involved?'

Isabel suppressed a sigh. Bea had very specifically asked her to do something, and now she seemed uncertain. 'You asked me to,' she replied.

Bea sounded apologetic. 'I know, I know. But I've been thinking, and it occurred to me that this man Tony might be difficult. We don't know much about him; what if he were to turn against you? What if he found out that you were interfering in his scheme?'

'If he has a scheme,' said Isabel.

'Yes, if he has one. What then?'

'We deal with that when and if it arises,' said Isabel. 'But listen, if you don't want me to go ahead, I won't.'

Bea was silent. At last she said, 'The problem is that I feel wretched. I've already put one person in a position where things may not turn out well for her, and now, with you, I'm putting another person in the firing line.' She paused. 'The original mistake seems to be growing arms and legs.'

Isabel felt a certain exasperation. Bea, she thought, was flailing around. She had not given sufficient thought to her introductions – introducing people she barely knew, or did not know at all – and now, with the materialisation of a risk that anybody should have been able to foresee, she was uncertain what to do.

She decided to be firm. 'You asked me,' she said, 'and I said that I would do something about it. I do not intend to change my mind.'

It sounded rather formal, even pompous, and Isabel smiled at herself. *Do I really say things like that?* she thought.

The effect was immediate. 'You're right,' said Bea. 'I shouldn't interfere. You've agreed to help me, and I should be saying thank you rather than putting you off.'

'Well, there we are,' said Isabel. 'That's all settled. Now what I need to get from you is Rob McLaren's telephone number.'

Bea had provided that, and now Isabel sat at her desk and dialled the number. There was no response at first, and she had almost put the receiver down when a voice came on the line. Rob McLaren listened to her and then agreed to see her later that morning. Isabel suggested the neutral ground of Cat's delicatessen; if they met there then she would be in a position to bring the meeting to an end should it show signs of going on too long. One could always just announce that one had to go on somewhere else: it was not easy to do that in one's own house. Anxious glances at one's watch could be effective in shifting a guest who overstayed his welcome, but not in every case: the thick-skinned sometimes failed to notice such things, or were happy to ignore them.

Cat was surprised to see her when Isabel arrived at the delicatessen shortly before eleven. 'Have I made some mistake?' she asked. 'Were you due to come in?'

From behind his end of the counter, Eddie answered his employer's question. 'No, she's not due to do a session until next week. You're going to the dentist – remember? Isabel said she would help out.'

'I haven't come to work,' explained Isabel. 'I was going to meet somebody for coffee. Although if you need any help, I'll be happy to do what I can.'

Cat eyed a large Milanese salami on a plate beside the meat slicer.

'I could do that,' said Isabel, picking up on Cat's glance.

She took off her jacket, donning the white coat that Eddie fished out of a drawer. Then there were the latex gloves that Isabel always wore when she handled meat – not that Cat and Eddie bothered.

She picked at the string stocking in which the salami was clad. Eddie, standing beside her, was clearly keen to demonstrate his own method of dealing with this. 'If you cut the string stuff like this,' he said, running a knife down the side of the salami, 'then it peels off quite easily – you see.'

He demonstrated the removal of the string and then handed the heavy salami back to Isabel. 'Watch your fingers,' he said.

She started the machine. There was a hum, and then a whining noise as the circular blade began to spin. As Eddie uttered his warning, she remembered the butcher in Newington from whom they had bought meat in the days when she and her father were living alone in their large

Edinburgh house. It had been a time when she missed her mother terribly – and she still did, of course, but it was particularly hard then, as she was a teenager and experiencing all the anxiety and uncertainty that blights the teenage years. The butcher, whose name was Mr Hogg, had one finger missing from his left hand and two from his right. They had all been lost at the knuckle and when she first set eyes on these mutilated fingers, Isabel, who was then not yet fifteen, had been unable to take her eyes off them. Mr Hogg was used to being an object of interest to children, and made light of his misfortune. He would stick the stump of a finger into an ear, giving the impression that a much longer digit was inserted. Then he would turn his fist, as if he were operating a screwdriver. Isabel had cried out in alarm, and he had quickly withdrawn his finger to reassure her. But the image had stayed with her, and now made her look with horror at the blade. It would require only the smallest slip, a wrong movement over an inch or less, to become nine-fingered. And that, of course, applied equally to so many other situations in life: the car shooting past pedestrians who were no more than a stumble from its lethal path; the half an arm's length that separated two approaching trains from one another; the couple of yards of runway that made the difference between a safe landing and disaster. She picked up the salami and began to slice it.

'Isabel?'

She looked up. As she did so, the salami slid past the finger-guard, and for a moment her hand might have brushed against the blade. But it did not. She reached for the switch and silenced the machine.

It had been Eddie. Now he said, 'I'm sorry. I didn't mean to distract you . . . '

She glanced at the blade. 'Don't worry. No harm done.'

Eddie gestured towards the end of the counter. 'That chap asked for you.'

Isabel looked down the counter, and knew immediately that this was Rob McLaren. It was not just that she had arranged to meet him round about this time; it was also something to do with the name. This was clearly a Rob McLaren.

He was a man somewhere in his early forties, she thought – possibly a bit older. Although the day was fairly warm for the late spring, he was wearing a tweed jacket and a rather dashing ochre waistcoat. He had no tie, but the breast pocket of his jacket sported a blue bandana-size handkerchief, protruding enough to draw the eye. If she had looked for a single adjective to sum up his appearance, it would, she thought, have been 'jaunty', or even 'raffish'. But it was the name that did the work: to be called Rob McLaren implied solidity and reliability, spoke of a world of douce Borders towns and the quiet farms that surrounded them; it reassured. There had been a famous rugby commentator called Bill McLaren, she remembered, and perhaps that was why the name resonated – at least for her – in that particular way. That Bill McLaren had been a familiar voice on the radio, even to those for whom rugby commentary was as otiose as the shipping forecast; yet, like the shipping forecast, which spoke of poetically named sea areas – Dogger, Fisher, German Bight and so on – Bill McLaren's pronouncements on rugby had a certain timelessness about them that spoke of a rural hinterland of solid values, of quiet perseverance, of uncomplicated decency.

Slipping her hands out of the cloying latex gloves she made her way to the other side of the counter. They introduced themselves and as they did so she noticed his eyes, which were a light blue. His gaze upon her was intense, but not in any troubling way. It seemed to be anticipating something – an expectant gaze, she thought.

They sat down. He was gentlemanly in his manner, waiting until Isabel had taken her seat at the table before he lowered himself into his. Isabel saw that Eddie was watching them, and she sipped at an imaginary cup of coffee to make the request. Eddie nodded.

'Eddie over there does a very good cappuccino,' she said.

'Perfect,' Rob replied.

Isabel signalled again to Eddie, who was already at the hissing coffee machine. Cat was off to the side, busy with a customer, but she glanced over towards Isabel, clearly interested in what was going on.

Isabel went directly to the point. 'I need to talk to you about something rather sensitive,' she said.

He brushed an invisible fleck off his jacket sleeve. 'I know,' he said. 'Bea told me you'd be getting in touch.'

'Do you know her well?' asked Isabel. 'I was at school with her, you know.'

Rob smiled. 'She mentioned that.'

'I don't see very much of her these days,' Isabel continued.

'She said that too.' His voice was low key and modest. The accent, which was not very pronounced, had the gentle burr of the Scottish professional classes. This was an accent that would score highly in those tests of reliability that newspapers liked to carry out – those surveys that tended to reveal that a mild Scottish accent in a bank manager or financial adviser inspired more public trust than any other voice. By the same token, although the surveys were never so tactless as to point it out, people were reluctant to take investment recommendations from a person with a very strong Irish accent. There was no objective reason for this, of course, even if Ireland had created a property bubble of gargantuan proportions in the days of easily borrowed money. These views were tied in with old perceptions, and were slow to change, even in the face of hard evidence.

'It was about this person, Tony MacUspaig. Did she tell you I wanted to talk to you about him?'

Rob looked around the room. His body language was almost imperceptible, but Isabel noticed it; something was frightening him. When he answered, his tone was tense. 'She said that she had spoken to you about him.'

'We can speak quite freely to one another,' said Isabel, her voice lowered. 'I understand about confidentiality. I take it very seriously.'

He visibly relaxed, sitting back in his chair, his shoulders less hunched. 'I suppose you do. Bea tells me you're a philosopher.'

'I am,' she said. 'Not that I practise it.'

He looked interested. 'How does one practise philosophy?'

'You teach it,' she said. 'Or you write about it. Many people do both. People think of it as a somewhat ivory tower occupation, but it's not always like that. Philosophers play a part in the real world too . . . ' She paused, as she thought of Professor van der Pompe and his hostility to anything that saved lives. Was he anything to do with the world of real problems – a world that was full of human suffering? The thought made her feel cross again. Did van der Pompe himself never accept any medical help? Did he ever travel by road or cross one of those bridges he said should not be there? And what about Professor Lettuce and Dr Christopher Dove, both of whom she suspected were only very marginally interested in the problems of other people? They were not as extreme as van der Pompe in any respect, but she still doubted whether they really understood, or even cared about, the struggles that ordinary people had in living their daily lives – their battle to make ends meet, to pay the bills, to raise their children, to keep a roof above their heads.

Rob was looking at her. He had addressed a remark to her that she had missed because she was thinking of the shortcomings of her *bêtes noires*.

'I'm very sorry,' she said. 'I was thinking of something. People accuse me of daydreaming . . . and I'm afraid they're right.'

He smiled. 'Bea told me you're the editor of some rather impressive journal. I was just wondering about it.'

She made a dismissive gesture. 'I'm not sure how impressive it is. We have what most people would consider a pretty tiny circulation. In fact, I sometimes wonder just how many people read the articles we publish.'

He seemed interested. 'What? Ten thousand? Something like that?'

Isabel's eyes widened. 'That would be beyond our wildest dreams. Even one thousand would be a vast improvement.'

'Surely—'

She interrupted him. 'No, you see we're very academic. Although we mostly deal with applied ethics and although we are, in a sense, quite practical, we still have a tiny circulation. Most of the copies go to university libraries. We have about thirty private subscribers – people who are interested enough in philosophy sign up for a subscription, but they're a real minority.'

'But then people must read them in libraries?'

She grimaced. 'I wish that were true. But walk into the current periodical section of an academic library, and what do you see? Row upon row of periodicals – every one of them the latest issue in any number of titles. The review of this, the journal of that: every subject under the sun, and some others, will be there.' She paused. 'And in philosophy alone – just in philosophy – there'll be about forty journals, more if the university in question is well funded. So the question I ask myself is this: are there enough people to read all these journals, and, if so, who exactly are they?'

'Students?'

She considered this. 'Sometimes. But I'm not sure that students read specialist academic articles. And so . . . '

He was looking at her sympathetically.

'And so, I suppose what we publish,' she continued, 'is only read by a handful of other philosophers. And I suppose the friends and relatives of the people who write the papers.'

This clearly surprised him. He raised an eyebrow. 'Then why do you continue?'

She did not answer immediately and he looked contrite. 'I'm sorry, I didn't mean to be rude.'

She forced herself to smile. His question had disconcerted her. Why did she continue with the *Review* if it had so little impact on the world? Was there any point in continuing to publish purely for the edification of people like van der Pompe and all the others whose main objective was to see their name in print, to get tenure in their posts, or simply to give vent to their preoccupations? She thought that, but gave expression to none of it. Instead, she said, 'Maybe it's worth doing something even if the effect is very tiny.'

His face lit up. 'Yes!' he exclaimed. 'Yes, that's exactly right. I have a couple of projects myself that don't make a massive difference to the world, but that I happen to think are worth persisting with. Small things, but . . . '

'But small things are worth doing,' she said. 'Of course they are.'

She wondered whether she should ask him what these projects were, but she reminded herself that the point of their meeting was to find out about Tony MacUspaig, and so far she had only got as far as mentioning his name.

'This man, Tony MacUspaig – how well do you know him?'

He became tense once again. 'Not all that well,' he said.

She waited for him to continue, but he lapsed back into silence. Eddie had brought their coffee over by now, and Rob was taking a cautious sip of his.

'How did you meet him?'

This time he answered without hesitation. 'We were at university together. St Andrews. I was studying history and he was a medical student. As you may know, the medical students at St Andrews go off to do their clinical years elsewhere. They do anatomy and so on at St Andrews and then go off for the hospital bit. He went to Manchester, as all of them did in those days.'

'And then he came back to Scotland?'

Rob looked up at the ceiling. He had the air, Isabel thought, of one who was searching the dusty corners of memory. 'Not straight away. As far as I know he worked in hospitals in London, and I think he was somewhere in Africa – I think it was Zambia. In fact, I'm sure it was Zambia because I met somebody else who was in my year and he had seen him in Lusaka. He mentioned it.'

'He became a plastic surgeon?'

Rob nodded. 'Yes. When he came back to Scotland, he came to a year reunion we had up at St Andrews. The university published a small booklet with a note on what everybody was doing, and I remember reading his entry. He said that he had specialised in plastic surgery in London and was now back in Scotland, working at a hospital just outside Edinburgh, I think. It didn't say much more.'

Isabel asked if that was the extent of his dealings with Tony MacUspaig. It was not, he said. 'As it happens, he took up with a woman I knew vaguely. Apparently he had been married when he was in London – somebody from Glasgow, I think, who was working down there – another doctor. Anyway, they divorced and she went back to Glasgow. Then Tony came up to Scotland and started to see a woman called Andrea Murray. They were together for less than a year, and then it fell apart.' He paused. 'She tried to commit suicide.'

Isabel had not been prepared for this. She had her cup of coffee halfway to her mouth; she put it down, spilling a small amount on the table. She reached for a paper napkin and spilled some more in the process.

'Here,' said Rob. 'Allow me.'

While he dabbed at the coffee, she composed herself. She found suicide ineffably sad, even just to hear about it like this, let alone to encounter it. How alone, how abandoned, could people feel to take that final step? What desperation, what utter wretchedness could drive people to negate everything; and yet they did, daily, hourly, throughout the world, in the far reaches of despair people took their own lives.

'Because of him?' she asked.

Rob folded the soggy paper napkin and laid it neatly by his own cup. The action of an obsessive, thought Isabel.

'I don't know,' he said evenly. 'It's the usual *post hoc, ergo propter hoc* question. I've never asked her. I used to see her now and then, but I haven't been in touch with her for a while.'

'And then?' said Isabel.

'He took up with somebody else.'

Isabel waited.

'She was a few years younger than he was. Late thirties. He must have been, what . . . forty at the time? Yes, he would have been, because he was in my year, as I've already said. He would have been forty because it was three years ago.'

'Who was she?' asked Isabel.

'Her name, as far as I recollect, was Tricia. Tricia somebody or other. I didn't know her, but somebody I knew did. I have a friend who's a lawyer in town. He knew this woman because she was a client of theirs. He told me that Tony MacUspaig had started seeing his client, and he was a bit worried. Those were his actual words: "I'm a bit worried." I asked him why, and he said that their client was very wealthy and although they tried not to be too protective, they felt a bit concerned about the motivation of any suitors. He said . . . ' He stopped. 'You know, there's a bit of a problem here. You mentioned confidentiality.'

'Yes, I did. But I really do assure you – I give you my word – I won't reveal any of this to anybody. This conversation we're having is strictly confidential.'

He smiled wryly. 'The Edinburgh definition of "strictly confidential" being: tell only one person at a time?'

Isabel grinned. 'No, not that. I really mean it.'

'I'm sure you do,' he said. 'But it's not confidentiality as far as you're concerned that worries me – it's what I said to my lawyer friend. I told him that I wouldn't tell anybody what he told me about his client. And here I am about to tell you. That's what worries me.'

Isabel realised that she was now bound by her own assurance to him. She could hardly stress the importance of confidentiality in relation to anything he told her, and then, in the same breath, go on to urge him to break a promise of confidentiality that he had given somebody else.

'The principle of confidentiality isn't an absolute one, you know,' Isabel said.

'Meaning?'

'Meaning you don't have to keep quiet if some other value is threatened.' She wondered what the most apposite example would be. 'If somebody came to you and said, "Don't tell anybody, but I'm planning to plant a bomb in a shop on Princes Street," of course you'd have to tell the police.'

'Of course.' He thought for a moment. 'Unless you're a priest. Don't they keep what is said in the confessional a complete secret?'

'I think so,' said Isabel. 'But that's a special case. In more normal circumstances you can ignore confidentiality if you're protecting somebody from harm.'

'Provided the harm is serious enough?' asked Rob.

'Yes.'

He thought for a moment. 'What's the harm here?'

'Financial exploitation,' said Isabel. 'Separating people from their money.'

Rob smiled. 'Isn't that what normal business does?'

She conceded the point. 'Yes, but that's governed by rules – at least in enlightened capitalism.'

He seemed to savour the phrase. 'Enlightened capitalism . . .' And then he suddenly said, 'All right, I can hardly mention something to you then suddenly clam up, can I?'

Isabel was about say *No, you can't* but stopped herself. That would not be the real justification for his telling her, and she wanted him to make a properly defensible decision.

Rob folded the table napkin over on itself, and then once more, making a compressed postage stamp of it; a fussy gesture, Isabel thought. As he did so, he explained, 'The lawyer told me that alarm bells rang when Tricia made a substantial transfer of funds to Tony. The lawyers knew about it because they handled the money. It was fifty thousand pounds.'

'Ah,' said Isabel.

'Yes,' said Rob. 'Ah.'

'Did they know what it was for?'

Rob shook his head. 'No. They just knew that the money had been paid over.'

'And did he – the lawyer – ask Tricia about it?'

'He did, and Tricia became all defensive. She more or less told the lawyer to mind his own business.'

'But maybe it was his business.'

Tony considered this for a moment. 'To an extent, I suppose. He was a trustee, but ultimately the money's hers as the beneficiary. The lawyer couldn't stop her using it for whatever purpose she wanted, as long as the capital was preserved.'

Isabel said that people gave gifts to lovers. Or maybe they were buying something together – a flat, perhaps, and this was her share of the deposit.

'Who knows?' said Rob. 'But whatever it was, it didn't stop them separating three months later.'

'I see. Well, I suppose that puts a somewhat dubious complexion on it.'

'Doesn't it just,' agreed Rob. 'Especially when you bear in mind that the previous two women friends had been conspicuously well off. His wife – the woman from Glasgow – was the daughter of a ship-owner. Andrea Murray, whom he took up with in Edinburgh, had inherited an engineering company – and then there was Tricia. All three of them were, not to put too fine a point on it, seriously wealthy.'

'And Connie?' asked Isabel. 'The woman he met at Bea's dinner party?'

Rob sighed. 'Rich as Croesus,' he said.

A line of poetry came to Isabel's mind. *Your gift survived it all: the parish of rich women, physical decay* . . . It was Auden, of course – in his poem about W. B. Yeats. It was such a striking image: a parish of rich women. Not a *cluster* of rich women, or a *group* of rich women – a *parish* of rich women.

'He seems to have a parish of rich women,' she said, almost to herself.

'So it would seem,' said Rob.

7

There was a new dog in their lives – a rumbustious, enthusiastic black Labrador, burdened with a Russian name that Isabel knew she would find difficult to remember. The days when dogs bore names like Bobby or Hero seemed to be over; now dogs were given names from Icelandic sagas or, with playful irony, named after philosophers, actresses, or obscure football players. This Labrador, a recent addition to the household of Isabel's friends, Peter and Susie Stevenson, had been given the Russian name Lubka; their previous dog, Murphy, having had an Irish one. Another Irish name would be too much of a reminder of what they had lost: Murphy had not been an intellectual – few Labradors are – but had been loyal and loving, and was sorely missed.

Her visit to the Stevenson house in the Grange, that quiet, well-kept quarter on the south side of the city, was overdue. Susie had been keen to meet Magnus and Isabel had promised to bring him round sooner rather than later; yet he was already three months old and it was only now that she was standing in the hall of West Grange House, being introduced to the overactive bundle of fur, sinew and enthusiasm that was Lubka.

'And here he is,' said Susie as she leaned forward to examine Magnus, still fast asleep in his reclining pushchair.

What was there to say about babies? That was the question that Jamie had posed – not in a spirit of antipathy towards babies in general, but out of puzzlement that people appeared to be able to discuss any baby at length.

Isabel had pointed out that when babies were talked about, it was never babies in general terms; discussion of babies tended to be about a particular baby, and almost always about one whose parents were known to those participating in the conversation. People, she suggested, had a great deal to say about their own babies or their children's babies; there was endless interest in their everyday doings, in their progress towards physical control of the head, in their sleep patterns, in their reactions to the world: a baby might do nothing at all and yet be considered fascinating.

And now Susie, examining Magnus with unforced interest, pronounced on his appearance. 'The image of Jamie,' she said. 'The absolute image.'

Isabel would have been only too happy to agree. That one should be the image of Jamie would be a good start in life, but how could anybody see this in features that still had the malleability of early infancy? All babies, she remembered her father saying, look like Winston Churchill. And yet they did not look quite the same, because people could pick their babies out in the crowd; she would certainly not mistake Magnus for another baby. So what made the baby face recognisable? As if in answer to her unspoken question Susie said, 'The eyes are the same, aren't they?'

Isabel gave a non-committal reply. 'Perhaps. But it's difficult to tell with babies, I find.' Then she added, 'I'll tell Jamie. I'm sure he'll be pleased.'

As she spoke, she found herself looking at Lubka, who had momentarily stopped wriggling and was sitting down, his liquid brown eyes fixed on Isabel. There was something in the dog's gaze that struck her as familiar, but she was unsure what it was. Then it came to her: Peter. The look in the dog's eyes was reminiscent of Peter's gaze – which was absurd, of course. Dogs were often said to resemble their owners because of unconscious factors at play in the choosing of dogs; pit-bull terriers were not owned by thin aesthetes, but by stocky, aggressive types, mesomorphs almost without exception; poodles were often to be seen with fashion-conscious owners; mongrels attracted comfortable, home-loving people who were not too bothered with grooming, either canine or human. But that was as far as it went, and that a dog should somehow have the eyes of its owner was fanciful anthropomorphism.

They went inside and Susie led them into the kitchen at the rear of the house, a comfortable room complete with a piano and a view of the monkey-puzzle tree that dominated the lawn. Peter appeared, took a look at the still sleeping Magnus, and gave Isabel a kiss of greeting.

'He looks just like his father,' he said, smiling.

Susie made a face. 'He says that about every baby.'

'Reassurance,' said Isabel. 'And tact. One could hardly remark on the fact that a baby looked nothing like the putative father.'

Susie busied herself with the teapot. 'You must have your hands full,' she said. 'Charlie, and now Magnus . . . '

'Jamie's very hands-on,' said Isabel. 'And there's Grace, of course. I still manage to get time for other things.'

Peter was watching her. 'You aren't—' He broke off. 'You aren't *getting involved* again, are you?'

She sighed. 'I didn't seek this one out.'

Peter laughed. 'But you never do. People come to you. In spite of your never breathing a public word about what you do, they come, don't they?'

Isabel made a gesture of acceptance. 'I know, I know.'

Peter laughed. 'It's amazing how they know. They don't even have to search for you on the Internet – because there's nothing there, anyway, to encourage people to ask for your help. You're too modest for that, aren't you?'

'You've looked?' asked Isabel.

'Of course I have,' said Peter. 'Not to look for one's friends on the Internet is actually a breach of civility.'

Isabel found herself thinking of when she had last searched online for a friend's name: yesterday.

'If you don't look for somebody,' Peter continued, 'then you're actually implying that they aren't interesting enough to have much of an online presence.' He was smiling at her, and Isabel was not sure whether he was entirely serious.

'And to look for oneself?' asked Isabel.

Peter shrugged. 'Most people do that, even if not many admit to it. But of course you should be careful; it's like reading a recommendation that somebody's written for you: you might not like what you see.' He thought for a moment before continuing. 'As often as not, what people find when they do a self-search is stuff they've written themselves – about themselves.'

'Our narcissistic times,' said Isabel. 'I just don't see what the attraction is in leading one's life in public. Yet so many people do it. They put all the details of their lives up on social media, every last little thing. With photographs. "Here's me waiting for the train." "Here I am making sandwiches." And so on.'

Peter nodded. 'Selfies.'

'Have you ever taken one?' asked Isabel.

'No. Not really.'

She smiled ruefully. 'Nor have I.' And added, 'Does that make us out of date?'

'Probably,' said Peter. 'Everybody seems to take selfies now. It's made being the Pope or the Prime Minister a very demanding job. The moment you meet somebody they want a selfie, and you have to get up close to your new friend and grin into the camera.'

'I suspect there's a protocol about that.'

'Not one that the public observes,' said Peter. He was going to add to this, but Magnus had awoken, and was being lifted up admiringly by Susie.

Peter turned to Isabel. 'Shall we talk?'

She nodded. She felt slightly reluctant to burden them with the issue, but they had never objected in the past. And, she thought, they half expected it.

'Do you know somebody called MacUspaig?' she asked.

Susie looked up. 'Mac what?'

'MacUspaig. Yes, it's a very rare name, apparently – originally from the Hebrides. He's a doctor – a plastic surgeon.'

Peter shook his head. 'No. I don't. Susie?'

'No,' Susie replied. 'It's a name one would remember, don't you think?'

'Or a woman called Connie Macdonald,' Isabel continued. 'Constance Macdonald.'

Peter shook his head again. 'No. Of course there are thousands of Macdonalds . . . '

'Or Bea Shandon?'

He looked thoughtful. 'I think we may have met her.' He looked across the room, to where Susie had Magnus in her arms. 'Bea Shandon, Susie?'

Susie looked up. 'It rings a vague bell. I think we've met her, but I can't remember where . . . or when, for that matter.'

Isabel thought: *the Village of Edinburgh*. She turned to Peter. 'May I tell you the full story?'

He listened attentively as she explained. When she'd finished, he surveyed her with one of his characteristic looks: a look that said that he understood the issue and could see why she felt she should do something, but at the same time made it quite clear that it would be far better for her not to be involved. It was a complex look.

'So,' said Isabel. 'There you have it.'

Peter sighed. 'Or there you have *part of it*.'

'Meaning?' asked Isabel.

'What I mean is that you've heard about all this from one source. And when you hear about something from one source, it means that you have one person's view of things, with all the filters that one person has.'

She was a philosopher; it was the very beginning of philosophy, that question: how we know what we think we know.

'All I'm suggesting,' Peter continued, 'is that you consider the possibility that none of this may be true.'

She frowned. 'But of course,' she said. 'Anything we hear may not be true, but we can't be too sceptical. We have to assume the truth of at least some of the things we hear, otherwise . . . well, otherwise how would we live?' She paused. 'It's what I'd call a necessary assumption.'

'I like that,' said Peter, savouring the expression. 'A necessary assumption.' He appeared to consider this for a moment before he went on, 'You mentioned an Andrea Murray? I assume it's the same Andrea Murray we know.'

'I don't know anything more about her,' said Isabel. 'I know only what I told you.'

'I think it must be the same person,' mused Peter. 'It would be interesting to hear her side of the story.'

'What do you know about her?'

'Not much. She was friendly with a friend of Susie's.'

Susie joined in from across the room. 'My friend saw quite a lot of her. They played bridge together, but then I think they lost touch with one another.'

Isabel remembered what Rob had told her about Andrea's attempt at suicide. She wondered if Susie had heard of what had happened.

Susie looked astonished. 'I don't think so,' she said. 'I'd heard that she had some sort of bust-up with a man, but I was told that she was the one who got rid of him.'

'Perhaps your friend got it wrong.'

'Or,' said Peter, 'perhaps you did.'

They looked at one another, each uncertain what to say. Eventually Isabel broke the silence. 'I could speak to her,' said Isabel.

Peter frowned. 'Are you going to ask her about all this? About what happened with this MacUspaig character? It could be very painful for her.'

'I could speak to one of the others,' said Isabel.

'Possibly,' Peter replied. 'If you can track them down.' He scratched his head. 'But just let me work out why you would want to do that – to satisfy yourself as to whether what you've heard about Tony MacUspaig is true? Is that it?'

Isabel replied that she thought it might be useful to have evidence that she could use to warn Connie about Tony's past.

'You couldn't just tell her what you know?' asked Peter.

'She didn't respond very well to Bea when she tried that,' said Isabel. 'I think she's going to need to be confronted with actual testimony from one of the women he's been involved with.'

'And you're going to go to all that trouble?' asked Peter. 'Why doesn't this Bea person sort out the mess she created in the first place?'

Isabel shrugged. 'She feels out of her depth.'

'Is that an excuse?' asked Peter.

'No, but it's an explanation. The poor woman's very anxious. Sometimes we create situations for ourselves that just seem too ... too overwhelming. I can understand how one feels the need to turn to somebody else and say, "Please sort it out."'

Peter accepted this. 'But the problem is,' he went on, 'that you seem to be asked to do that rather often.'

Isabel looked out of the window. How quickly she found herself sucked into these affairs; how easy it was to take the first step and then discover that small step had mired one in further complications. It was so easy to engage; so difficult to extricate oneself.

'I promised Bea I'd help her,' she said quietly.

Peter pressed the fingers of his hands together, like a man beginning to pray; it was a gesture of conclusion. 'In that case,' he said, 'you have no alternative. Promises ... '

'... must be kept,' said Isabel, completing the adage. '*Pacta sunt servanda*.'

Peter smiled. 'Latin adds dignity, doesn't it?'

'It helps,' said Isabel. 'Or put it this way – it discourages people from disagreeing with you. Spout Latin to them and they tend to throw in the towel.' But *festina lente*, she thought; was *pacta sunt servanda* a firm rule or was it a recommendation that could, in some circumstances, be ignored? It seemed to her that more and more people in public life were prepared to ignore their own promises. Politicians did that all the time, sometimes requiring no more than a few weeks to change their tune entirely and forget the things they had just solemnly promised. Not that they actually *forgot* their promises – they just ignored them. Presumably they had no personal mottoes preventing them from doing this – a motto such as *Do what you said you'd do*, or *My word is my bond*.

Of course there were still people who made mottoes for themselves, and tried to live according to them. *Never give up. Be kind. Help the weak. Courtesy always.* There were any number of family mottoes that could be seen in heraldry books. Slowly these expressions of intention were beginning to look more and more threadbare – quainter, even, in an age of selfishness and individual self-indulgence – but they were still there.

Peter cleared his throat. 'One thing I'd say, though,' he began, 'is that if this man is who he is said to be – if he really has been on the hunt for wealthy women, then that means he could be dangerous. I imagine that if you got too close to him, and if he thought you might be on his track, then he could be . . . ' He seemed to search for the right word.

'Awkward?' suggested Isabel.

'More than that,' said Peter quietly.

She opened her mouth to protest, but Peter held up a hand to stop her.

'I mean it,' he said. 'You see, Isabel, you live in a rather rarefied Edinburgh. You mix in academic circles – you rub shoulders with musicians, philosophers, artists, all of those.'

Isabel winced. She did not like to hear this. She considered herself to be unexceptional; she would never have sought to confine herself to any particular circle, and it hurt to be seen as out of touch with the ordinary life of the city. *I am not an elitist*, she said to herself. *I simply am not.*

Aware of her discomfort, Peter's tone was gentle. 'I'm not suggesting that there is something less *real* about your world. But there's another, very different Edinburgh.'

She drew in her breath. 'I know that, Peter. You don't have to tell me.' She sighed. 'I find it strange that people think that just because I lead what some would see as a comfortable life—'

'Which it is,' he interjected.

'All right – which it is. But just because I'm fortunate, it doesn't mean that I don't know what life is like for others. That's really unfair.'

Her point struck home. 'No, I'd never say that. I'm just saying: be careful.'

'He's a doctor,' she said flatly.

'Doctors are people – like anybody else.'

'I'm sure I can look after myself.'

'You sure? What does Jamie think about this?'

She hesitated. She knew that Jamie worried about her, and she wondered now whether she should not pay more attention to his concerns. She had sometimes felt he was being over-protective, but was a husband not entitled to feel that way? And would it not have been worse had he felt indifferent? She wondered what it would be like to be married to somebody who did not care what you did; who never waited anxiously if you were late coming home; who never said 'Take care' when you left the house or started a journey; who just said 'Goodbye' and nothing more. Of course you did not want your husband to say too much; it was unnecessary for him to say 'Love you' at the end of every telephone conversation, as so many people now did when talking on the phone to those close to them. That had become the equivalent of saying 'Goodbye' and it could be awkward if it became too automatic. If you became too accustomed to saying 'Love you' then you might just say it at the wrong time, like when you were saying goodbye to your bank manager on the telephone, or to your child's teacher, or the plumber. That could lead to misunderstandings. And what about those whom you did not like very much? Would people start to say 'Not too keen on you' when they ended conversations with them?

She realised that Peter was waiting for an answer. 'I'm sorry,' she said. 'I was thinking.'

'About something that made you smile?'

'Yes.' She returned to his question. 'Jamie? He worries. Not all the time, but sometimes.'

Peter said he was not surprised. 'I can see why. You see, this man might not take kindly to somebody getting in his way. If he's after this Connie's money – and that's a distinct possibility – then he's not going to like you queering his pitch, is he?' He answered his own question. 'No, he's not. So he could do something unpleasant.'

'To scare me off?'

'Yes. Precisely.'

She thought Peter sounded a bit melodramatic, and told him so.

'In the cold light of day, perhaps,' Peter retorted. 'But it does get dark, doesn't it?'

'Oh, come on, Peter,' protested Isabel.

'Don't frighten her,' said Susie.

They lapsed into silence.

Peter looked apologetic. 'I didn't mean to worry you,' he said. 'But what I said is true, you know.'

'And I'm listening to what you say,' said Isabel. 'I'll be careful.'

'Very careful,' said Peter.

'Yes. Very careful. I promise.'

He smiled. 'Another promise.'

Magnus started to cry.

'Back to you,' said Susie, handing the baby over.

Isabel cuddled him, his soft skin warm against hers, breathing in his milky, babyish smell. All animals, she thought – all mother animals know the smell of their offspring. He was hungry, and she would need to feed him. Like so many women, her life seemed to be all about the needs of others. Auden had said something about that, she reminded herself – something witty. We are here on this earth to help others, but he had no idea why the others were here.

She went over their conversation as she made her way back towards Bruntsfield. She valued Peter's advice – over the years she had discussed various problems with him, and he had often got her to see things that she had missed. She was cautious in her assessments, of course, and tried not to leap to conclusions, but it suddenly occurred to her that she had often got things wrong. *I am meant to be a philosopher*, she reproached herself, *and yet I must be ignoring some of the most basic rules about being sure that you really did know what you claimed to know. Perhaps I should take an introductory course in epistemology all over again; go back to school, remind myself of the basic rules of how to draw supportable inferences, how to question propositions, how to proceed from premises to conclusions in a way that did not offend any of the rules of logic. Perhaps I am just a failed philosopher . . . a failed philosopher who happens to have been in a position to get myself into an influential position as the editor of a journal of applied ethics by simply buying the journal.*

It was a self-deprecating line of thought, but as she walked down the slope towards Holy Corner, the intersection where three churches surveyed three of the same sets of traffic lights, while Mammon, represented by a branch of the Bank of Scotland, glowered over the fourth, Isabel found herself wondering whether other people saw her as nothing more than a well-off dilettante. The thought lowered her spirits.

Sensing the negative direction of her thinking, she suddenly stopped, and stood immobile where she was on the pavement. A young man, who had been immediately behind her, had to swerve to avoid collision. As he walked past, he threw her an irritated glance. She muttered an apology that he did not hear. Apology changed to reproof – in her head: *I'm entitled to stop walking if I wish. There's no rule about standing where you happen to be and looking up at the sky or just breathing in and thinking . . .*

She remembered something she had seen many years ago, on a visit to New York. She had been there with one of her aunts from the South, and she had noticed a street sign that said *No standing at any time.* The sign obviously referred to vehicles, but could be read just as easily by pedestrians, and she had been struck by its unintentional humour. What was one to do when confronted with such a sign? Was one to sit down immediately, right there on the New York sidewalk, obedient to the point of immobility?

There was no point in muttering at people in the street, she decided, and she resumed her walk. Magnus was asleep, but there was no sign saying *No sleeping at any time.* That, at least, was something that officialdom allowed us to do – even in a heavily regulated society one might drop off if one wished – other than when one was driving, or doing something else that required full awareness. Judges sitting in court were expected not to drop off to sleep during proceedings, although every so often one did, and this came out during an appeal. The fact that the judge, or indeed any member of the jury, had been asleep could be fatal to a conviction. And quite rightly so, Isabel reflected.

This curious line of thought stayed with her almost all the way to Holy Corner. Was it in any way wrong to go to sleep at the theatre? People did just that, of course; a glance at the audience, especially during a tedious play, would often reveal people who had nodded off, some superficially out for the count, but others clearly enjoying a fairly profound sleep. Nobody paid too much attention to that, as long as there was no snoring – that changed everything, and those sitting about the sleeping member of the audience were fully entitled to tap the offender on the shoulder or even to administer a dig in the ribs. The justification for that, thought Isabel, was our entitlement to enjoy the performance free of disturbance from those who noisily unwrapped mints or chocolates, or who started to snore.

It occurred to her that there might be sufficient ethical issues involved in sleep to justify a special issue of the *Review.* She saw the cover and its title – 'The Ethics of Sleep: A Discussion'. This could be accompanied by a picture of somebody lying asleep in bed, or perhaps one of those representations of the sleeper in art – Michelangelo's *Night*, for instance, or any of those sleeping nymphs the pre-Raphaelites liked to paint. The Victorians approved of those, because the Victorians liked the idea of the elegant swoon and were always aspiring to the well-timed and graceful collapse into unconsciousness.

And what would go into the special issue on sleep? She was less sure of that than she was of the cover; there were issues, she imagined, around entitlement to sleep: there could even be a right to sleep set out somewhere in the list of recognised human rights. If we had a right to a reasonable amount of leisure – which we certainly did – then surely there was a right to get our necessary seven hours, or whatever it was, of sleep each day. That meant that employers could not expect their employees to work long hours that prevented their getting adequate sleep. That was a real problem, she knew, because there were many instances where people were expected to work ridiculously long hours or follow work rotas that must disrupt normal sleep patterns.

The ethical issues, she thought, were flooding in, and she was now thinking of the wording of the announcement and call for papers. *Ever since Edison invented the electric light bulb, human sleep patterns have been under threat* . . . She wondered whether that was too melodramatic, and decided that it was not. Electric light had changed everything; without it we were creatures of the cave, housebound by darkness, unable to do all the nocturnal things that we now took for granted. So that wording was not too extreme – human sleep patterns were indeed under threat, even if Edison might not have foreseen that when he first flicked that switch of his. But then at the time of invention people often failed to see the implications of the things they had dreamed up. The Wright brothers would not have foreseen the massive movement of peoples that would result from their invention, nor aerial combat, nor the living hell endured by those who had their homes directly under airport flight paths. Nor would Marie Curie have imagined Hiroshima.

She had reached Holy Corner. Her thoughts about sleep had lifted her spirits, and the doubts that had assailed her after her conversation with Peter were dispelled. She would return home, feed Magnus, cuddle Charlie – if he was back from nursery and in a mood to be cuddled – kiss Jamie, put out the recycling bin for collection, and sit down at her desk to draft the announcement of the special issue. That was quite enough for anybody, and if she had any thinking to do about this difficult situation that Bea Shandon had dropped her into, then those thoughts could be put off for a while. She would decide what to do the next morning, and would allow herself two days, at the most, to do whatever needed to be done. That was the key to dealing with matters like this – as indeed with most matters: you set a time limit and then you stuck to it. In theory.

8

Putting Charlie to bed that night took longer than anticipated as there had been numerous questions about the bedtime story. Why, Charlie asked, did people not like porridge that was too cold? He saw nothing wrong with cold porridge, and were these Scottish bears because Scottish bears would probably not like to put sugar on their porridge. And then there was the question of beds: did bears really sleep on beds or did they prefer to sleep on the floor? She answered patiently until eventually Charlie allowed her to turn out the light, give him his goodnight kiss, and go downstairs, the door having been left slightly open, for light and comfort.

Jamie was in the music room, experimenting with chords at the piano. He looked up as Isabel put her head round the door.

'Do you like this?' he asked.

He played a chord, followed slowly by a second, and then a third.

'Is it meant to be going somewhere?' asked Isabel.

Jamie nodded. 'It resolves like this.' Two more chords followed, and the music died away.

She asked him what it was.

'Nothing,' he replied. 'Just notes.'

She came into the room and stood beside him. He reached up and touched her arm gently. She put her hand on his. He looked down.

'Every piece of music is *just notes*,' she said.

'Yes. But put them together, give them shape, and it becomes something different. It then says something.'

She moved her hand to his shoulder. 'Do you remember that song you sang recently – a couple of weeks ago?'

He frowned. 'What song?'

'It was a folk song. A modern folk song. Something about a tortoise that regretted a hare. I forget how it went.'

Jamie smiled in recognition. 'Oh, that's by James Yorkston. He's Scottish, you know. It's called "Tortoise Regrets Hare". It's all about the end of a love affair.'

'That must be one of the commonest themes, surely.'

Jamie agreed. 'Yes, loss. Do you know what loss sounds like? I'll show you.'

He played a few notes. They were in a minor key, descending, fading away.

'That's loss,' he said, grinning.

Isabel smiled. 'This tortoise . . . '

'I suppose it's about incompatibility. Hare has gone off with somebody else – she's the fast one. Poor tortoise is left behind and regrets his lost lover.'

Isabel caught her breath. For a moment she thought, *I could be tortoise. I'm fourteen years older than him. He's my beautiful, lissome hare.*

His hand moved to the keyboard, and he began to sing. She closed her eyes. Tortoise regrets hare; fox takes hare. Who would be the fox to take her hare?

He did not finish the song.

She looked at him. 'Is that all?'

He shook his head. 'No, there's more. But I don't want to sing it.'

She understood, and she moved to be closer to him. She leaned forward and put both her arms about him. She realised that he was crying.

'Jamie . . . '

She felt his shoulders heave beneath her. He was making an effort to stop his tears.

'Why, Jamie? What's wrong?'

He spoke indistinctly, the words half swallowed. 'I went to see the doctor today.'

Her heart skipped a beat. 'You didn't tell me.' It was not what she had intended to say, but these were the words that emerged – and they sounded like an accusation. She did not mean to reproach him, but she could not imagine why he had not told her. They concealed nothing from each other – or so she liked to believe, but perhaps she had been naïve.

'No, I didn't.'

She waited, but he did not say anything more. He lowered his head.

'Jamie, darling, what's wrong?'

'They have to do some more tests. He took some blood.'

She gasped. She was light-headed; there was a strange, whistling sound in her ears, as if somebody, somewhere, was blowing across a pipe or a tube.

She asked him again what was wrong, but he simply shook his head. 'I don't want to talk about it.'

'But you must. You can't say something like that and then not tell me.'

He shook his head. 'I really don't want to. It could be nothing.'

'But there must be some reason why you went.' She paused. 'Did the doctor say why he needed to do a blood test?'

He had his hands folded in his lap and he was looking down at them intently. For a moment she wondered whether it was something to do with his hands; that would be serious for a musician. What went wrong with hands? Arthritis?

She tried another tack. 'Why won't you tell me? Is it something . . . something private? Something embarrassing?'

'No. It isn't.'

'Then why won't you speak to me about it? We don't have any secrets from one another, do we?'

She kept nothing from him and she had always assumed that this was the same for him – but had she assumed too much? For a moment she felt something rather like anger. His failure to be open about this was insulting to her; it was as if he did not trust her with this secret – if that was what it was – about his health.

He was struggling to say something. She let him try for a few moments before she spoke again.

'I can't understand why you won't tell me about it. Is it something awful? Is it?'

She was pleading with him now, her heart cold within her. It was; it was something terrible, something untreatable, and she was going to lose him. Everything, everything was going to come to an end, as we all secretly feared, because we all knew, in our heart of hearts, that the thread by which life hung was such a thin and tenuous one. It did not take much to snap it – a few cells deciding that they would multiply in the wrong place, in the wrong way, and the whole body, resilient until then, would start its inexorable dissolution. We were tenants, not owners, even if we had no idea what the term of our lease would be.

He was saying something.

'What was that?'

He repeated himself. 'It's not something awful. I'm not going to die.'

She held him closer. She was in an awkward position, half beside him, half behind him, and he was still seated on the piano stool. He moved his hands to the keyboard and several notes, unconnected and discordant, sounded. She clutched at the lifeline.

'So it's nothing serious?' she stuttered.

'I don't want to talk about it,' he muttered.

She released him. She did not know what to think. At least he had told her that whatever it was – and now she knew that it was not what she feared – was not going to kill him. At least he had said that. She looked at him, looked down on the top of his head. What was he thinking of to give her such a fright? He was normally so considerate and yet here he was being almost unbelievably thoughtless . . .

'Can we talk about it over supper?' she asked. 'It'll be ready in half an hour.'

He did not answer.

'Did you hear me, Jamie? Can we talk a bit later?'

Now he shook his head. He stood up and faced her. She saw the reddened eyes and her anger abated.

'Do you mind if I don't have dinner?' he asked. 'I think I'll just go and listen to something. I don't really feel like eating.'

All she could think of to say was, 'Listen to what?'

'Stravinsky,' he said.

He held her gaze, and she saw in his eyes something like agony. He was not telling her the truth, she decided; it *was* serious.

She turned to leave the room. As she did so, he reached out to her and caught her by the forearm. She felt the tightness of his grip.

'I'm sorry,' he said. 'I'm really sorry. I've been so stupid.'

She spun back to face him. 'Oh, Jamie, this is so ridiculous . . .'

'Of course it is. I've been really stupid.'

'No, you haven't. You've been upset. You're human, that's all . . . But you need to speak to me about it – whatever it is.'

'He thinks it's gout.'

For a few moments she was speechless. Then, when she had recovered her composure, she blurted out, 'You?'

'Yes, me. Gout.'

She was unsure what to say. She had been imagining something infinitely more serious – a cancer that had already widely metastasised; some other disease about which nothing could be done. Now she had to adjust to a disease that seemed utterly unlikely – a disease that some people even seemed to treat as comic. Gout was something that men – and it seemed to afflict men more than women – had in their sixties and beyond, a condition associated with excessive consumption of red wine, or particularly of port. It had all the wrong associations for somebody like Jamie, who was young and active, and who actually avoided port because it gave him a headache.

Jamie was now describing his symptoms. 'I had this really painful big toe,' he said. 'On my right foot.'

Isabel stared at him. 'Toe?'

'Yes, my big toe. It was as if somebody was putting needles into it – it was that sore. Red hot needles.'

She could not help herself: she was smiling. 'Your big toe?'

Jamie's frustration showed. He looked at her reproachfully. 'It's not funny.'

She struggled. Toes had always struck her as vaguely comic appendages, even if she knew how important they were for balance and for walking. She understood, too, that there were some people for whom toes had an erotic charge; she had never been able to understand that – but that was the whole point about the various fetishes that people entertained; they thrived in corners of the mind that were beyond the comprehension of others.

'No, it's not at all funny,' she said, and then laughed. She could not help herself.

Jamie glowered. 'You see. You see what it's like. People think that gout's a joke.'

She made a supreme effort. 'I don't. I really don't.'

'Then why did you laugh?' he asked accusingly.

She found it difficult to explain. It was not so much the comic aspects of toes that had amused her, but the words she herself had used: *it's not at all funny.* For most people, to have to say that something is unfunny raises an often irresistible temptation to smile or laugh. That might be because we know that the statement *it's not at all funny* is in itself funny, the humour being in our need to conceal our true feelings.

Jamie waited for his answer.

'It was spontaneous,' she said. 'Something serious can provoke a laugh. It's something to do with having to keep a straight face. The moment you do that, you lose your control and smile.'

'I don't see it.'

'Well, it happens,' she said. 'Haven't you seen those clips of newsreaders losing their self-control when reading the news on television? They have to report some dreadful event – a natural disaster, or something like that – and then they start to giggle uncontrollably.' She paused. She remembered seeing a film clip of a Dutch television presenter chairing a discussion of people who had been the victims of medical accidents and starting to laugh at the strange voice of a man he was interviewing. It was not at all funny: his guest had been left with a falsetto, and when he remonstrated with the interviewer, pointing out that he saw nothing funny about the situation, this had only made matters worse. It had cost the interviewer his job, but in one sense it had not been his fault – at times we cannot control laughter and one might as well fire somebody for sneezing at the wrong time.

Jamie sighed. 'All right, sorry. You didn't mean to laugh. But that's the whole problem: people smile when you say the word "gout". It's an old man's disease – and they think it's punishment for eating too much rich food and drinking too much wine.'

'And is it?'

He looked at her incredulously. 'Is it a punishment?'

'No, I didn't mean that. I meant: is that what causes it?'

Jamie shrugged. 'I read up a little bit. It's to do with an excessively high level of uric acid in the blood. That's to do with diet. There are high levels of things called purines in some foods.'

'And if you eat those, you can get gout?'

'Yes. They make crystals which lodge in a joint. They're like tiny razor needles. Hence the pain.'

Isabel winced. 'I'm sorry. I was very insensitive.'

He seemed to accept her apology, and went further than that. 'I'm the one who should apologise. It was ridiculous not to tell you right at the beginning.'

'I thought you had something terrible. I thought it was cancer.'

He took her hand, holding it, pressing it gently. 'I wasn't thinking straight. I suppose I've been ashamed. I've never been really ill, you see. I'm used to being very fit, and now . . .'

Isabel could understand how he felt. Jamie, not yet thirty,

was at an age at which physical imperfection was more often than not the problem of others. He took pride in his fitness – he went for regular runs along the canal towpath, he played squash with an old university friend a couple of times a month; he occasionally went to the gym at Craiglockhart. He carried not an ounce of spare flesh and he never needed to consult the doctor – and now, gout . . .

'You don't need to feel ashamed,' she said.

He nodded. 'I know. And yet, I've been dreading what you'd think – and what other people would think too.'

'Unnecessary.'

'I know it's unnecessary, but . . . but I don't want to have gout.'

She asked him how they treated it.

'There's a pill that stops the action of purines. But you may have to take the pill for ages. Forever – if you want to avoid future attacks.'

She glanced down at his feet. 'I didn't see you limping.'

'I tried to conceal it, but it was very sore when I walked. It still is.'

'My darling . . . '

He brushed aside her concern. 'Let's not talk about it any longer. I want to go and listen to . . . '

'Stravinsky?'

'No. I don't know why I said Stravinsky.'

Jamie began to make his way towards the door. She watched his gait; was there anything different about it? She decided that there was.

'You still don't want dinner?'

He shook his head. 'I'm not hungry. I hope you don't mind.'

She did, but she did not tell him. Instead, she said, 'I'm so sorry you've been upset. Can we talk about it later? Tomorrow, maybe?'

He nodded. 'Yes. Meantime . . . '

She waited.

'Meantime, I'll go and listen to some Arvo Pärt.'

She asked him whether he would like her to listen with him. Again he shook his head. 'You go ahead and have dinner. I'll be all right – really I will. And I'm sorry I was so touchy.'

He turned to kiss her – a light kiss on the cheek. She appreciated the gesture, but it was not enough. He might have come to sit in the kitchen with her, as he usually did when it was her turn to cook. But he did not suggest that, and she felt rebuffed – and saddened. They very rarely, if ever, had any sort of disagreement or fight. This exchange between them left her feeling raw; Jamie was worried and upset, yet she did not feel she could do anything to help him. He would have to work through his feelings on his gout; he would need to come to terms with it. She could not make that any easier, she suspected.

She would never have expected that he would react so badly to being ill. This, she decided, was his Achilles heel – his particular vulnerability. He had always seemed so strong, so unassailable, and now a weakness – an ordinary human weakness – had been exposed. The shock of the sudden row began to abate. Jamie, in her eyes, was so overwhelmingly perfect that this little thing, this flash of petulance, would soon be forgotten. He had not shown himself to be selfish or greedy, or anything of that sort; she could be grateful for that. And there were plenty of women who made much more unsettling discoveries about their lovers or husbands – who discovered that they had done something appalling, that they had a murky past, or were seeing somebody else: at least this was nothing like that. The thought brought relief; men were peculiar – that was all there was to it. You thought you understood the male psyche, and then suddenly and quite unexpectedly it revealed a quirk you would never have imagined: in this case, a concealed pride in physical perfection. She smiled at the thought: the key to understanding men, a friend had once said to her, is to remember that the boundaries between the man and the boy within were often blurred, and not every woman knew where they were. Once you knew, then you would understand much more, and could look benevolently on the more difficult ways of men – on their moods, their silences, their need to spend time together in the pursuit of their male pastimes. You could even begin to understand rugby and football, and other things that made up the secret life of men.

She went into the kitchen. *The secret life of men* . . . Why was it that women were so keen to shine a light on that life, to force men out into the open? Why drive men out of their sheds and into the light, where their secret pursuits would be exposed for what they were – boyish enthusiasms that meant nothing very much and were never a threat to women. She found herself shaking her head. It was hard being a man – having to pretend to be strong, having to bottle up your feelings, having to be afraid to cry. Poor men.

She opened the fridge and took out cold roast chicken that she had bought that morning from the butcher in Bruntsfield. She would have some of this, she thought, with a salad and some new potatoes. She would pour herself a glass of New Zealand white wine and sit at the table, her plate of chicken before her, and let things return to normal. Then she would look up gout online and see what was said about it.

She glanced out of the window. A movement in the garden directly outside had caught her eye; the swaying of the boughs of a shrub in the wind, she thought, but no, it was a flash of red-brown fur, the swing of a bushy tail, a brief hesitation.

Isabel stood quite still. Brother Fox seemed to notice movement more than anything else, and now she saw his eyes, two small buttons of intelligent black looking directly into the kitchen. What did he see? A table? Something behind the table – another piece of furniture in his eyes, perhaps, but one supporting a plate on which something intriguing lay.

She wondered whether he could smell the chicken. Air entered the kitchen through the window sashes – she knew that because draughts could be felt if one sat too close to the glass – and if that were the case, then surely smells could drift to the outside. Olfactory porosity, she thought, and wondered if such a term existed. The mingling of smells was another way of putting it . . . As if in confirmation, she saw Brother Fox raise his nose to the air and sniff.

'Roast chicken,' she whispered.

She did not feed Brother Fox because there was opposition amongst the neighbours. 'We don't want to encourage them,' was a common point of view; foxes, they felt, did not belong in towns and feeding them was an interference in the natural order of things. 'Nobody feeds them in the wild . . . '

Isabel did not share this animosity towards foxes. They led difficult lives, she felt; harried by farmers who accused them of taking their lambs and chickens – which they did, of course; seen off by dogs; pursued across hillsides by mounted huntsmen; chased away by householders; few people seemed to welcome them, although Isabel did. Animals, like people, did not ask to be who or what they were, and to make life difficult for others simply for being what they were seemed to her to be fundamentally unkind. Of course there were times when interests came into stark conflict – as when a great white shark attacked a surfer or a grizzly bear mauled a hiker – but these were the results of territorial incursions and could hardly be unexpected. Surfers, she had noticed, tended to recognise this and would show surprising understanding of the sharks that nibbled at their surfboards. She had seen a report of one young Australian saying, from his hospital bed, the punctures from the shark's teeth vivid on his calf, 'I was in his element – what can one expect?'

She was sure that Brother Fox would never bite anybody unless provoked. She had seen his teeth, and she imagined he could administer a sharp enough nip, but why would he do that unless cornered and forced to defend himself?

'You wouldn't . . . ' she heard herself whispering.

The fox had taken a step forward and was now closer to the window. Again he lifted his nose and sniffed.

'You know, don't you?' said Isabel. 'And yes, it smells delicious, doesn't it?'

It came upon her quickly, and without announcement: a sudden surge of sympathy for Brother Fox in his *foxness*. It was more than a simple understanding: it was a sense of being somehow with him, a sense of having been vouchsafed an insight into what had been an utterly alien world; she recalled Thomas Nagel's philosophical essay, 'What is it like to be a bat?' One might ask the same question here, she thought: What is it like to be a fox? Somehow, she felt she knew the answer. She would never be able to explain it, of course, but she was sure that she felt it.

She made up her mind. Moving slowly, so as not to disturb her visitor, she edged towards the kitchen door. This gave out directly onto the garden, and she pushed at it gently, hoping not to alarm Brother Fox. He was just around the corner, and when Isabel stepped out, holding before her a large and greasy chicken drumstick, it was as if she were presenting to him a peace offering – something to reassure him that her intentions were pacific.

When Brother Fox saw her, he lowered his head in a cringe and then, almost immediately, raised it again. He had picked up the whiff of chicken, and was interested.

'For you,' whispered Isabel, holding out her offering.

She waved it about, and then dropped it to the ground in front of her. Brother Fox watched. He looked at her again, as if assessing her intentions, and then suddenly darted forward to snatch the manna before him. There was a crunching sound as his teeth bit into the bone and then he vanished into the undergrowth, as quickly and unceremoniously as he had made his first appearance.

Isabel returned to the kitchen, pleased that she had been able to relieve Brother Fox's hunger. It was a small part of her meal, but for him it must have been an immense treat, a succulent addition to a diet that must have consisted, for the most part, of small rodents and sundry scraps. The encounter had pleased her – not only because she always liked to see Brother Fox, but also because she felt that the simple act of sharing had somehow diminished the pain of this world; it was not much to throw a chicken bone on the ground, and yet what an effect it had. She did not think this as one who might congratulate herself on having done a good act; rather she thought of it as might one who simply kept a tally of good and evil, the simplest of all possible Benthamites, and rejoiced in any diminution of suffering, whether animal or human. That seemed to justify the sacrifice of a single chicken drumstick.

There was no thanks from Brother Fox, and for a moment she felt resentful at his matter-of-fact indifference to her gift. But that was an absurd feeling – animals could not be expected to understand the notion of gift; or could they ... She thought of the many instances where animals showed affection for humans for what they had done for them. Was that not gratitude? She thought of St Jerome and the lion; the lion could so easily have eaten the saint – and many saints had suffered that fate, dispatched and consumed by lions; she thought of Greyfriars Bobby, that great-hearted Edinburgh terrier who had refused to leave his master's grave for years after his death; she thought of elephants said to have remembered those who had shown them kindness. Brother Fox was not in that league; like all foxes, he would behave much as foxes in traditional stories behaved – deceptively, slyly, and with consummate style – although she felt that somewhere, beneath his shy glances, there lay a recognition on his part that she meant him well.

She went back inside and ate her solitary meal, briskly and without relish. She reproached herself for not giving more chicken to Brother Fox; he had made such quick work of the drumstick and it would hardly have done much to fill his stomach. She had more than enough for herself, as Jamie had said that he would not have any. Jamie . . . She tried to put out of her mind their earlier conversation – it had been so out of character on his part, she told herself, that she should dismiss it altogether. His visit to the doctor had touched a raw nerve – that was all – and everything would be back to normal the next morning. Yet she found herself dwelling on his sudden touchiness about his physical limitations and wondering why she had never guessed that it existed. Were there other things about him – other secrets – that she knew nothing about?

After her dinner, she went into her study. Unread papers, each submitted to the *Review* with the silent prayers of its authors, were scattered on her desk. There was Professor van der Pompe's unrealistic proposals; there was a book review by none other than Professor Lettuce, signed at the foot of the page with the magisterial *Lettuce* with which he concluded all missives ... It was a ridiculous affectation, thought Isabel; bishops signed themselves by the name of their diocese, but that was a long tradition and things done out of respect for tradition were in a different category. And bishops, of course, would add their first name, which made it seem rather friendly. Dukes, too, signed themselves with the name of their dukedom, as in *Montrose* or *Argyll*, but this was no encouragement for mere professors of philosophy, such as Lettuce was, to call themselves *Lettuce* and nothing else. She smiled as she remembered the professor of history from that academic novel who answered the telephone with 'History speaking'. Perhaps Lettuce could do something similar, saying 'Reason' or 'Logic' when he picked up the telephone.

She sat down at her desk, pushing aside the pile of papers as she did so, but immediately retrieving them out of guilt. Papers may hang over you, may hedge you in, but you could not dispose of them by simply pushing them aside like some remote and unaccountable bureaucrat.

She had noted Rob McLaren's telephone number on a back page of her diary, and she now dialled it. He answered quickly – after little more than an initial ring – and she imagined him at a desk somewhere, waiting for a phone call. She had felt that he was lonely, and this quick answer seemed to confirm that. Lonely people sat by their telephones, she imagined, waiting for calls that in most cases never came.

He seemed pleased to hear from her. 'I'd hoped you might get in touch,' he said.

At first she found this strange, but then she remembered that she had said something about letting him know how she got on with her enquiries.

'I wanted to contact somebody we talked about,' she said. 'Andrea Murray. I wondered if you had her address.'

There was a silence at the other end of the line. Then he said, 'Her address?'

'Yes. You said that you saw her from time to time.'

Again there was a pause before he said, 'Why do you want to get in touch with her?'

Isabel thought she had made it clear to him why she was taking an interest in Tony MacUspaig, but she told him again. Halfway through, he interrupted her.

'I can give you an address,' he said. 'I'm not sure if it's current, but I do have one.'

She thanked him. 'Do you have it to hand?' she asked.

'No,' he replied. 'But I could find it.'

'Could you get back to me?' asked Isabel.

He seemed to hesitate. 'I tell you what: could you meet me tomorrow?'

'I suppose I could. But wouldn't it be easier to do this over the phone?'

His reply came quickly. 'I'd prefer to meet,' he said. 'If that's all right with you. What about lunch?'

Isabel reached out with her free hand to fiddle with one of the papers on her desk. Lunch? She saw no reason for them to meet for lunch simply to exchange an address. But then she reminded herself that Rob was doing her a favour, and that if he felt they needed to meet for lunch then she should accept gracefully. He seemed pleased with this, and suggested the Café St Honoré, a small French restaurant tucked away in a lane off Thistle Street.

Once she had rung off, she turned her attention to the papers on her desk. She glanced at her watch, and saw that it was now nine o'clock. She wondered whether she should seek out Jamie – she heard snatches of music off in the distance – but she decided that she would leave him to his own devices.

She would give half an hour or so to the papers, and then go up for an early night. If Jamie came in while she was still awake she would talk to him about his medical issue – if he did not, then it could wait until the morning, when problems tended to assume more manageable proportions anyway.

She picked up Lettuce's book review and began to read it. 'New contributions to the debate on causation are always to be welcomed,' Lettuce began, 'as long as they have something fresh to say, which this one most decidedly does not.' She gave an inward groan. She did not like discourteous reviews, especially, as in this case, when the book under review was written by somebody whom Isabel liked. Yet if she went back to Lettuce and asked him to tone it down, he would object. 'Written by a friend of yours?' he would ask, and she would have to reply, 'Yes, but that's not why I'd like you to be a little kinder.' That would bring a laugh – Lettuce's characteristic snort-like laugh, that made him sound to all intents and purposes like a braying donkey.

She sighed, and put the review to one side. One possibility was simply to lose it. Papers got lost of course – they did – and it was always possible that something could get so thoroughly lost that it would not turn up again until after the deadline for the next edition of the *Review*. If that were to happen, then it could well be that the following edition would just be too full to allow for Lettuce's review – now miraculously found again – to be published.

She allowed herself a smile as she dropped Lettuce's review into the waste-paper basket. She let it lie there for a few moments, and then, with a sigh, she reached forward and retrieved it. The trouble with having a conscience, she said to herself, is that it never sleeps.

9

Isabel arrived at the Café St Honoré earlier than she had anticipated. She had with her a copy of that morning's *Scotsman* newspaper, and while she waited for Rob she busied herself with her two favourite features, the letters column and the crossword. The letters column, which occupied a double-page spread in the newspaper, was the spiritual home of the combative and the contrary, those who would write letters on the topics of the day, disagreeing with one another, challenging received opinions, and generally provoking debate. Certain themes formed a constant refrain: Scottish independence, or otherwise; the hypocrisy of politicians; national debt; and in the background a long-running argument between secularists and theologians. Certain names cropped up with great regularity, and these correspondents, writing from familiar suburban addresses, had built up a following almost as large as that of the paper's regular columnists.

One of these – a favourite of Isabel's – had written that day on the subject of statues in public places and of the need for more statues of people whom the public actually recognised.

'There are far too many statues of long-forgotten generals and the like,' he wrote. 'These should be melted down and the metal used to cast statues of people who mean something to us today. For example, the current manager of the Scottish football team has no statue erected to him . . . '

Isabel rolled her eyes. The manager of the Scottish football team was important enough, in his way, but she had no idea who he was. Perhaps a statue of him might help people like her to recognise him, but that was not the point of statues. And there was, she thought, a strong argument against erecting statues of living people; a statue cast a person in metal and was intended to be a permanent monument – but what would happen if the person in question were to fall into disgrace, as public figures could do? Would the statue be scrapped, or moved into an obscure position, as had happened to statues of Lenin and others: as the past became hated, so too did its symbols and mementoes, left to the tender mercies of iconoclasts.

But it was not just statues that could fall victim to revisionism: street names, portraits, and even personal names could all become unpopular because of the changes in attitude. Isabel remembered her friend, Neville Chamberlain, who had stuck to his name in spite of its association with appeasement – his parents had believed the earlier Neville Chamberlain had done his best to avert war. But if there were few Adolfs in post-war Germany or Benitos in Italy, then that was understandable; it was safer, by far, to avoid giving children names that had an association with public figures.

She had moved on to a letter about education and the threat to the teaching of cursive script. There were schools where children were no longer being taught to write – and this, the correspondent said, should not be allowed to happen in Scotland. Isabel agreed; she wondered how people would be able to sign their name in the future if they could not write – by mark, perhaps, or a cross, as had been common in the days of widespread illiteracy. She found herself sharing the correspondent's outrage, and was mentally composing a letter herself when Rob arrived.

'Something interesting?' he asked, as he sat down opposite her at the table.

'A letter to the paper,' she said. 'It's about how some children are no longer being taught cursive script.'

He frowned. 'So they print everything? In capital letters?'

Isabel nodded. 'Or type. They're still being taught to type.'

He shrugged. 'It'll be the end of letters.'

She thought that letters had already ended. 'Nobody writes to anybody any longer.' She looked at him and smiled, wondering whether he received any letters. She thought not; the loneliness she had sensed before was definitely present.

It was as if he had heard her question. 'I very rarely get a letter these days,' he said. 'At least, not a personal one. But then, I don't write any.'

'Well, you could try,' she said. 'It would be like casting bread upon the waters. You would write off to somebody – out of the blue, perhaps – and see if you got anything back.'

He looked puzzled. 'To people I don't know? To public figures?'

'Why not? Not all of them would reply, I imagine, but some might.'

'But what would I say?'

Isabel said that public figures were used to getting letters that gave them advice on what to do. Then they wrote back to say 'Thank you for your suggestion'. 'You could also try writing to them to tell them how much you admire what they do – they like that. In fact, everybody likes to hear that . . . '

She stopped. Rob was looking at her with a puzzled expression on his face; her flights of fancy were not for everyone, she realised.

'I don't think I should do that,' he said.

'No, maybe not.' She looked at the menu. 'Perhaps we should decide on our food.'

A waitress arrived and took their order.

'I'm glad you came,' said Rob. 'I like having lunch. I find it a much more sociable meal than dinner.'

'It can be more relaxed,' said Isabel. 'Now, Andrea Martin . . . '

He inclined his head. He did not seem to be particularly interested.

'I've discovered a new restaurant,' he said. 'It's in an old timber shop – very convenient for the Lyceum Theatre and the Usher Hall. You may know it.'

Isabel did. 'Yes, I've been there. You mentioned you could give me an address . . . '

This time he reached into his pocket and took out a small piece of blue paper, folded in two. 'It's there,' he said. 'And her phone number.'

Isabel opened the note.

'That's her Edinburgh address,' he said. 'She has a place outside town – out in East Lothian, but I don't think she spends much time there.'

Isabel tucked the piece of paper into the pocket of her blouse.

'I hope you succeed,' he said. 'I hope you succeed in getting Connie to see reason.'

'Not even reason,' said Isabel. 'Just to see danger.'

He nodded. 'Well, let me know how you get on.' He paused. 'But you must tell me a bit more about yourself. All I know is that you're a philosopher and you edit a journal.'

Isabel smiled at him. 'Which is more than I know about you.'

He raised a finger. 'You first.'

'All right. I've spent most of my life in Edinburgh. My father was Scottish, my mother American. I went to Cambridge. I studied abroad. I married an Irishman and then thought better of it. Then I married a Scotsman. I have two children – both boys. Is that enough?'

She found herself stressing the word *married*. There was something about this meeting that made her acutely uncomfortable. There had been no reason why he could not have sent her the details she wanted, rather than hand them over like a spy passing classified information. And why lunch? She had assumed that there was something more he wanted to tell her, but he had simply passed over the paper and then changed the subject. Now it occurred to her that he had some other agenda; that this, in his eyes at least, was a date.

He answered her question. 'It tells me something, but not all that much. What do you read? Do you like Italy? Have you ever been to India? Do you have another job? All those things that one wants to find out about somebody.'

She squirmed. 'But those are things that come out naturally – in the course of conversation. One doesn't lay it all out on the table.'

He appeared to accept this. 'Perhaps not. But perhaps you could answer just one of them – do you have another job?'

She shook her head. 'What I do may not sound all that taxing, but it keeps me busy enough, you know.'

He absorbed this and then said, 'But, forgive me for asking – how does your journal manage to keep going? You told me it had a very small circulation – how does it pay its way? You must take a salary, I assume . . . '

She answered before she had time to think. 'I support it . . . ' She trailed off.

'Ah,' he said. 'You're the backer.'

'You could call it that, I suppose.'

He adjusted the cutlery before him so that it was perfectly aligned with the pattern of the tablecloth.

'Every publication needs an angel,' he said. 'They all need somebody to support them. Newspapers, magazines – they have such a battle.'

'I suppose it helps in this life to have somebody to pay the bills.'

When she said this, she noticed that his face broke into a smile. 'If only . . . '

She laughed. 'I could do with that.'

He threw her a sideways glance. 'Surely not. Surely you don't need that.'

She looked away. She decided that there was something about him that she did not like and she was trying to decide what it was. On the surface, he was good company – easy in his manner, softly spoken, good to look at; but underneath that there was something else, and she decided that it was intrusiveness. He was one of those people who seemed just a little bit too interested in you, a little bit too prying.

The waitress returned with their orders. He had asked for a glass of house wine, and this was now poured for him; Isabel could not take wine at lunchtime if she wanted the afternoon to be productive. He seemed disappointed by this. 'Surely a little drop? Something light?'

She shook her head. 'No, thank you. I find if I have a glass of wine at midday, it makes me sleepy. Then the afternoon is ruined.'

'Come on,' he urged. 'Special occasion.'

She stared at him. 'I'm sorry – I'm not with you. Is this really a special occasion?'

He looked at her coyly. 'Well, a lunch *à deux*. This place.'

She moved back in her chair. She had been holding her water glass, and she put this down on the table with a thud.

'I'm sorry, but I think there may be a misunderstanding.'

He remained impassive. He reached for his glass. 'This is a white Burgundy. Do you like Burgundy?'

She pushed herself further back. 'I really must be going,' she said. 'I have a young child, you see.'

He was staring at the tablecloth. He began to say something. 'Please don't think that . . . '

His tone was wretched – like that of a boy caught red-handed in some misdemeanour.

She hesitated, and almost changed her mind. But then she decided: there was no sense in prolonging an encounter that had got to this point.

'You've been very kind,' she said. 'I wouldn't want you to think me rude.'

He shook his head. 'I don't. Of course I don't. I'm the one who has been rude.'

He was still seated, and she was looking down on him.

'My life is a bit lonely,' he said. 'I'm not looking for sympathy, but . . . but the fact of the matter is I'm on my own and sometimes I wish it could be different.' He looked up at her. 'I don't expect you'll know about that.'

'Loneliness? Of course I know what loneliness is. But there are ways of dealing with it.' She paused. 'Listen, Rob, you don't ask married women out to lunch. You just don't.' She paused again. 'Surely you must realise that?'

He looked at her helplessly. 'I'm bad at these things.'

She wanted to laugh, and she did. 'Well, at least you see it.'

The tension of the previous few minutes now dissipated. The irritation that Isabel had felt now disappeared, to be replaced by a sort of pity – a fond pity. She sat down again.

'Let's eat our lunch,' she said. 'I think we both know where we stand, so there's no reason why we can't enjoy our meal on civil terms.'

He nodded eagerly. 'Thank you,' he said. 'And I hope you'll accept my apology for my . . . for my thoughtlessness.'

'Let's forget it, yup. Now, I told you a bit about myself – you tell me about you.'

'It's not very interesting, I'm afraid.'

'I'm sure it is.' She took a sip of water. 'I think there are very few personal histories that are devoid of interest. So try me.'

'My father was a diplomat,' said Rob McLaren. 'He came from up north – from Forres – and studied German in Edinburgh. He was good at languages – he had Russian and Arabic too, and so he got into the diplomatic service when it was pretty competitive. He met my mother at university and they were married when they were both quite young. They had me, and then my sisters – both of whom married Dutchmen; their husbands are cousins. One lives in The Hague and the other in Amsterdam. They're both lawyers – the husbands, that is.

'My father was posted all over the place. You'd think that because of his German and Russian they would have sent him to Bonn or Moscow, but no, that's not the way the Foreign Office works: we were in Delhi, Jakarta, Asunción – all sorts of places. I was actually born in Jakarta, then we went to Delhi when I was three.'

Isabel watched him as he spoke. She saw that he had cut himself while shaving that morning – there was a small nick on his chin and a fleck of blood on his collar. She found the sight curiously poignant: people prepared themselves for the world – combed their hair, washed their face, chose their clothing – all of this because of human vulnerability and the desire to be approved of by others, to fit in, to be loved.

'Do you remember India?' she asked. 'Were you old enough?'

'I was six when we left, and yes, I do remember a bit. Not very much.' He sat back in his chair. 'What about you? What was your first memory?'

'Oh, when I was three or four, I think. I remember throwing a doll out of the car window.'

He laughed. 'Really? And you felt . . . '

'Guilty,' said Isabel. 'It was my first experience of guilt.' She smiled. 'I've been feeling guilty ever since.'

'Really?'

'Well, I exaggerate, I suppose. But I do feel guilty about things – about not doing enough, about not answering letters as quickly as I should, about letting my study get out of control. All the usual things.'

'You shouldn't feel that way,' he said.

'I try not to,' said Isabel. She wanted to get off the subject of herself. 'But carry on – what do you remember about India?'

'I remember having a birthday party in the garden. I remember one of our dogs being shot by the vet because they thought he had been in contact with rabies. I remember the vet coming and not wanting to give him an injection because he didn't want to risk being bitten. I remember his taking a revolver out of his bag and shooting the dog. I wasn't meant to see it, but in the excitement nobody noticed me around and so I witnessed the whole thing. I must have been about five, I suppose.'

Isabel winced. 'What a terrible thing for a child to see.'

Rob nodded. 'I suppose it was. And that's why I remember it, when I've forgotten so much else.' He was staring at the tablecloth. 'I remember other, better things, of course. I remember a toy plane I had, made out of pressed tin. It was painted yellow and through the windows you could see the one-dimensional people inside and also the pilot, who had a tiny painted moustache. I wanted it to fly, I wanted that so much, but it was an earthbound toy. It could be propelled along the ground by its clockwork motor – perpetual taxi-ing.

'I started going to school in India. I went to a place for the children of diplomats. I remember very little about it other than that it smelled of sick. The children were sick in the corridor and although they cleaned it up, there was always a lingering smell. Even today, that smell triggers memories for me of that school and of the way the sun used to slant in the windows at an angle and of how there was a picture of Gandhi in the corridor.

'Of course, as I got older it became more difficult for me to be schooled in the places where my father was posted. So when I was eight I was sent to a small prep school in East Lothian. I was rather young for it, but I was actually rather happy there.'

'Eight is terribly young to go off to boarding school.' She imagined sending Charlie off four years from now; she could not see herself doing that.

But Rob said he thought he'd thrived there. 'It was a kind place. They allowed us all sorts of treats – I suppose because they must, at one level, have felt sorry for us. We were encouraged to take up all sorts of hobbies – woodwork, collecting things, birdwatching. They kept us busy.

'Then, when I was twelve, I had to go off to senior school. My parents were doing a second tour of duty in India then – my father was looking after the consulate in Madras, as it was then.

I went out just before I was due to start at my next boarding school. I remember it as a sad trip. I was aware that something was coming to an end, but I wasn't sure what was next. I asked if I could stay in India. I didn't want to return to this country. I remember weeping and weeping, but to no avail. I dreaded the thought of what lay ahead, but my parents just tried to jolly me along. They said that everything would be fine, that I would enjoy the next place and that before I knew it the time would have arrived to come back for the summer holidays. They said we could go up to Shimla together or even make a trip out to the Andaman Islands. I was inconsolable, though, and wouldn't be bought off with promises.'

Rob paused. 'I can't imagine you'll be interested in all this.'

'But I am,' Isabel assured him. 'I'd like you to go on.'

He seemed uncertain. 'I don't know if I want to.'

She was not sure how to respond to that. She had formed the impression that there was something he wanted to talk about, but that he was finding it hard to let go. There were, she thought, years of repression to overcome and that would hardly happen over lunch in the Café St Honoré. And Rob, she decided, was not straightforward; he was a vulnerable and evidently lonely man, one who was desperate for affection but who misread social signals. Everything about him suggested that she should keep her distance.

'It's up to you,' she said. 'I don't want to press you.'

He seemed to make up his mind. 'No, I'll tell you. But stop me if you like.'

She nodded her assent. I've started this, she said to herself; this is my fault.

'The school I went to,' he continued, 'was in Perthshire. It's one of those expensive Scottish boarding schools where everybody wears a kilt on Sunday and where there are compulsory outings into the hills and mountains. It was an all-boys school in those days; it's different today – different in every respect.'

He stopped. 'I don't think I should burden you.'

Isabel opened her mouth to say something, but he had already continued.

'But you did ask me. I wouldn't otherwise . . . '

'Of course not. But don't if you feel awkward. I wouldn't want to upset you.'

'It's too late for that,' he said softly. 'What happened, happened.'

She said nothing; the casualties of past cruelties were still there amongst us; the least we could do was to listen to them.

'Not a day goes past – not a day – that I don't think of that place. Of what happened there, of what they did to us.'

She still said nothing. She had never understood why men – or boys – in groups were so inventive about finding ways of hurting one another.

'I've tried to make a go of my life,' he went on. 'And I know that there's no point in going over the past – rehashing it. I know that one should just get on with living. I really have tried, you know.'

'Of course you have.'

Then he said, 'Sorry. I didn't mean to . . . ' He was finding it difficult to talk.

'We all have painful memories,' she said gently. 'Every one of us, I suppose, has something that's just very painful to us.' She thought of John Liamor, and of what he had done to her – the deception, the indifference to her feelings. She thought of how she herself, as a twelve-year-old, had joined in the teasing of a girl called Morag Maclean, who wore her hair in plaits and had a speech impediment. They had called her M . . . M . . . M . . . Morag and had tied a notice to one of her plaits saying, *Pull here to get a word out.* She added, 'And shameful, too. Shameful things we've done ourselves.'

'I know. I know.'

She could see that he was struggling to remain in control of himself. It had been the same with Jamie and that sad little episode over his visit to the doctor: it was exactly the same, she thought – these were both instances of the loneliness of men and their battle to be strong. On a sudden sympathetic impulse, Isabel reached out and placed a hand on top of his, on the table. It was a gesture of solidarity between the sexes; a woman who knew, and felt, what a man was going through and wanted to say: *We understand.*

A young woman walked past – she had been lunching in the downstairs section of the restaurant. She paused as she passed their table, glancing at Isabel. Isabel tried to remember where she knew this woman from, but it would not come to her. She was, thought Isabel, somebody she had come across incidentally – somebody with whom a brief conversation had been shared at a party; somebody who was a friend of a friend, or a member of a committee. She did not think that she knew her other than in that casual way.

Isabel was thinking of Rob's story. For her part, the woman appeared to think that perhaps she was mistaken in thinking she recognised Isabel; she moved on.

'I shouldn't have told you all this,' said Rob. 'I'm not looking for pity.'

'No, I'm sure you're not. And you know, talking through things is often the best thing to do.'

'Maybe,' said Rob.

'No, definitely,' said Isabel.

She took her hand away.

10

Jamie had been busy with bassoon lessons all day and was tired when he came back that evening.

'I had to teach that boy again today,' he said. 'Gordon Christie. I don't want to be uncharitable, but he's utterly hopeless. It's something to do with his ear – he can't seem to hear any differences of pitch. Everything sounds the same to him, or so it seems.'

Isabel had heard Gordon Christie being complained of before. 'Is he tone deaf?'

Jamie scratched his head. 'I'm not sure if there's such a thing as complete tone deafness. I suspect that just about everybody can tell that notes are different, even if they can't work out which is which. No, I don't think he's hearing properly.'

Isabel wondered whether he had spoken to the school nurse, but he had not.

'It occurred to me his ears might be blocked,' Jamie continued. 'So I discreetly tried to take a look. And you know what? I noticed that there was wax – I saw it. You could actually see the wax in his ear.'

Isabel shuddered. She was squeamish about wax – and ears, now that she came to think of it. 'Did you say anything?'

He shook his head. 'I didn't want to. Wax in the ears is a bit personal, don't you think?'

'I do. Somebody was talking about ear candling the other day. I didn't enjoy the conversation. And I didn't know even that "candle" was a verb ... but I suppose anything can be a verb these days.'

Jamie was intrigued. 'Ear candling?'

Isabel explained. 'You lie on your side and stick the end of a long hollow candle into your ear. Then somebody lights the candle, and it draws air up through its hollow centre, creating a suction effect.'

'Which gets the wax out?'

Isabel nodded. 'So people claim. But there are those who claim it's nonsense and that what you think is ear wax is actually candle wax. It's a bit like homeopathic medicine – highly unlikely and with no empirical evidence to support it.'

'But there's always a placebo effect, isn't there?' Jamie was thinking of an uncle of his, who always swore by homeopathic remedies. He was now dead.

'I don't see how a placebo can clear your ears of obstruction,' Isabel pointed out.

'Oh well ... ' He smiled at her. 'Let's not talk about Gordon Christie's ears. What about you? What did you do today - apart from look after your two children, organise the house, run the *Review*, think great thoughts, and so on?' His smile broke into a broad grin. 'I'd never accuse you of having too little to do.'

'This and that. Nothing special. Grace helped with the boys. She wants to monopolise them.'

She flushed as she spoke. She had told Jamie about her

previous meeting with Rob, but this last occasion had been very different, coloured by the fact that he had entertained those embarrassing hopes of an affair. She could have told Jamie about this, but somehow she felt awkward about it. It would in no way reflect badly on her that she had been the recipient of unwelcome attentions, but she just did not want to talk to him about it. And that fact itself added to her discomfort: she had reproached Jamie for not talking to her about his visit to the doctor, and now here she was doing much the same thing – keeping something from him.

It was still open to her to qualify her reply. She could have said, 'Nothing special. Apart from lunch with Rob McLaren.'

She could have done that; she had lunch with various people from time to time, particularly with people associated with the *Review*. Rob had nothing to do with that side of her life, of course, but it was relevant to this other thing she was doing – this other thing that Jamie knew all about.

'A day in your study,' said Jamie. It was a statement, not a question, yet she answered it.

'Yes, mostly.'

Now it was too late, and she frowned as she thought of what she had just done. *I have lied to him*, she thought. *I did not spend the day in my study.* And then she asked herself why she had done this. It crossed her mind that it was some form of subconscious revenge for his having gone to the doctor without telling her; often our conscious acts are that petty – stratagems pursued to compensate for the things that have happened to us – small acts of getting even, acts of punishment.

She pulled herself together. 'Actually, I did go out. I went out to get hold of an address. It was to do with this Connie Macdonald business.'

Jamie did not show much interest. 'Progress?' he asked, although she could tell that he was not especially keen to hear just what progress – if any – had been made.

'Rob McLaren,' she began. 'He gave me . . . '

But Jamie was taking off his jacket. 'I'm feeling very sweaty,' he said. 'I don't know why, but I always come back from the Academy feeling a bit hot and sticky. I'm glad that it's the end of term.' He tossed his jacket onto a chair. Men, thought Isabel, never hang up their clothing.

'He's a bit odd . . . ' Isabel began.

'Plenty of people are a bit odd,' said Jamie. 'But I'm going to take a shower. I'll cook this evening, if you like.' He moved off. 'I hate feeling sticky like this – I really hate it.'

She watched him leave the room. At least she had told him, even if she had said nothing about Rob's surprising behaviour. She could not bring herself to do that, but she still imagined that it would make no difference to anything. There must be many women, Isabel thought, who failed to mention to their husbands that somebody had made a pass at them; and many men, as well, who would not mention it if a woman showed an interest in them. Jamie, she imagined, must have people giving him second glances every day, but he never mentioned this. Perhaps he thought it unimportant – part of the background noise that went with being as good-looking as he was. She remembered that Auden had said something about that – about the blessed not caring what angle they were regarded from, having nothing to hide.

This conversation took place in the kitchen. Charlie was on the floor, constructing something from a set of plastic building bricks; Magnus, who had just woken up, was in his cot, preoccupied with a colourful mobile of fur-covered blocks.

'If Daddy's going to have a shower,' said Charlie, 'then I

want one too. I want to shower with Daddy.' And then he added. 'And with Mummy.'

'We could all have a shower together,' said Jamie. 'And Magnus as well. We can't leave little Magnus out.'

Jamie caught Isabel's eye. 'Bonding exercise,' he whispered.

'Magnus smells,' said Charlie. 'But all right: all of us.'

It took time to get the water temperature right, and then, holding Magnus to her, Isabel stepped gingerly into the shower. Jamie held Charlie at first, but then the small boy wanted to stand on his own, clinging to his father's leg. The water fell upon them, gathered in rivulets, then disappeared amongst feet and toes. Jamie smiled at Isabel. 'What families are all about,' he said.

She returned his smile. 'A family that showers together, stays together.'

He laughed. 'That's probably true,' he said.

'It's definitely true,' she said.

From down below, Charlie made his contribution. 'Let's put Magnus down the drain,' he said.

Cat asked her to help in the delicatessen again the following day. She was apologetic about it – as she always was – and Isabel agreed to put in three or four hours – as she always did. It suited Grace, of course, for whom it would be an excuse to lavish attention on Magnus. She had found a café in Church Hill that particularly welcomed mothers and infants, and had taken to wheeling Magnus there in his pushchair and joining in the discussions that took place on diet and teething and sleeping patterns. Grace was an expert in all of these things, and announced to the other customers of the café that she was a governess. This was not true; Grace was a housekeeper, but took a liberal view of her position and occasionally described herself as, variously, a house manager, a 'butleress', and a life-style assistant. Her job included aspects of all of these, at least in so far as she had expanded it over the years, and Isabel was perfectly happy for Grace to announce herself as she wished. Isabel wanted Grace to be happy in her work and if it helped her to enhance the description of her job, then that harmed nobody. It was a common enough practice, after all, and had led to an inflation of position resulting in the disappearance of many established roles; salesmen had long since vanished, to be replaced by sales or retail consultants; clerks had become IT operatives; and bank tellers were account advisers or associate managers. It was all obfuscation, of course, but it was, Isabel decided, *generous* obfuscation.

Cat needed help because she had been invited to a salami fair in Glasgow. 'Don't laugh,' she said. 'It's a sort of trade fair for salami people. It's important.'

'I'd never laugh at those who profess to love salamis,' said Isabel.

Cat looked at her sideways. 'I'm not joking,' she said.

'Nor am I,' said Isabel. 'There is nothing wrong in dedicating yourself to salamis.'

This brought a reproachful look from Cat. 'I don't think you take this seriously enough . . . '

'Take salamis seriously enough? Of course I do.'

'You sound very condescending, you know.'

Isabel refuted this. 'I am *not* condescending. And I'd remind you that I *have* agreed to help you out today, but if you'd prefer me not to . . . '

'Oh no,' said Cat quickly. 'I'm grateful to you – I really am. It's just the way you go on about salamis makes me think—'

'Let's forget about it,' said Isabel. 'Tell me what's going on today. Who's on?'

'Eddie's coming in shortly and there's a new person.'

'A new employee? Full time?'

'Yes,' said Cat. 'You know how you were telling me I was understaffed? Well, I've found somebody. Peg. She started yesterday.'

Cat gave Isabel a triumphant look before continuing, 'She's very good. She has a degree in history. She's going to be in charge of the pastas and the filled rolls.'

It was typical of Cat, thought Isabel, to conflate history with pasta and filled rolls. 'Well, her degree in history will help,' she said, and then, noticing her niece's dismayed expression, added quickly, 'I wasn't being condescending. I really wasn't. I just meant to say that it's good to have well-educated staff in any business involving people. It just helps, doesn't it?'

Cat made a non-committal noise.

'Where did you find her?' asked Isabel.

'I met her,' said Cat. 'We were chatting and she mentioned that she was looking for a job. It was that simple.'

'Where did you meet her?' asked Isabel.

Cat ignored the question. 'She's got a natural feeling for filled rolls.'

Isabel smiled, wondering how such a feeling manifested itself. Perhaps it was in the eyes; perhaps in the way one *looked* at filled rolls.

'Where did you meet her?' she asked again.

'Oh, somewhere or other,' said Cat. 'I can't remember.'

Isabel noticed that as she answered, Cat's cheeks became red. It was as clear a sign as any that her niece knew her answer was unsatisfactory. While it was true that we might forget where or how we met old friends – friends we had had for years, for decades – that was not the case with friends of a more recent vintage. Cat remembered perfectly well where she had met her new assistant, but did not want to tell Isabel. Such reticence, annoying as it was, was nothing new: there had been other occasions on which Cat had been reluctant to reveal even the most insignificant piece of information – such as where she had bought a particular item for the delicatessen – and had claimed not to remember it. Isabel thought this entirely unbelievable amnesia was something to do with power: knowing something, but yet not disclosing it to another, made one feel stronger than the person denied the information.

'I look forward to meeting her, anyway,' said Isabel. 'I've always thought you made life more difficult for yourself by being short-handed.'

Cat nodded absently. 'Maybe. Anyway, if you could show her anything she needs to know. She's still finding her feet.'

Isabel confirmed that she would be happy to do this and set about the task of cleaning the work surfaces. This was something that Cat was lax about, and Eddie disliked doing. Yet it was high on the list of must-dos in running any food business, and Isabel was very conscious of safety issues. She read copies of the trade magazine, the *Grocer*, which she found lying about in Cat's office and paid particular attention to the occasional report of a health-related prosecution. She left the magazine on Cat's desk, turned, in warning, to the relevant page, but she was not sure whether the message had been received and, if it had, whether it was ever acted upon.

Eddie came in as she was finishing the wiping of the cheese boards. He had not been expecting Isabel to be working that day and his pleasure at finding her there showed itself in a broad grin.

'I'm glad you're helping out today,' he said to her, his voice lowered so that Cat might not hear. '*She* expects me to do everything while *she* goes off to Glasgow to meet all those salami freaks.'

Isabel suppressed a smile. Eddie's language could be adolescent, but it was sometimes acutely descriptive. *Salami freaks* ... She could see what he meant: they must be odd – they had to be – to take such a strong interest in sausages. In fact, it was glaringly obvious to anybody who had the slightest inkling of what Freud would have said on the subject.

Eddie was tying on his apron, wiping his hands on the material.

'Eddie, I wonder whether you shouldn't wash your hands rather than wipe them ... '

It was the gentlest of reproofs, and it failed to meet its target. 'They're not dirty,' he said. 'I'm fine, thanks.'

Isabel tried again. 'I didn't say they were dirty, it's just that—'

Eddie interrupted her, leaning forward to whisper into Isabel's ear. 'Have you heard about Pig?'

'Pig?'

'Yes, Pig – or at least that's what I call her. She calls herself Peg. She's the new assistant.'

Isabel glanced across the shop to see if Cat could hear the conversation. But she was now on the phone, and Isabel heard the word *salami*. Cat would not overhear what she and Eddie were saying.

'I don't think that's very kind.'

'Well, it's accurate, even if it's not all that kind. Wait until you see her.'

Isabel frowned. 'What do you mean?'

Eddie lowered his voice even further. 'I mean she looks just like one.' He pointed to a large cured ham on the chilled counter.

Isabel stared at him disapprovingly. 'You're being really juvenile, Eddie.'

He shrugged. 'I can't help it if I notice these things.'

She tried another tack. 'I take it you don't like her?'

'No, I don't. Not really. She keeps telling me what to do. She thinks that she's senior to me because she's a few years older – that's all. And she doesn't know anything, Isabel – I swear she knows hardly anything.'

Isabel pointed out that Cat took the view that Peg was good at making filled rolls. It was an important part of their business, and if she had a talent for that, then surely that was something.

'Anybody can make filled rolls,' said Eddie scornfully. 'But can anyone slice meat really thin? No, they can't. I'd like to see her try.'

Isabel tried again. 'Perhaps she doesn't know she's being bossy. Sometimes people don't realise that, and others get the impression they're trying to tell them what to do, when they aren't.' She paused. 'I think that maybe you should give her a bit more of a chance.'

'It won't make any difference and . . . ' He looked out of the large display window. 'And here she is. Look – see that girl who looks like a pig? That's her.' He leaned forward again. 'And here's another thing: Cat thinks Pig's the best thing since sliced bread. You should see the way they look at one another. You should just see it.'

He turned away, and the door opened. Peg stood in the doorway for a few moments before approaching Isabel.

'You're Isabel, aren't you?'

Isabel smiled at the young woman standing before her. She judged her to be a few years younger than Cat – perhaps in her mid- to late twenties. She was attractive, with an open, slightly freckled face and a slightly retroussé nose, and was dressed in dark blue jeans and a white cheesecloth blouse. The blouse was decorated with a line of delicately embroidered flowers around the collar. Eddie's comments about her appearance were, thought Isabel, not only immature but inaccurate.

'I'm sorry I'm a bit late,' said Peg. 'My bus broke down. They had to get another one.'

Isabel reassured her that she was not late, she herself having arrived only a few minutes earlier.

Eddie's muttered comment was just audible. 'Yes, but you're not paid.'

Isabel turned to glare at him, and he looked away guiltily. Isabel glanced in Peg's direction, wondering whether she had heard. She decided she had not – either that, or Peg was not going to show that the provocative comment had reached her.

Cat came out of the office and greeted Peg. Isabel saw that Eddie, although busying himself with a task behind the counter, was watching the two young women.

Cat reached forward and took Peg's right hand. She gave it a squeeze. 'Everything all right?' she asked.

Peg nodded.

'Isabel will be able to help if you need to find out about anything,' said Cat, smiling at Isabel. 'She knows everything.'

'Well, hardly,' demurred Isabel.

'Just ask her,' said Cat. 'You'll be fine.'

Isabel saw the effect that this had on Eddie; she realised that he would resent the implication that Peg should turn to her for advice rather than ask him – and yet he was a full-time employee who had put in far more hours than Isabel had.

'I'm sure Eddie will be able to help too,' Isabel said.

Cat turned towards Eddie. 'Oh, yes, of course. There's Eddie too. Of course. Eddie's dealt with most things.'

Too little, too late, thought Isabel. She thought that Cat had been tactless, but then she had always shown a lack of tact in her dealings with people.

Cat nodded towards her office, and Peg followed her. The office door closed.

Eddie caught Isabel's eye. 'See?' he whispered.

It was a busy morning. While Eddie and Isabel dealt with a stream of customers, Peg spent her time preparing the filled rolls that were the staple of their lunchtime trade. Isabel surreptitiously inspected one of the rolls; it had smoked salmon, boiled egg and lumpfish caviar at its centre. Cat was right: it had been made by someone with a real feeling for filled rolls – and yes, it looked good. At eleven o'clock they entered their slack period – too late for morning shoppers and yet too early for the lunchtime rush. Isabel suggested a coffee break, and when Peg accepted, asked Eddie to look after the counter.

He agreed to do this, but not without a reproachful glance at Isabel. She ignored it; she was still cross with Eddie for his remarks about Peg. And yet she had to agree that the greeting Cat had given Peg was warmer than she might have expected. That was no excuse, though, for Eddie to coin a hurtful nickname, nor did it justify the slightly huffy, slightly distant attitude towards Peg that he had maintained since her arrival that morning.

After Isabel had made coffee for both of them, they sat down at a table by the window. They were far enough away from Eddie to be able to talk freely, and Isabel decided to broach the subject of Eddie's attitude right away.

'You may have noticed that Eddie's a bit sour this morning,' she said.

Peg's expression gave nothing away. 'Oh,' she said.

Isabel persisted. 'I don't know if Cat told you anything about him.'

'A bit.'

'He's a nice young man, but he's had a tough time in the past. Things are much better now. But he's still a bit insecure.'

'I see.' And then, after a few moments, she added, 'I'd picked up his negativity. But it doesn't matter.'

Isabel took a sip of her coffee. 'Have you and Cat known one another long?' she asked.

Peg played with her spoon. 'A few months, I suppose. Not long.'

Isabel tried to sound casual as she posed the next question – the one that Cat had avoided answering. 'How did you meet?'

Peg put down her spoon and lifted her coffee cup to her lips. Isabel waited. The coffee cup was placed back on its saucer. 'Oh, I forget. I think it was through somebody, but I can't really remember.'

But you can, thought Isabel. It's just that you don't want to tell me.

She was now intrigued, but she understood that she would get nowhere with any further questions on that topic. There were other avenues to be explored, and now she asked Peg about where she was from. Surely that could not be classified information, and she could hardly say that she had forgotten.

'Haddington,' she said.

Haddington was in East Lothian – the centre of a rich farming area. It was the sort of town to which well-heeled Edinburgh people drifted on their retirement while its own young people migrated in the opposite direction. It was a comfortable, safe place, sure of itself and its values.

'You came to live in Edinburgh when you went to university?'

Peg looked at her quizzically. 'Cat's told you about me?'

'Yes,' said Isabel. 'Not very much, but she did mention that you studied history.'

Isabel noticed that Peg now relaxed, the information that Cat had not told Isabel very much seeming to reassure her.

'I studied here in Edinburgh,' Peg said. 'Scottish history. Then I had a job as a researcher in the Scottish Parliament. I did that for three years.'

Isabel asked what that had entailed.

'Anything the members wanted to find out. They asked for all sorts of stuff. Crime statistics, trade figures, sea temperatures off Orkney in the winter . . . ' She smiled. 'A lot of it was pretty obscure, and I can't imagine they used it for anything very much. But sometimes you heard the facts and figures you'd unearthed being spouted in parliament. I enjoyed it.'

'But you gave it up?'

'I wanted to try something different. So I took a job with a television company. They made historical documentaries – sometimes rather good ones. I really enjoyed that, but . . . '

Isabel waited. 'But?'

'But it didn't work out in the end. So that was that.'

There was a note of finality in her voice, and Isabel realised that she was not being encouraged to enquire further. 'So this job cropped up?'

'Yes. Cat told me she was looking for somebody and I was free. So here I am.'

It was a brief *curriculum vitae*, adequate as far as it went, but Isabel felt there was nothing personal in it. There was so much she wanted to know, including where Peg lived. Now she asked her.

Peg took a sip of coffee. 'In the New Town.'

Isabel nodded. 'Nice.'

'Yes.'

There was nothing more; at least, nothing more was being offered. Peg was now gazing out of the window, as if looking for something in the street. Isabel felt a sudden desire to wave a hand in front of her in a crude attempt at attracting attention. 'Whereabouts?' she asked.

Peg continued to stare out of the window. She did not answer Isabel's question but said, instead, 'I like this part of town. I like the small shops.'

'Oh yes,' said Isabel. 'Small shops . . . ' She felt a sudden irritation. Conversation was not only an art – it was sometimes a duty. If you were drinking coffee with another, then you had a right to attention: for them not to engage properly was a discourtesy.

She decided to give it one more try. 'Do you share a flat down there?' she asked.

'Yes.'

That was all: yes. There was still nothing about where the flat was, nor about whom she shared it with. But then it occurred to Isabel that this reticence on Peg's part had arisen because she understood why Isabel was prying. If Peg knew that these seemingly innocent questions – small talk really – concealed an intrusive agenda, then she might feel entitled to give monosyllabic answers. *And what exactly is my agenda?* Isabel asked herself. The answer embarrassed her in its simplicity: to find out whether there was a boyfriend. She wanted to know that because she had tried over the years to understand Cat and her difficulties with men and it was possible that the key to understanding that issue had evaded her – just as it might have evaded Cat herself. She wanted Cat to be happy; of course she did, and if there had been anything in her attitude or her expectations that had made it difficult for Cat to find that happiness then she was truly sorry.

'We should get back to work,' said Isabel.

'Yes,' said Peg, standing up to take the two coffee cups to the small kitchen behind the delicatessen.

Eddie came over to Isabel. 'What were you and Pig talking about?' he whispered.

'Don't call her that.'

'All right then, Peg.'

Isabel gave a non-committal answer. 'This and that.'

'You know what I think?' said Eddie, sniggering. 'She and Cat are an item.'

Isabel looked him in the eye. 'So?'

He seemed surprised. 'What about all those men of hers? And what do they do in the office? Why do they close the door?'

Isabel shrugged. 'None of this is our business.'

She was aware, though, that it was. If Cat and Peg were lovers, then Isabel wanted her to know that she did not disapprove. But she was not sure how she could do that. She would ask Jamie. And she would also ask him to speak to Eddie, because Eddie listened to him.

She glanced towards the far end of the shop, where Peg, having returned from the kitchen, was beginning to stack packets of pasta on a shelf. Peg had noticed Eddie whispering in Isabel's ear and was looking uncomfortable.

'I can't work out,' said Eddie, his voice barely lowered, 'what Cat sees in Pig. Sex, I suppose.'

Isabel turned to Eddie. 'Eddie,' she muttered, 'if you can't behave in a civil, adult way, I'm going to speak to Cat about you.'

He gasped. 'I only . . . '

He got no further, but burst into tears.

Isabel caught her breath. *What on earth am I doing?* she asked herself. All this crying! Three men had been in tears, or close to tears, in her company, within the space of two days: Jamie at the piano, in tears about his visit to the doctor; Rob, at the very edge of tears when remembering his boarding school; and now Eddie, suddenly weeping when threatened with dismissal by somebody who was not even his employer and had no right to fire anybody.

Then she remembered Charlie and Magnus – both of them had cried in the last twelve hours, although of course they were still very young, of an age at which male crying was expected, permissible and not the subject of shame, as it still was, in spite of everything, for so many men.

11

Isabel left the delicatessen shortly after lunch. The afternoon was usually considerably less busy than the morning, and Eddie and Peg would be able to manage perfectly well by themselves. The atmosphere, though, was prickly; Eddie was taciturn and from time to time gave Isabel a reproachful look; Peg was clearly aware of the tension, but avoided addressing either Isabel or Eddie directly, at one point retreating into Cat's office to attend to a task that neither Isabel nor Eddie could divine. Eddie broke his silence to whisper to Isabel, 'What right has *she* got to go into *her* office?' Isabel did not answer; for her part, she had decided that there was nothing she could do to ameliorate the situation, which was Cat's problem rather than hers.

She did, however, apologise to Eddie for threatening to speak to Cat. 'I over-reacted,' she said, 'and I'm sorry that I upset you.'

At first, Eddie said nothing. Then, in a somewhat grudging tone, he said, 'All right.'

'Friends?' said Isabel.

'Sort of,' said Eddie, and then returned to slicing a large Milanese salami with more than usual vigour. Isabel felt like warning him that one should never use cutting equipment of any sort while in an emotional state. *Never approach a salami in anger,* she thought, and smiled. Salamis . . . she wondered how the salami conference was going in Glasgow. Did people move from stand to stand tasting salamis and noting down their qualities, as at a wine tasting? Of course, at a wine tasting you spat out the wine into a conveniently placed spittoon, avoiding the swallowing of too much alcohol – would one do that at a salami tasting to avoid excessive calories? It was an unattractive thought – even more unappealing, perhaps, than an olive-oil tasting where you might try to spit it out but would inevitably succeed only in leaving a slick of oil across one's chin and one's front. She smiled again.

'What's so funny?' muttered Eddie. 'I don't see the joke.'

'Just thinking,' said Isabel. 'Not about you, Eddie; something else altogether.'

Eddie turned away. 'You do that all the time, you know. You think about things that have nothing to do with what you've been saying – or what other people have been talking about – and then you start smiling.' He turned back to look at her accusingly. 'It's rude. It's really rude to other people.'

She was taken aback by the sudden onslaught. Eddie was usually mild – inoffensive to a fault – but his tone now was heavy with grievance. And it occurred to her that he had a good point: it really was rude to allow oneself to daydream while somebody was talking to you. In a way, it was every bit as discourteous as taking a telephone call while engaged in conversation with another; or closing one's eyes and drifting off to sleep in a concert in full view of a performer. And yet how did you prevent thoughts coming into your mind? And once they were there, how did you stop yourself from entertaining them? The answer was that you had to make an effort; you had to concentrate – and she would try.

'Eddie, I didn't mean—'

'Yes, Isabel, you don't realise, do you, that other people know you're thinking about them – judging them, laughing at them. But they do.'

'I don't laugh at other people . . . '

'You do. You laugh at them all the time.'

She felt herself becoming angry. His comment on her smiling was reasonable enough, but she did *not* mock people in the way he was suggesting.

She defended herself. 'This is ridiculous. And anyway, you're one to talk, Eddie. Who called Peg "Pig"? Who's sniggering over Cat's private life? You, Eddie.'

'I didn't snigger.'

'You did.'

'I didn't.'

Isabel sighed. 'I think we should both leave it right there. There's no point trading insults. You did, I didn't, and so on.' She took a deep breath. 'I said: friends. Remember? I'm going to say it again. Friends?'

Eddie hesitated. 'Will you stop laughing at me?'

'I never laughed at you, but if it makes you feel better, I'll promise not to laugh at you.'

'Promise?'

'Of course – I've just said it.'

'All right then.'

She tried to recall the last time she had had such a juvenile exchange. There had been a girl at school who'd accused her of trying to steal her boyfriend. It had been a completely unjustifiable accusation but had resulted in a screaming match that had escalated until both of them had suddenly seen how ridiculous the argument was and had both lapsed into giggles. The memory made her smile . . .

'There you go.'

She tried to sound firm. 'I'm not going there, Eddie. I'm not going to have to justify my every facial expression. I'm sorry, but I'm not.'

And they had left it there. Peg had slipped out to the chemist and they could see her crossing the street on her return.

'Try to be nice to her,' said Isabel. 'It won't cost you anything, Eddie. Be kind.'

Eddie said nothing, and Isabel decided to try a parting shot. 'You might remember, Eddie, that people were kind to you when you first came here. Cat was, and I think I did my best to help you too. Think about that.'

The point struck home. He stared at her open-mouthed, and Isabel left him in that state as she untied her apron and prepared to leave the delicatessen.

The address that Rob had given Isabel was in Colinton. This had originally been a village on the south-western outskirts of Edinburgh, now partly overtaken by the outward march of the city but still retaining much of its village feel. It was, in fact, next door to Isabel's own suburb, described, whenever it was mentioned in the press, as 'leafy Merchiston'. There were trees, Isabel accepted, but other places had trees too and were not always called *leafy*.

She decided to walk and to make the journey back by bus. It was a fine afternoon, and after being cooped up in the delicatessen all morning, she wanted the fresh air. The quickest route was also the one with the most traffic; a slower route would take her along the canal towpath, across the aqueduct over the

Water of Leith, and then along the river banks to Colinton itself. It would take her a good forty minutes, but she had no need to be back home until late in the afternoon, as both Grace and Jamie were there to look after Charlie and Magnus.

She felt, though, a slight pang of guilt at being away from Magnus for so long. But then she reminded herself that there were plenty of working mothers who spent the whole day at work while their children – some even younger than Magnus – were looked after in a crèche or nursery. She was a working mother too, although her job did not require her presence in some distant office or factory; she did her editing in her study, within earshot of Magnus, and could intersperse working sessions with childcare. Her spells in the delicatessen, of course, were different – she could be recalled if there were an emergency – but there she was out at work in a proper sense. And that led to another thought: in the last week or so she had put in three sessions at the delicatessen; that day, in fact, she had been there for a full morning. It seemed to her that the centre of gravity of her working life was subtly shifting in favour of the delicatessen – to the point that she should perhaps describe that as being her principal occupation. *Shop assistant* . . . she liked the sound of that because it was suggestive of a simpler life. A shop assistant would not have to worry about printers' deadlines, nor demanding authors, nor people who seemed intimidated when she revealed that she was a philosopher. There was something appealing about merging into the anonymity that came with very ordinary occupations. Had Lawrence of Arabia not signed up as an ordinary aircraftman at the height of his fame? There was more to that, she thought, than a simple desire to escape attention, but there were other examples of people who had left challenging or distinguished positions for a simpler existence – Horace, she thought, had done that when he retired to his Sabine farm, to raise cattle and make wine and do the other things that Roman farmers did – or, rather, ordered their slaves to do. Of course all of this involved the romanticising of simplicity: assistants in shops worked long hours, had to endure the rudeness of customers, and had to accept the diktats of management; farmers lived with crop failure, with drought, with poor prices at market. She imagined they would love to edit philosophical reviews and spend the occasional morning in their niece's delicatessen.

Some might sneer at the way in which she exchanged her study for her place behind the counter at the delicatessen. Everyone, she thought, should bear in mind Marie Antoinette playing at being a milkmaid in the grounds of Versailles . . . She blushed at the thought that there might be those who looked at her delicatessen work in the same way; but let them think what they liked – the judgement of others was often more about them than the one they were judging.

The canal towpath was busy. People were walking dogs, runners were working up a sweat, and here and there young mothers crouched with their children as over-indulged ducks gobbled up pieces of dry bread flung in their direction. There were a few cyclists, too, mostly well behaved, although Isabel was almost forced into a clump of nettles by an aggressive young man who shot past with scant attention to other users of the pathway. Her displeasure was quickly replaced by reflection on what actually went through the mind of somebody like that. She wondered how they thought of their act: did they see their actions for what they were – selfish, thoughtless, hurtful – but did that understanding have no impact on them? You could harm another, knowing that you were harming somebody, but just not care. That was a failure of something very deep and essential in the psyche – sympathy. It was what psychopaths lacked – they simply did not feel regret or shame – and yet it was unlikely that the young man on the bicycle was a psychopath. So what was he? Thoughtless, perhaps; inattentive to her existence rather than hostile – inattentive because he was too consumed by himself or by his own projects, as eighteen-year-olds can be. At that age you were immortal, you were at the centre of the universe, you were . . .

There was a sudden cry, and then a splash. She spun round; a few hundred yards behind her the cyclist had veered off the path and had ended up in the canal, the top of his bicycle showing above the surface, a twisted wheel, a set of handlebars. The canal was not deep and he was standing, soaked and muddy, chest deep in the water, holding on to his bicycle with one hand.

On the towpath a dog barked, unattended by any owner, and Isabel realised that this must have been the cause of the accident: the dog must have run out of the bushes, dashed across the path, and caused the cyclist to serve. Once on the slippery verge, he must have lost control and plummeted over the edge into the canal.

She ran back towards him. The cyclist was already clambering up onto the bank, dragging his damaged cycle behind him. Isabel reached out to offer him a hand.

'Are you all right?'

He looked up at her. 'Yes. I'm all right.'

He took her hand. The rise from the water to the bank was only a couple of feet, but she was able to help him negotiate it.

'What happened?' she asked.

He looked shaken and did not answer immediately, but as he rose to his feet, the water dripping off him, he shook his head. 'That dog.'

She looked round; the dog had disappeared back into the undergrowth.

There was a small frond of weed on his shoulder; Isabel took this off. He moved away as he felt her hand brush against him. 'I'm all right,' he muttered.

She stood for a moment, uncertain what to do. His bicycle was still in the water, although he had moved it to the side. She noticed that he was staring at its buckled front wheel, and that his expression was one of pain and regret. She thought: *this bicycle was his pride and joy; now it's wrecked and he may not be able to afford a new one.*

'That'll be expensive,' she said.

He turned to her and spoke in a tone that was close to a snarl. 'Of course it's expensive, what do you think? And I don't know where I'll get the money.' He swore, coarsely, and without inhibition.

Isabel spoke on impulse. 'From me.'

He frowned. 'What?'

'I said you can get the money from me. I'll pay for your bike to be fixed.' She paused, noticing his expression of astonishment. 'You said that you would find it hard to find the money – well, I can pay for it. I can easily do this for you.'

He opened his mouth to say something, but no words came.

'I really do mean it,' said Isabel.

'But it wasn't your fault,' he stuttered.

'No, I know that. But I happen to be able to afford it.'

The young man scratched his head. 'But why?'

'Because I want to,' she said, smiling. 'I just want to.' She did not explain the theory behind her offer – it was far too complicated and he might not understand if she started to talk about moral proximity. But that was what lay behind it:

Isabel's private theory of moral proximity, the basis of those obligations that came into existence when we found ourselves close enough to others to be able to witness or feel their needs, or when we were in some other way linked to their plight. We could not deal with all the suffering or need in the world, but we could – and should – deal with that sliver of suffering that was reasonably close to us. We could not ignore the needs of our immediate neighbour, with whom we would obviously be in moral proximity; when it came to the needs of people whose identity we did not know, with whom we had no dealings, and whom we did not actually *see*, then any moral obligation to them would be harder to justify – other, of course, than a general duty not to harm them.

Jamie had been intrigued by the notion of moral proximity when she had explained it to him one afternoon on the lawn.

'All right,' he said. 'There are those beggars who sit on George IV Bridge or on the pavement in Bruntsfield. You know the ones – they have a few blankets and they sit on these and mutter, "Any loose change?" to passers-by.'

Isabel saw them whenever she went into town. Many of them came from Eastern Europe – from Romania, in particular. She nodded. 'Yes, I know which ones you're talking about.'

'Am I in a relationship of . . . what do you call it? Am I in a relationship of moral proximity with them?'

It was not a simple question to answer. She had walked past a beggar earlier that day and had been troubled by it. 'Not necessarily,' she said.

'So what does that mean? That I can ignore them?'

Isabel sighed. 'These things are never simple.'

'No, but we still have to know what to do. Can I ignore them, or does the fact that I can *see* them make a difference?'

'It might.'

Jamie was not going to let it go. 'But if I switch on the television and see a picture of a person in need in, say, an obscure corner of China, do I have a duty to help? Is there moral proximity there? Remember, I can see the person, even if it's only a picture.'

She was sure that there was no duty to help a person that far away. And anyway, China was rich; they had money in abundance and first and foremost it was the duty of wealthy Chinese people – rather than outsiders – to do something.

Jamie returned to the case of the Romanian beggars. 'You know how they're always sticking their legs out? They lean against the wall of the building and stretch their legs out in front of them.'

Isabel nodded. 'Some of them are intrusive.'

'Well,' continued Jamie, 'what if I stumble over a beggar in the street. What then?'

'I would say that you could be morally engaged,' said Isabel. 'Moral proximity might exist in such a case.'

'But why?'

'Because of physical closeness.'

Jamie looked doubtful. 'But why? What difference does physical closeness make?'

'It's just one way of restricting the number of situations in which we have to act. It may be arbitrary, but it acts as a sort of filter. You can't do everything – but you still want to do *something.* So you say, "I only need act in cases that arise close to me." That cuts it down to manageable proportions.'

And now she had been present when the young man fell into the canal. She had spoken to him and he had revealed his need. She had responded because of moral proximity.

He was staring at her. 'What makes you think I need your

money?' he asked. There was an edge to his voice; an edge of resentment.

'You said . . . ' she began, but did not finish.

'You're all the same,' he muttered. 'You can keep your money.'

He turned his back on her, leaving Isabel standing, shocked by the rejection and the unasked-for hostility. *You're all the same* . . . She wondered what that meant – liberal do-gooders, busybodies, the middle class, women, pedestrians who got in the way of cyclists? It was impossible to tell.

She drew back. There was something in the young man's demeanour that worried her – the dangerousness that one senses in those on a short fuse. Such people could lose their self-control very easily and explode in anger. They were the ones who escalated the minor disagreement into a fracas, who suddenly produced knives – and used them.

She began to retrace her steps but had not gone more than a few yards before she heard him call out after her, 'Where do you think you're going?'

She did not turn around at first, but continued to walk.

'I said: where do you think you're going?'

She stopped and assessed her situation. She was beyond the busy part of the towpath and was now on a relatively deserted section, not far from the bridge that would take her over the canal into Colinton Dell. The bank to the right sloped down sharply, through a tangle of brambles, nettles and dock leaves, until it reached the fence that marked the rear of a suburban garden. There were several houses, in fact, but they were all a few hundred yards away and she was not sure whether any cry for help would be heard. In one of them she noticed a tall aerial structure rising at the back of the garden, a rickety, wire-rigged tower. She recognised it as a ham-radio enthusiast's aerial, and she thought, inconsequentially, that its owner could send his signals thousands of miles but she could not send a plea for help a few yards.

She was surprised at her own calm. She would turn around and try to take the heat out of the situation; an apologetic tone might achieve that – provided, of course, his anger abated. He was humiliated by his undignified accident; he was looking for somebody other than himself to blame; this was like being a metal pole in a lightning storm.

And then, from around the corner, she heard a voice shouting something unintelligible. Cutting sleekly through the water, a rowing scull appeared, its crew of four moving backwards and forwards in their sliding seats, their oars dipping in and out of the water in perfect unison. On the towpath, wobbling as he held his megaphone in one hand and steered his bicycle with the other, was the coach.

Isabel did not wait, but swiftly resumed her journey. The young man would not follow her, she thought, and she would, anyway, soon be off the towpath altogether. Behind her, conveniently, the scull slowed as the crew took a rest. That was perfect from her point of view. Under the eyes of four muscular young men – all students at the university, judging from the crest on the boat – the disgruntled cyclist would not try anything.

Her heart was still beating faster than usual. It had been a shocking incident, and she felt curiously dirtied by witnessing this display of threatening behaviour. This was not the Edinburgh she normally inhabited; this was a city that concealed crude violence under the surface; a city she barely recognised, but that she knew existed.

She tried to put it out of her mind. That was the only way to deal with things that would derail her from her ordered life. If she pondered them, then such things could consume her, dragging her down, ending the equanimity that prevailed at the centre of her world. She had a firewall, and she would keep it in good repair. This young man and his threatening talk had not penetrated it; it was still intact.

By the time she reached Colinton Village she had largely recovered from the incident. Her walk along the Water of Leith had been calming, and there had only been one moment of anxiety when, in the disused railway tunnel through which the path led, she had imagined footsteps behind her. That had been illusory, although there was somebody coming towards her in the tunnel – a woman with a small, snuffling dog. The woman had greeted her and made a comment about the wild garlic that was growing in profusion in the woodlands at either end of the tunnel.

'It scents the whole glen,' the woman said. 'And it makes my mouth water.'

'I know what you mean,' said Isabel, grateful for this comfortable exchange after the encounter with the cyclist. 'I must pick some.'

'So must I,' said the woman. 'I must pick some before it goes.'

'Things go so quickly,' said Isabel.

She had not intended to prolong the conversation, but this last remark seemed to interest the woman. She opened her mouth to say something more – perhaps about the transience of life – but the snuffling dog was tugging hard on his chain and she had to continue her walk.

Ten minutes later, Isabel was at the end of Andrea Murray's street. It was a quiet road that followed the contours of the hill overlooking the river's course. The houses that lined it on both sides were substantial, mostly Edwardian but with here and there a more modern example of twentieth-century domestic architecture. One of them, she thought, looked as if it was the work of Robert Lorimer, whose influence was felt extensively in that part of Edinburgh as well as in numerous country houses in the Highlands.

She checked that she had the right road – Ardkinglass Road – and then confirmed the number: 23. From the numbering of the first two houses, she could tell that this would lie on the north side of the street, the side overlooking the river, some fifty yards below. She located number 23; it was set back from the road, and had an impressive set of wooden gates for vehicle entrance along with a small pedestrian gate to the side. This gate opened readily, and she found herself on a short path leading up to the house. The surface of the path was covered with fragmented tree bark that gave a pleasant, soft feel underfoot.

The house itself was a two-storey building of the sort favoured by the well-heeled edges of Scottish cities – spacious and well set, with an oak front door and oak window casings. The garden surrounding it was tidy, but perhaps rather too orderly for Isabel's taste. There were none of the rhododendrons that Isabel liked but, rather, lines of lavender and juniper flanking well-tended herbaceous beds. Isabel assumed that there was a professional gardener – certainly it had that feel to it.

She rang the bell and heard it sounding somewhere within the house. She waited; there was no response. Then she rang again, and from inside there came the slamming of a door. A few seconds later, the front door opened.

Andrea Murray was younger than Isabel had imagined she would be – there were ten years between her and Rob, Isabel thought. Rob was in his early forties, Andrea must have been in her early thirties.

She was an attractive woman, with high cheekbones and bright, almond-shaped eyes. Her skin was clear, and there was an air of health and vigour to her – not something that Isabel had expected. Having heard the reports of Andrea's attempted suicide, she had imagined somebody who looked more drawn. Not this bright-eyed woman standing before her.

Andrea waited for Isabel to introduce herself.

'My name is Isabel Dalhousie. I know Rob McLaren. He suggested I should come to see you.'

'Rob McLaren? Well . . . ' There were a few moments' hesitation before she invited Isabel in. 'I'm in the kitchen,' she said. 'I'm pickling things, so there's a rather vinegary smell. I hope you don't mind.'

Isabel mentioned the dill pickles she had put into the jar two weeks ago. 'The jury is still out,' she said. 'We have yet to try them. My husband has a weakness for them.'

Andrea led the way into the kitchen. This was on the other side of the house, overlooking the weir that halted the Water of Leith on its journey to the sea. Isabel remarked on the view.

'I look out on rhododendrons from my kitchen,' she said. 'Rhododendrons, and occasionally a fox.'

Andrea laughed. 'I can watch the river for hours – especially when I'm meant to be doing something else.' She switched on the kettle and then turned to Isabel. 'Distractions . . . Do you mind my asking . . . '

'Why I've come to see you? No, not at all.'

'You said you were a friend of Rob McLaren's?'

Isabel nodded. 'Well, I know him. Not very well, but I've met him recently.'

There was something in Andrea's look – something Isabel was not quite able to interpret. It could have been a look of amusement, she thought – or was it something else?

'But I haven't come to talk about Rob.'

Andrea was impassive.

Isabel had decided to be direct. 'There's a man called Tony MacUspaig.' She paused, waiting to gauge the effect of her mentioning the name. She was half expecting a dramatic reaction, or at least a shadow to pass across Andrea's face, but this did not happen.

'Tony?' said Andrea. 'You know him too?' The tone was bright, and there was nothing to suggest anything other than mild surprise.

'I haven't actually met him,' confessed Isabel.

Andrea waited politely.

'You might be wondering why I wanted to talk about somebody I haven't met,' said Isabel.

Andrea laughed. 'Well, I've been wondering about why you're here at all,' she said. 'I'm all for social visits, but it's not every day somebody comes to see me to talk about men . . . '

If tension had been building up, then this had the effect of dispelling it. Isabel now began her explanation, telling Andrea about Bea's concerns over unfortunate matchmaking and her doubts about the suitability of Tony MacUspaig. She did not raise any question, though, of the doctor's monetary motives.

After she had finished, Isabel looked at Andrea expectantly.

'But what's this got to do with you?' asked Andrea. 'Sorry to sound rude, but what business is this of yours?'

'Bea asked me to help.'

Andrea looked doubtful. 'Why can't she do it herself?'

Isabel shrugged. 'Embarrassment, perhaps.'

This did not impress Andrea. 'She started the whole thing. Surely she should clear up her own mess – if it's a mess, which I don't think it will be.'

This interested Isabel. 'Oh? Why not?'

They had been standing during this conversation, and now Andrea gestured to two chairs at the kitchen table, inviting Isabel to sit down. As she did so, Isabel noticed a magazine on the table. The cover was familiar, and she saw that it was one that she herself received from time to time, the magazine of a Scottish child charity. A picture of a young boy on the cover, a bit of an urchin, his face smeared with what looked like jam, gazed out at her. *URBAN POVERTY*, the inscription below read in large red letters.

'I don't think it'll be a mess,' Andrea explained, 'because I can't see why anybody should think Tony unsuitable for . . . ' she made an expansive gesture '. . . for anyone.'

This was not what Isabel was expecting, and she frowned. 'I heard you and he were together.'

'Yes,' said Andrea evenly. 'We were. Then we parted.' She looked up at the ceiling. Isabel thought she looked wistful rather than evasive or regretful. Cat, by contrast, closed her eyes whenever the name of a former boyfriend was mentioned – a form of denial, Isabel had decided. There was no denial here.

'I see.'

'Yes,' Andrea continued. 'I decided that I was better on my own. You know how it is? You sometimes feel that . . . well, that your life is less complicated if there's just you.' She paused. 'Do I sound selfish?'

'Not at all,' Isabel said quickly. 'A lot of people reach that conclusion.'

'I'm glad you agree,' said Andrea. 'If you're single, you get used to pity, you know. People assume that you want somebody and that you can't find him. They try not to show their pity, but it's there – it really is. You feel it.'

Isabel knew what she meant, and told her so.

Andrea looked at her with interest. 'Are you by yourself?' she asked.

'No, I'm married. But I wasn't always. I had quite a few years on my own.'

'So you'll know what it's like.'

Isabel nodded. 'I'd heard something about you and Tony,' she said. 'I'd heard that he'd broken up with you.'

Andrea smiled. 'Where did you hear that?'

Isabel gave a vague answer. 'You know how this city is. People spend half their time talking about one another.'

'You could say that about anywhere,' said Andrea. She seemed to muse on Isabel's remark. 'They were one hundred and eighty degrees wrong, you know. I was the one who brought it to an end. He was actually quite upset.'

'People!' exclaimed Isabel.

'Yes, people. You'd think that if they were going to talk about others, they would at least get their facts right.'

'Quite,' agreed Isabel. 'But there was something else that somebody said. I feel a bit uneasy telling you about it.' Even as she spoke, she knew that this was not something you should ever say. You should never tell people you knew something unless you were prepared to share it. It was a lesson that was usually learned very early – well before the age of ten.

Andrea looked uncomfortable. 'I don't know whether I want to hear it, but . . . ' She trailed off.

Isabel was now committed. 'It's nothing much, and it certainly doesn't put you in a bad light.'

'That's a relief.'

Isabel swallowed. 'There was some suggestion that Tony took advantage of you financially.'

The effect of this was immediate. Andrea stiffened. 'What?' she exclaimed. 'Took financial advantage? Of me?'

'That's what I heard,' said Isabel. 'I didn't immediately assume it was true.' She felt she could say that honestly; she had had her doubts, even if they were not large ones.

'Just as well,' said Andrea. 'Because it's utterly false. Tony would never do something like that.'

'Are you sure?'

'Of course I'm sure,' exploded Andrea. 'I knew him very well. He's completely honest. Completely.'

Isabel sighed. 'Gossip,' she said. 'I should have known.' She held Andrea's gaze. 'So there's no truth in the allegation that he got you to make money over to him.'

Andrea's voice rose. 'Of course there's no truth in it.' She hesitated. 'None at all. Except . . . '

Isabel waited.

'Except for the money I gave him for medical purposes.'

Isabel thought quickly. Tony MacUspaig was a plastic surgeon and might well have a practice in cosmetic surgery. Such surgery was not common in Scotland, where the ravages of age were accepted with a certain insouciance, but there were one or two surgeons who would nip and tuck if asked. If he were interested in money – and she had heard that he was – then that is exactly the sort of thing he would do. Burns and grafts may have been the staple of National Health surgeons, but the state system of free medicine did not pay nearly as well as the lucrative tightening of ageing skin. As discreetly as she could, she studied Andrea's face. There was no sign of the smooth, slightly lustrous skin that followed the elimination of wrinkles. Certainly there was none of the mask-like artificiality that followed a significant face-lift. That could make people look like a masked actor in a Japanese Noh play or one of those leggy plastic dolls with which small girls played.

'I wouldn't want to pry,' said Isabel.

Andrea laughed. 'Oh no, not for me.' She touched her face gingerly. 'Did you think I was a candidate for that sort of thing?'

Isabel was quick to reassure her.

'It was for a clinic he runs,' said Andrea. 'A medical volunteer place.' Tony MacUspaig, she told her, was a trustee of a clinic in Marrakesh that performed plastic surgery procedures. He usually went out there twice a year – for a few weeks on each occasion – during which he would give his services, unpaid, as a plastic surgeon. He had persuaded other surgeons to volunteer, and they now had a regular roster of Canadian and Australian doctors joining their Scottish and English counterparts there. But these schemes cost money, she said, and he raised quite a large sum himself, as well as volunteering to perform the actual surgery.

'I gave him a fairly large gift for the clinic. He had showed me a picture of a little girl whose hare-lip he had repaired.' Andrea looked incredulous. 'Do you think that's what people have been talking about?'

'Possibly.'

This was greeted with disbelief. 'You know, when I saw the photographs of what he had done – a man who had suffered from a terrible growth on his jaw – before and after, it was amazing. That little girl standing there with a perfectly ordinary smile. I was very moved.'

'Who wouldn't be?' said Isabel. She had made a bad mistake – again; she, a philosopher by training, had believed what she had been told without question. You had to be sure of your premise – you simply had to. After all, even the fundamental truths of physics could be questioned, let alone stories you'd been told second or third hand. Rob McLaren may have believed what he told her, but may have been quite wrong. 'I can see that there's been a misunderstanding.'

'There certainly has,' said Andrea. 'Tony is the nicest, kindest, most gentle of men. I still feel very strongly about him even if I thought we should go our separate ways.'

'I'm so sorry,' said Isabel. 'I've been misled.'

There was now a note of anger in Andrea's voice. 'You should tell that woman, Bea or whoever she is, that she's got it quite wrong and that anyone who goes out with Tony MacUspaig is really fortunate. Tell her that.'

'I shall,' said Isabel, rising to leave.

'Good,' said Andrea firmly.

She saw Isabel to the door. The atmosphere was now less warm, and Isabel did not want to overstay the little welcome that she had. She shook hands with Andrea at the door and as she did so she noticed something that she had missed earlier. On her left wrist, irregular and at an angle, were two railway-line scars.

Isabel averted her eyes. She walked out onto the street without looking back, then made her way up the slope towards the end of Colinton Road. As she passed the boys' boarding school, she was overtaken on the pavement by two of the students, dressed in the school's uniform, both fair-haired boys of fifteen or sixteen, walking with their hands deep in their pockets, more or less oblivious of Isabel's presence.

She overheard a snatch of their conversation.

'I said to him that I didn't do it,' said one of the boys. 'I told him.'

'And he didn't believe you?' asked his friend.

'No,' said the boy. 'I suppose it's because I'd told so many lies in the past.'

They were almost out of earshot now, but she just managed to hear the final exchange. 'Poor you. It must be awful not to be believed . . . '

12

That evening, Isabel and Jamie went to a concert in the Queen's Hall. The last time Isabel had been there – a few weeks earlier – Jamie had been playing; she had sat in the back row, paying scant attention to the music, being distracted by thoughts of Magnus. It was the first time that Grace had babysat for them in the evening – at least for Magnus – and she was experiencing the anxiety that any parent would experience in such circumstances: the first dinner *à deux* in a restaurant, the first cinema outing – these are not easy, relaxed occasions for any new parent, no matter the care being lavished on the baby at home. Grace, of course, was completely reliable, and had already looked after Magnus for long periods during the day. She knew where everything was, she checked up frequently – perhaps rather too frequently – on both Charlie and Magnus when they were sleeping, and she had Isabel's mobile number should anything be required. Even in a concert, with the mobile set to silent but ready to vibrate should a call come in, Isabel checked it from time to time, just in case Grace should call her and the phone for some reason fail to alert her. Of course there had been nothing, and there had been no reason to summon a taxi at the end of the concert rather than walk back, as she and Jamie usually did.

This evening there was no such anxiety, and as she and Jamie set off, Isabel found herself looking forward to a concert where she would listen to the music rather than sit and worry. For Jamie, too, it was something of a treat. Most concerts he attended were ones in which he was playing, and no matter how confident he felt about the music, it was still work – and demanding work at that.

Waiting for the concert to start, Isabel ran her eye down the programme. It was Jamie who had suggested that they come to this particular performance; he knew several of the musicians in the ensemble, he said, and there was a new piece by a young composer from Glasgow with whom he had worked.

'There it is,' Jamie said, '*Butter Yellow.* That's Laurence's new piece.'

Isabel read the programme note. 'Laurence Mave composed *Butter Yellow* after a trip he made to Colombia. This is its first performance.' She looked at Jamie. 'So he went to Colombia?'

Jamie glanced at the programme. 'So it says.'

'And it inspired him?'

Jamie shrugged. 'Possibly.'

'But it must have,' said Isabel. 'It says that he went to Colombia and then he wrote *Butter Yellow.* It must have been something he saw in Colombia. Butter, perhaps.'

James gave her a sideways look. 'Not necessarily. And I don't think we should be too literal. Music doesn't have to be representational.'

'I see. So we shouldn't think about Colombia? Or butter?'

Jamie seemed distracted. He had seen somebody. 'Probably not.'

Isabel was thinking. 'What's that condition you get when your senses get confused? You hear something and it makes you see something. Syn . . . something or other.'

'Synaesthesia,' said Jamie. 'We had a lecture on it at music college. Some people see colours when they hear music. Or they think of numbers having particular colours. Two is green, three is blue, and so on.'

'So perhaps your friend, Laurence, saw butter yellow when he wrote this new piece.'

Jamie agreed that this was a possibility.

'But why Colombia?' asked Isabel.

A door opened at the side of the hall. 'Later,' whispered Jamie. 'We can discuss it later.'

The musicians entered. It was a chamber ensemble, and Isabel recognised one or two of them as people with whom Jamie had worked before. The viola player was somebody who occasionally came to the house to collect a score, and the young woman who was playing the cello . . . Isabel struggled with the memory. She had definitely seen her before, and had seen her again recently, somewhere or other. She looked down at the programme to read the names of the players. *Cello* . . . Stephanie Partridge. *Partridge* . . . had she met somebody called Partridge? There had been that woman called Sheila Grouse who had stood for the Liberal Democrats in the council elections and who had called at the house with an election pamphlet. Isabel had remembered her name because the day she had called had in fact been the beginning of the grouse season – the 'Glorious Twelfth', as it was known – and Isabel had been half listening to something on the radio about it. Then the doorbell had rung and there was a woman who introduced herself as Sheila Grouse. Isabel had said, 'Is it safe for you to be out in the open today?' and the woman had looked at her in astonishment. A good opportunity for a humorous remark – sent to us like manna from providence – could be wasted if the person to whom it was made did not get the reference. Your name, Isabel had thought. *It's not a good name to have on the opening day of the grouse-shooting season.*

'I'm here on behalf of the Liberal Democrats,' said Sheila Grouse.

'Of course,' said Isabel, and thought, *Not to complain, of course . . .*

But now it was partridge rather than grouse. She turned to Jamie. 'The cellist,' she whispered.

'Stephanie?'

'Do you know her?'

'Yes, of course. We did that recording for Paul Baxter – remember?'

'Vaguely.'

The musicians took their places.

Partridge? Partridge?

The ensemble was ready to begin. 'Gavin Bryars,' whispered Jamie, pointing to the first item on the programme. 'Remember him? *The Sinking of the Titanic*?'

Isabel's memory for composers was not as good as Jamie's, but she remembered the performance of that haunting piece of music, performed beside a large swimming pool with some of the audience in the water, swimming or holding on to floats as the musicians played. Jamie had explained it to her on the way to the concert. 'It's actually going to be beside the pool,' he said. 'And it's meant to be the orchestra on the *Titanic* playing as the ship went down. It's gorgeous, evocative music. And they get fainter and fainter towards the end, when the band was playing at an impossible angle on the tilting ship.'

She had been unable to say anything.

'And Marconi,' Jamie continued, 'developed a theory that sound never dies – that it would always be there, but infinitely faint. So if you take that view, the sound of the band playing that hymn on the deck of the *Titanic* is still out there in the water. Still there, but very, very faint.'

'Oh.'

'Yes. And Marconi thought if only he could develop sensitive enough equipment he could hear all the sounds that had ever been made in the past. He hoped that we would be able to hear the Sermon on the Mount – actually hear the words, still echoing out there somewhere.'

'And hear Caesar saying, "*Et tu, Brute?*"'

Jamie smiled. 'If he ever said that, yes. And hear the rumble of Vesuvius and the impact of the meteor that caused the extinction of the dinosaurs. And President Kennedy saying, "*Ich bin ein Berliner.*"'

'And that would settle that,' mused Isabel.

'Settle what?'

'You know what a Berliner is?' asked Isabel. 'It's a jam doughnut. Some people say that Kennedy said he was a jam doughnut. If you wanted to say "I live in Berlin" you'd say "*Ich bin Berliner*", without the article "*ein*". So some people laughed at him and said that he'd solemnly announced that he was a jam doughnut. But they were wrong.'

Jamie raised an eyebrow in mock seriousness. 'He wasn't a doughnut?'

'He wasn't a doughnut. Apparently if you want to say that you identify with a group of people and are not actually a member of the group, you can put the indefinite article in. So he was being grammatically correct. And if we could hear it again, we could check up that nobody laughed.'

'Because laughs never die away entirely,' said Jamie. 'At least, if you believe in Marconi.'

'A nice thought.'

'Nor do tears,' said Jamie. 'But I suppose that's a question of evaporation rather than the fading of sound.'

Isabel closed her eyes. 'Just think of all of humanity's tears. They would make vast lakes, wouldn't they? Dantean lakes.'

Now, in the Queen's Hall, she remembered how she had felt at the end of that piece of music. The swimmers in the pool had lingered, barely moving, holding on to floats, and then slowly they had come out, and Isabel had seen how moved they had been.

The ensemble began to play and Isabel's attention wandered. She tried to concentrate on the music – she liked Bryars but she was thinking about something else he had written. He had come across a tramp at the railway station singing, in a frail and cracked voice, 'Jesus' Blood Never Failed Me Yet'. Bryars had put that on a tape loop and played it time and time again, slowly bringing in the swelling sound of an orchestra, and that had somehow lent great dignity to the faltering tones of the tramp. It did not matter that he was feeble and broken down; he had an orchestra behind him, and it made him and his song, for those moments at least, glorious. The kindness of music, thought Isabel; the kindness.

Partridge, she thought. *Partridge?* She watched the cellist; she watched the tremor of her fingers over the vibrato notes. She saw how she had tied her hair back so that it would not get in her eyes as she bent to the music. She saw that the strap on one of her shoes had come undone. And then it came to her. This was the young woman she had seen in the Café St Honoré.

She was surprised that she had not realised this straight away, but it was something to do with context.

For a few moments she felt satisfaction in the fact that she had now put a name to the face, but then, in a sudden moment of chilling realisation, it occurred to her that this person had seen her having lunch with Rob and, at that precise time, Isabel had put her hand over Rob's on the table. It had been a gesture of comfort and reassurance – nothing more than that – but now it occurred to her that it might have looked very different to Stephanie Partridge. What she would have seen was two people at a table, holding hands over lunch; not an unusual sight in a romantic restaurant such as the Café St Honoré undoubtedly was, but – and here a chill touched Isabel's heart – Stephanie must have known that she was married to Jamie because otherwise why would she have stopped and stared in recognition?

Isabel caught her breath. It had not occurred to her that her innocent gesture would be interpreted in this way, but of course it was entirely understandable that somebody should do just that. At the back of her own mind, of course, there had been a certain hesitation about telling Jamie about her meeting with Rob; she knew that it would sound odd to meet him just to get an address, and of course she should have told him at the outset, and she had not. And then she had given him an incomplete, ambiguous account of her day precisely because of her feeling of embarrassment. She should have told him then and there: she should have said that she had met Rob over lunch because he had more or less insisted, and that he had made an inept pass at her and she had almost walked out. That was all believable – and besides, it was the truth.

She stared at the musicians, oblivious of the music, agonising over the possibilities. Jamie always liked of go to the bar at the Queen's Hall after a concert, specifically to talk to his fellow musicians. She was sure he would be planning to do that this evening, as Laurence would be there and he was bound to want to congratulate him on *Butter Yellow.*

The Bryars came to an end. There was a brief silence, followed by a burst of enthusiastic clapping. Isabel watched the members of the ensemble stand up to acknowledge the applause. Stephanie Partridge, balancing her cello with one hand, pushed back a wisp of hair that had strayed across her brow. She was smiling as she looked up towards the gallery; she knew somebody up there, and inclined her head in greeting. A lover, thought Isabel; her lover is with her and she has been playing for him.

Jamie nudged Isabel gently. 'Didn't you enjoy that?' he whispered.

'Yes. I did. Of course I did.'

'Then why aren't you clapping?'

She put her hands together, but the applause was dying down and the ensemble was preparing for the next piece. This was *Butter Yellow.*

The leader of the ensemble, a tall man with heavy-rimmed spectacles, stood up to say something.

'Ladies and gentlemen, this next piece is the world premiere of a new piece by a composer we have enjoyed working with over the past few years – Laurence Mave. *Butter Yellow* has presented technical challenges for us – as good music often does – but we are immensely excited by this piece and we would like to thank Laurence for showing confidence in us by writing this specifically for us.'

There was more applause, and the leader sat down. *Butter Yellow* began. Isabel closed her eyes and tried to stop thinking about Stephanie Partridge. But she could not; she now imagined herself in the bar after the concert and Stephanie Partridge coming up to her and saying, in Jamie's presence, 'I see you like the Café St Honoré too.' And Jamie would say, 'We haven't been for ages,' and Stephanie would look puzzled and say, 'But I saw you there the other day.' Or would she? If she thought that Isabel was there with a lover – and there was a strong possibility that this is what she thought – then only malice would prompt her to mention their meeting. It would be an act of deliberate sabotage, and there was no reason to think she would stoop to that.

But what if Stephanie and Jamie were old friends, as was perfectly possible. They might have been at music college together – Stephanie looked as if she was the right sort of age for them to be contemporaries – and in that case she might feel protective towards Jamie, as old friends so often can be. An old friend might well reveal the apparent unfaithfulness of a friend's spouse because of uneasiness over the deception.

Of course, it was possible that Stephanie had not noticed that Isabel had her hand over Rob's, and had assumed that they were meeting for lunch in an entirely innocent way. Rob could be a cousin, for instance – a cousin who had come into Edinburgh from the country and was being taken out for lunch. That less compromising conclusion might mean that she would not hesitate to make a casual reference to having seen Isabel in the restaurant, and Isabel would then have to explain to Jamie why she had been there and why she had not mentioned the lunch to him.

She felt her stomach turn. It was a ridiculous situation for her to find herself in, and it was entirely her fault. She should admit to Jamie that she had misled him out of a feeling of awkwardness and embarrassment. He trusted her and surely he would see that she was telling the truth. And yet, at the same time, might he not ask why she had kept the meeting back from him in the first place? That was the bit that did not make sense.

She tried to put the matter out of her mind. She began to concentrate on the music. Yellow butter – could she see it? Were these chords the chords of yellow butter? She found herself thinking of Colombia. She had never been there but she had known a Colombian at Cambridge. He had been studying for a postgraduate degree in linguistics, and he had told her about research he had done in the Amazon basin. He had been bitter about what he saw as the hijacking of his country by *narcotraficantes*. 'There used to be a country called Colombia,' he said to her. 'But no more.'

At the end of *Butter Yellow*, Isabel made sure that she applauded. 'Beautiful,' she said to Jamie as the applause rang out and the composer was invited up onto the stage.

'Possibly,' muttered Jamie.

'You didn't like it?' she asked.

'Too fluid,' he said.

She was not sure that she understood. 'How?'

'Difficult to get hold of,' said Jamie. 'It slid around . . . ' He shuddered. 'Butter's slippery, I suppose.'

The composer was bowing to the audience. At the back of the hall somebody hooted out appreciation – a sort of yelp that would have been more at home on the sports field. 'Groupies,' whispered Jamie. 'Even composers have them.'

At the end of the concert, Jamie turned to Isabel and said, 'Bar?'

Isabel did not answer immediately but eventually said, 'Do you really want to?'

Jamie looked surprised. 'We normally do.' He glanced at his watch. 'It's still pretty early.'

Isabel was on the point of saying that she had a headache and would prefer to go home when she stopped herself. She did not have a headache, and a further lie was no solution to an earlier one – or to an earlier half-truth.

'I suppose so,' she said.

Jamie encouraged her. 'You always enjoy it. You like the crowd.'

'The crowd' was an expression that Jamie often used to describe his fellow musicians. Isabel found it amusing, conjuring up, as it did, a joyful throng – perhaps a little loud, perhaps a little over-enthusiastic. She imagined the crowd finding it difficult to get reservations in restaurants – *Too many of you, I'm afraid* – or being too large to fit into a single taxi; or walking boisterously along, filling the pavements to overflowing.

'The crowd,' she muttered.

'Yes,' said Jamie. 'A lot of them are here tonight. Laurence is popular.'

She nodded mutely – and miserably. 'All right.'

But Jamie was now worried. 'Are you sure? If you're not feeling up to it, we can go home, but—'

She cut him short. 'No, I'm fine. Let's go before the bar gets too busy.'

He seemed pleased. 'You can grab one of the tables, if you like.'

'I'll stay with you,' she said.

By the time they reached it, there was already a knot of people around the bar. Jamie, though, immediately saw a friend who offered to buy him and Isabel a drink.

'Joe's going to get us something,' he said to Isabel as he cast an eye around the room. 'And there's Laurence over there. Let's go and speak to him.'

Isabel asked him what he was going to say. 'Are you going to be truthful?'

He looked askance at her. 'I'm not going to criticise it, if that's what you're asking.'

'I suppose I am asking that,' said Isabel. 'You said that you found it too fluid.'

His glance was intended to silence her. 'I can't say that.'

'But you did.'

'That's different. You can't tell somebody who's *made* something that you don't like it. You just can't. You have to say you enjoyed it.'

'But I thought you didn't.'

He sighed. 'What I said to you was private. We can have private reservations about a person's work, but that doesn't mean to say that we have to spell those out to him. It's called tact, Isabel!'

The reproof was administered gently, but it was a reproof nonetheless. Jamie, though, had more to say. 'You're the same, you know. What about van der Pompe? Did you tell him his paper was rubbish? You didn't, did you?'

She realised he was right. 'I'm sorry,' she said. 'You're quite right. Why hurt Laurence's feelings?'

'Precisely,' he said. 'And even if I said it was too fluid, that doesn't mean to say that it wasn't intelligent – or thought-provoking. Excessively fluid pieces can have their merits, after all.'

She had no stomach for further debate. 'Of course,' she said, looking towards the group of people in whose direction they were heading.

'See,' said Jamie. 'He's over there. He's being kissed.'

Isabel followed his gaze. A neat, rather muscular-looking figure was in the centre of a circle of admirers. The woman kissing him was Stephanie Partridge.

They joined the group. Jamie reached forward to shake the composer's hand. 'Really great,' he said.

The composer had a broad smile on his face. 'You like it?'

'Sure,' said Jamie. 'I think everybody did.'

'Yes,' said somebody standing nearby. 'The guy next to me said he'd never heard anything like it.'

'Well, that's a bit ambiguous,' joked Laurence. 'But I shall take it as a compliment.'

Jamie laughed. 'No, they liked it all right. I saw that chap from the *Herald* – he was smiling. And the *Scotsman*, too. I saw Susan Nickalls. She looked as if she was enjoying it.'

'If the critics are happy,' said Laurence, 'then I'm happy.'

This reminded Isabel of a fridge magnet she had seen a few days ago. There had been a kitchen scene printed on the surface of the magnet; a well-padded mamma-type figure, arms folded, gazed over her brood of children. The inscription read, *If Mama ain't happy, then nobody ain't happy.* She had thought of the persistence of stereotypes, but had then laughed. *Disapproval first*, she thought, *then laughter.* It was a play on Brecht and his 'Grub first, then ethics' – a proposition with which she had always been in profound disagreement. Grub *was* a matter of ethics and one could not detach the business of survival from the realm of ethics . . . But that raised issues altogether too complicated for the world of fridge magnets.

A thought came to her: 'The ethics of fridge magnets' – a special issue of the *Review of Applied Ethics*. Should you display a fridge magnet that perpetuates inequality, or intolerance, or selfishness . . . People did, of course: there were grossly insensitive fridge magnets about; there were fridge magnets that belittled men, even if few of them belittled women (who, by and large, chose fridge magnets in the first place). There would be so much to discuss.

Laurence turned to Isabel. 'You're Isabel, aren't you?' And to Jamie he said, 'Jamie, you never introduced me to Isabel.'

Jamie smiled. 'Sorry,' he said. 'But you're right, this is Isabel.'

Laurence shook hands formally. Isabel glanced about her. Where was Stephanie?

'Congratulations,' she said. 'I think your piece went down very well.'

Laurence bowed his head. 'Thanks. I was a bit nervous. You know how it is.'

'The programme said you were in Colombia,' she said.

'Yes. I was there just before I wrote this piece.'

'Inspired by it?' asked Isabel.

'Yes. I went to a dairy farm. I was going to stay in this fantastic old hotel – you know, Spanish colonial style – and I took the wrong turning and ended up at a dairy farm. They were very friendly.'

'They let you stay?'

'No, although I expect they would have, if I had asked. But they insisted on showing me round. Then they gave me some of their butter. They were very proud of it.'

'Hence *Yellow Butter*.'

'*Butter Yellow*,' corrected Jamie. 'It's *Butter Yellow*. The order makes a difference, I think.'

'Sorry,' said Isabel. 'I suppose you're right. *Yellow Butter* would be about butter, whereas . . . '

'*Butter Yellow* would be about yellow,' supplied Jamie.

'Yes, that's right,' said Laurence.

'But you were thinking about butter?' asked Isabel. 'Or were you thinking about yellow?'

'I suppose it was yellow,' said Laurence. 'But somehow it progressed beyond the title – and beyond yellow, I think.'

'There's that song about yellow,' said Jamie. 'About the mellowness of yellow. About being mad about saffron.'

'But she was a person,' said Isabel, 'not a spice. And I think that song was about synaesthesia.'

Jamie glanced at her. 'Don't start to dissect the lyrics of songs. Look at "American Pie". What's that about?'

Laurence laughed. 'Everyone has a theory about that,' he said. 'Except the composer.'

Isabel suddenly looked to her right and saw that she was standing next to Stephanie Partridge. She caught her breath. She looked at Jamie. He was facing Laurence, but now he turned and saw Stephanie. He seemed surprised.

Stephanie looked back at him; she did not seem to notice Isabel.

'You played brilliantly,' Jamie said. 'As usual.'

'Thank you. Laurence's piece was not easy.'

'I warned you it wouldn't be,' said Laurence. 'You were a consenting adult. You agreed to play it.'

Stephanie did not look at Laurence as he spoke, but had her eyes fixed on Jamie.

Jamie touched the sleeve of Isabel's dress. 'This is Isabel,' he said.

Stephanie looked at Isabel, as if for the first time. 'Hello.' Her tone was quite flat. She was uninterested. She looked back at Jamie.

Isabel felt a surge of relief. She's forgotten. So I was worrying about something that would never happen. She turned to Jamie; she wanted to hug him, publicly. She reached for his arm and gripped it tightly in a gesture of solidarity and affection. He glanced down at her hand upon his sleeve but he did not say anything. Nor did he look at her.

Somebody tapped Isabel on her shoulder. She swung round to see her friend, Iain Torrance, the theologian. She had not seen him for some time and she eagerly engaged him in conversation. Iain was keen for Isabel to see Dr Neil's Garden, in Duddingston – a secret corner of Edinburgh, facing the very loch on which the Reverend Robert Walker, the skating minister painted by Raeburn, had braved the ice. They talked for a few minutes before Isabel noticed that Jamie was now engaged in what looked like an intimate, whispered exchange with Stephanie. She froze, her earlier relief now turned to despair. She was telling him; Isabel was sure of it.

'Iain,' she said. 'I have to go.'

He inclined his head. 'Of course.'

'I'm not being rude; I just have to get back. The children . . .'

'I understand.'

She made her way to join Jamie. As she did so, Stephanie half turned towards her but did not so much look at her as through her. Isabel faltered, but now she felt angry. Jamie was *her* husband and it was not for this woman to look at her as if she was intruding upon a conversation. She moved forward briskly, tempted to brush Stephanie aside, but actually only coming slightly between her and Jamie.

'Sorry to interrupt,' she said, to Jamie rather than Stephanie, 'but we'll have to get back to the children.'

She glanced at Stephanie. 'We have two children.'

'Oh,' said Stephanie.

'Yes,' said Isabel. 'Two.'

The silence was awkward, but Isabel had the impression that Jamie, like her, was eager to get away. This was puzzling.

'I can't remember – did you bring a coat?' asked Jamie as they began to leave the bar.

'No. Nothing.'

She looked at him, trying to read his mood. He seemed anxious.

'Are you all right?' she asked.

'Of course I'm all right,' he answered quickly.

She knew, though, from his tone that something was amiss, and from that moment she was certain that Jamie was now aware of her deception. She took his arm as they left the hall by the back exit, making their way down the narrow lane that led onto the Meadows. The easy companionship of an arm-in-arm walk was missing; he seemed stiff and uncomfortable in his movements, as if he wanted to be somewhere else.

'We need to talk,' she said. 'Can we walk back the long way? Through Buccleuch Place, perhaps?' She looked up. Although it was close to ten, the night sky was still light – as it would be, at their latitude and in mid-summer, until after eleven.

'I don't really feel like talking,' said Jamie. 'Do you mind?'

The rebuff brought a stab of almost physical pain. 'I'm sorry,' she said. 'But we really have to.'

He was silent, but it was a silence of assent.

'Let's cross here,' said Isabel.

A car went past, and from its window came a snatch of music. 'Mozart,' muttered Jamie. 'That car was playing Mozart.'

She squeezed his arm gently. 'I love it when cars play Mozart, don't you? Usually they play heavy rock.'

'Not in Edinburgh,' he said. 'Our cars love Mozart. And Bach too.'

She felt the tension ease. How our bodies reflect our souls, she thought – in their little movements, their tics, their attitude.

'I need to talk to you,' he said.

She winced. 'I've been really stupid,' she said. 'I don't know why I did it. I suppose I was embarrassed . . . '

He stopped, and they stood together on the pavement. A passer-by, a student in a dirty tee-shirt and a pair of frayed jeans, walked past them, throwing a mildly curious glance.

'What are you talking about?' said Jamie.

'About the Café St Honoré.'

He shrugged. 'We can talk about restaurants some other time. I want to talk about that girl.'

'That's what I mean,' said Isabel. 'You see—'

He cut her short. 'Look, Isabel, I don't know what you think, but there's nothing – absolutely nothing – between me and Stephanie.'

She stared at him blankly.

'I can see you don't believe me,' he went on. 'The truth of the matter is this: she's been coming on to me. It's been pretty obvious. We were at a recording session a few weeks ago and she said to me that there was something she wanted to discuss. I thought it was something to do with an audition – something like that – and so I agreed. She said it would be easier to talk over lunch.'

'Lunch?'

'Yes, at that French place in Bruntsfield, *la Barantine*. The bakery place. I agreed, but I didn't tell you. I sort of forgot – a lot was going on.' He paused. She saw that he looked miserable. 'It was the day that you went off to get some information about that business you're looking into – that matchmaking stuff.'

Isabel gasped, and Jamie misinterpreted her response.

'Yes, I know,' he continued. 'I just wasn't thinking. You know how you do something thoughtless and then it becomes difficult to get yourself out of it. I had lunch with her and of course she started to go on about how she thought we had so much in common. I realised that things were getting out of control and so I played it cool. But I don't think she took the hint.'

Isabel wanted to laugh. This, she thought, is a perfect symmetry of embarrassment.

'And so I had to spell it out to her again back there.'

'In the bar?'

'Yes. I had to actually spell it out. I told her that I was married, full stop. End of story.' He sighed. 'I don't like hurting people's feelings.'

She threw her arms around him. 'Of course you don't, you lovely, wonderful person. Of course you don't.'

His relief was apparent. 'You've forgiven me?' Then he added quickly, 'Not that I did anything, of course, but for not telling you something I should have told you. You've forgiven me for that?'

'Let he who is without lunch cast the first stone,' said Isabel.

'What?'

'Let me tell you,' said Isabel, taking his arm again and leading him gently on the next stage of their walk. 'There are coincidences, you know, and then there are extraordinary coincidences. I want to tell you about something that is an extraordinary coincidence. Don't interrupt, just listen . . . '

They made their way down Buccleuch Place, not walking on the pavement, but on the cobblestones of the road itself – there was no traffic. Skirting the great bulk of the university library, an angular monument to modernism that was in such stark contrast to the human dimensions of the tenements of Buccleuch Place, they wandered down onto the path that circled the Meadows. By the time they had reached Middle

Meadow Walk, the forgiveness, on both sides, was complete. It was easy, Isabel observed, because, when looked at dispassionately, there was nothing for either of them to forgive.

'Not that it makes much difference,' said Isabel. 'Often when people ask for forgiveness, it is they who need to forgive themselves.' She smiled at Jamie. 'Am I making sense?'

He evidently did not care that they were in full view of a cluster of dog-owners walking their dogs. He stopped and took her in his arms, kissing her passionately and urgently.

Then he drew back and looked into her eyes. 'You've always made sense,' he said. 'Even when I find it difficult to follow what on earth you're going on about, it seems to me that you make sense.'

'Good,' said Isabel. 'So we misunderstand one another perfectly.'

A dog raced past them, a bundle of fur and wagging tail. Their laughter excited him, and he gave an enthusiastic bark.

'That dog is composed of pure goodness,' said Isabel.

'How can you tell?' asked Jamie.

'By looking at him. That's how you tell.'

13

She telephoned Rob McLaren the next morning. He sounded weary when he answered – a late night, he said.

She apologised for the early call. 'I'm sorry if I woke you up, but I wondered if you could give me some information.'

His weariness became wariness. 'Possibly.'

'You mentioned that you'd heard a story from a lawyer. It was about another of these women who had got themselves mixed up with Tony MacUspaig.'

There was a brief silence. Then, 'Yes. I heard something, but I think I told you everything I know. I didn't hear much.'

'But the lawyer would know?'

He made a clicking sound. 'Lawyers won't talk about their clients.'

'This one did. You told me he spoke to you about money that had been paid to the good doctor.'

'Yes, but . . .'

'I'd like to speak to the lawyer. I'd like to find out who the woman was. You said that she was called Tricia – I take it you don't know her surname?'

For a few moments he said nothing, then, 'No, I don't know it. But if you contact him, he'll know that I've spoken to you about something he told me in confidence.'

She assured him that she would not mention his name. 'I'll leave you out of it. I'll simply say that I've heard from somebody. I won't say who.'

'I don't think he'll talk.'

'Perhaps you could let me see,' said Isabel. 'You may be right. He may clam up. But at least let me try.'

There was further hesitation, and then Rob gave the lawyer's name, and the name of his firm. It was a well-known firm that had its offices in the Georgian New Town. They were a private-client firm, adept at dealing patiently with the affairs of well-off Scottish families. The firm's motto was 'Preserve', which made it quite clear that their energy and talents were directed to the keeping of things exactly as they were. This drew comment from rivals, who saw them as being too conservative. '"Preserve" is an entirely suitable motto for a jam-making company,' said one. 'Marmalade and so on – I'm not so sure it's quite right for a firm of lawyers.'

And there it was: *PRESERVE*, written in italic capitals underneath a framed photograph of the founding partner, a comfortable-looking Edwardian figure wearing a wing-tip collar and a pair of unframed spectacles. Isabel stared at the picture from her seat in the waiting room and reflected on destiny and its effect on our appearance. A person who looked like that could not have been a farmer or a fisherman; he was a lawyer as conjured up by the casting department. And in so far as he had any message to impart, it was surely 'Preserve'.

It had been simple to arrange her appointment. She had telephoned the lawyer whose name had been given to her by Rob McLaren and he had been amenable to an appointment later that morning. A meeting he was due to attend had been cancelled. 'We settled,' he said.

Isabel liked that expression. She knew that lawyers used it in a technical sense to refer to an agreement not to pursue a claim, but it seemed to her that it was a word that could be used in many other contexts. One might settle with one's friends when there had been a misunderstanding or a tiff; one might settle with a neighbour after arguing over the height of a hedge; one might settle with the weather when one decided to stop complaining about it.

The lawyer came into the reception area.

'Isabel Dalhousie?'

Isabel stood up.

'My name is Tam Fraser.' He extended a hand. 'We've actually met, you know. My little boy's in your son's nursery class. You have Charlie, don't you?'

She tried to place him. She thought that she knew most of the parents of Charlie's playmates, but she could not remember this man.

'I picked him up one afternoon,' he said. 'My wife was in London and I was holding the fort.'

She was still looking blank when he told her, 'My son's Douglas. The little redhead.'

Now she knew: Douglas was collected by a woman who always arrived punctually, spent very little time chatting to the other parents, and then disappeared in a small blue car. 'Of course,' said Isabel. 'I'm sorry I didn't put two and two together.'

'There was no reason for you to do so,' said the lawyer. He

gestured towards the corridor. 'My office is down there. Shall we?'

He ushered her into a surprisingly large room. In the days when the building was a private house, this would have been the drawing room, with its three large windows spanning almost the whole distance between floor and ceiling. The view from these was over the bank that dropped down to the gorge below. The higher branches of the broad-leaf trees that clung to the descending slope were just below the lower level of the window – a sea of dark green that moved slowly in the wind. Drawn to the view, Isabel crossed to the window and looked out over the treetops.

'It's a great distraction for me,' said Tam. 'You'll see that I have my desk facing the other way. It's the only way to get any work done.'

Across the gorge, beyond the roof line of the terraces on the other side, was a thin sliver of silver sea and the hills of Fife. The sky was largely cloudless, a pale blue intersected by the thin cotton-line of a vapour trail. Tam noticed her looking up. 'I wonder where those jets go,' he said. 'Somewhere far away, I suppose. Iceland. America. Helsinki.'

She turned away from the window, allowing her gaze to fall on the lawyer's face. She saw that he had grey eyes and that these eyes were kind. Waiting in the reception area, she had flicked through a news magazine that had been lying on the table for clients to read while waiting for their appointment. On the cover there had been a picture of a well-known politician, a man famous for his rudeness and aggression. She had looked at the eyes – the piercing, accusing eyes, and had seen only an impenetrable, defensive anger. Nothing – no forced smiles nor rehearsed protestation of concern, could cancel out the cold selfishness of those eyes. *The eyes are the window of the soul* . . . it was such a well-worn adage, a cliché by now, but Isabel had read that neuroscience, which was validating so many intuitive, ancient beliefs about who we were and how we lived our lives, now confirmed this insight too. The part of the brain that was most closely associated with self-awareness, the ventromedial prefrontal cortex, lay directly behind the eyes. So that was where we were located – that was where the soul was to be found, if it were to be found anywhere.

Tam's eyes were the polar opposite of the vain politician's, and Isabel felt a strong sense of security in his presence. This was a man who would understand what she said to him – not just in a superficial sense, but at a much deeper level.

'Now then,' he said, as she sat down. 'What can I do for you, Ms Dalhousie?'

She felt encouraged to be direct. 'I want you to break a professional confidence.' She might as well start with his likely objection, she thought.

His mouth fell open. 'Did I hear you correctly?'

Isabel smiled. 'You did.'

He recovered his composure. Now he looked bemused. 'You can hardly expect me to do that.'

'I know,' said Isabel. 'But there must be exceptions to the rule.'

He thought for a moment. 'Occasionally. You know, I serve on the Law Society of Scotland committee that considers matters of that sort. We were discussing the issue the other day, as it happens.'

'And?'

'And we reaffirmed the rule that there were certain circumstances – certain very limited circumstances – when the very strong obligation to keep matters confidential may have to ... how shall I put it? May have to yield to a greater good of some sort.'

Isabel was on familiar ground. A few issues ago, the *Review* and one of the contributors had given close attention to the *Tarasoff* case. Isabel had been intrigued.

'Have you heard of the *Tarasoff* decision? It's an American court case.'

Tam shrugged. 'No,' he said. 'But remember: the law in the United States is very different from ours here in Scotland.'

Isabel knew that, but the case was still an important illustration of an issue that could arise anywhere. 'The things that happen are more or less the same everywhere.'

'True enough, but ... '

Isabel continued, 'Miss Tarasoff, you see, was a student at the University of California. This was back in 1967.'

'A heady time out there,' said Tam.

Isabel smiled. 'Yes, it was. Haight-Ashbury. The summer of love. Flowers in your hair ... '

'Of course.'

'But not everybody was happy,' Isabel said. 'There was a student from Bengal, a Mr Poddar. He became friendly with a fellow student, Miss Tarasoff. She didn't realise that she might have misled him as to her feelings. He didn't really mean very much to her. It was a time when people were very friendly.'

'It was 1967 after all,' said Tam wryly.

Isabel nodded. 'A time of innocence.'

Tam allowed himself a glance out of the window. 'I was exactly two.'

'And I didn't exist,' said Isabel. 'It's odd. I think of myself as having been alive in the sixties, but I wasn't.'

'It's because we know the period so well. We think we were there. Sometimes I imagine I remember the Battle of Britain.'

'A lot of people think that. We relive the war an awful lot in this country. I think the Germans find it a bit frustrating. They want to move on, and we keep making films that show them in the wrong.'

'Well they were,' said Tam. 'As were so many other people at various points in history. Lots of people, ourselves included, have done shameful things. At least the Germans have expressed their regret.'

'Yet there comes a time, surely, when you should refrain from mentioning the wrongs of others. Forgiveness may mean not mentioning the thing forgiven. You may have to draw a line under the past.'

He looked doubtful. 'It may be difficult to decide when to draw that line. We still talk about Culloden, don't we? That's still a live issue for some I could mention.'

'1746. Only yesterday,' said Isabel.

'Not to mention Bannockburn.'

'1314,' said Isabel. 'The day before yesterday, as far as much of Scotland is concerned.'

Tam shook his head in disbelief. 'Our countrymen have long memories.'

Isabel was about to say, *Yes, I agree*, but her response, when it came out, was quite different. 'Perhaps they do – but then that's better than having no memory.'

Her reply clearly intrigued Tam. 'Interesting,' he said, and then, smiling, continued, 'This is a rather unusual consultation, Ms Dalhousie. But rather welcome – on a day that was going to be somewhat mundane.'

'Perhaps I should return to Mr Poddar.'

'Ah, yes the unfortunate Mr Poddar from . . . '

'Bengal.'

'I can just see him,' said Tam. 'An earnest, serious young

man, expecting this California girl to return his devotion; not realising, of course, what he was up against . . . '

Isabel mentioned another detail. 'It was rather pathetic, in fact. This Poddar person was an Untouchable, as they used to be called. The word now is Dalit, I believe. It was pretty remarkable for an Untouchable to be given a scholarship to study abroad – unheard of, even. Imagine being somebody from the lowest drawer of Indian society – somebody outside their caste system, a pariah – and finding yourself in Berkeley just when free love and magic mushrooms and all the rest of it was in the air.'

'It must have been very confusing for him.'

'It was – so much so that he became unhinged. He started to stalk this Tarasoff woman – although I don't think that people used the word stalking very much in those days. But the behaviour existed and in due course he ended up seeing a psychologist employed by the university.'

Tam was absorbed in the story. 'This isn't going to end well, is it?' he said. 'In spite of flower power and all the rest, this story is going to end badly.'

'I'm afraid it does. Very badly.'

'Very badly for Miss Tarasoff?'

'Yes. For both of them, I suppose. Murder is bad for the victim but also for the perpetrator.' She paused. 'Like most bad acts.'

'I see what you mean.'

Isabel noticed Tam glancing at his watch. He was being discreet, but she saw it, and she blushed. 'I'm sorry if I'm taking up your time,' she said. 'I'll get to the point.'

He held up a hand. 'Please. There's no hurry – and I'm enjoying our conversation. Most of the time I sit here talking about very dull matters. Wills, executries, trust – that sort of thing. Tell me what happened.'

'Miss Tarasoff went off to Brazil,' said Isabel. 'While she was away, Poddar told his therapist that he was planning to kill a young woman. He did not mention her name, but from what he said she could be easily identified. The therapist was alarmed and told the campus police, who interviewed Poddar and took the view that he posed no real danger.'

'So when she came back . . . '

'When she came back, Poddar shot her with a pellet gun and then pulled out a knife and stabbed her to death.'

Tam winced. 'Not a pleasant tale.'

'No. But the point of the whole thing was that her parents felt that she – or they – should have been warned. They weren't, you see, because of the obligation of confidentiality. Doctors and therapists are told very firmly that what they hear in the course of treatment is not to be communicated to anybody else.'

'And priests,' said Tam thoughtfully. 'And lawyers.' He paused. 'I see where our discussion is going, by the way. But tell me: what happened? I take it that they sued the therapist?'

'They sued his employers, the University of California.'

'And what happened?'

'The Supreme Court of California said that there was a duty to warn. They didn't say that it applied in every case, but it did where there was a real danger of violence. So a psychiatrist – or a therapist – could ignore his duty of confidentiality in order to protect somebody at risk. Not only *could* he do that, but he *should* do it.'

Tam thought about this. 'And Mr Poddar? What happened to him?'

'He was charged with murder, but the conviction was set aside because of legal technicalities. He was then sent back to India where apparently he met a lawyer and was happily married.'

Tam sat back in his chair. 'I take it that the point of this is that you think I have confidential information that affects in some way the safety of somebody else. Am I right in thinking that?'

'Not safety, perhaps. But certainly welfare – and at a stretch that may affect safety.'

'How so?'

She felt that if somebody was capable of exploiting another, then that same person might be capable of harming them physically. This, though, seemed too tenuous a connection for Tam, who looked sceptical.

'I don't know of any client of mine who is planning to kill somebody,' he said.

'But you do know that one of your clients has been at risk.'

He frowned. 'You seem to have a good grasp of my business.'

'You have a client – a fairly wealthy woman, I gather – who made a transfer of money to a man she was seeing.'

Tam's eyes narrowed. 'These are client affairs, you know.'

'But you know what I'm talking about?'

He hesitated before replying. Eventually he said that he did, but his entire demeanour now was guarded.

'May I ask, how do you know about this?'

'I'm afraid that's confidential,' said Isabel.

Tam burst out laughing. 'But that's a bit rich. I don't mean to be rude, but don't you see a certain inconsistency here?'

Isabel did indeed. 'I know. I came in with the intention of asking you to break a confidence and then I claim . . . '

'You claim confidentiality yourself,' completed Tam; his tone was bemused now and the suspicion of a few moments ago seemed to have abated. He shrugged. 'Oh well, I suppose this place is as leaky as everywhere else in this city.'

Isabel sensed that this was her opportunity to make her request. Tam had obviously been interested in the Tarasoff story; he was well aware of the issues and she suspected that a public interest argument might not fall on deaf ears.

'I'd like to tell you exactly why I need to talk to you about that transaction,' said Isabel. 'There's a man in this city who I think may be preying on vulnerable women. Preying in the financial sense.'

Her instinct was right. Tam's expression tightened. 'Tell me more,' he said.

'This man has been introduced to somebody who is particularly well off. Now the person who made the introduction is really worried because she subsequently discovered there were two cases in which he appeared to have wormed his way into the affections of wealthy women. Both of these cases – of which one involves a client of yours – led to money being given to this man. I've looked into one of them . . . '

'And?'

'And I'm not sure about what happened. I was given an innocent explanation, but there's something that makes me feel that the story I was given by the woman in question may not be true.'

'Why? What puts you on your guard?'

'I think that the woman in question may have been suicidal. I think she's possibly trying to make the best of a bad situation and wants to avoid thinking the worst of the man. It's possible – I'm just not sure. So I really need to look at the other case – which is yours.'

'And then?'

'Then I'll know whether I can approach the woman who

I think may now be at risk. I want to be able to show her something concrete. Or, better still, get one of the victims to talk to her.'

Tam sat back in his chair. He thought for several minutes before he spoke again. 'You know something?' he said. 'One of the things that I feel strongly about – really strongly – is the protection of the people I look after. That's what I do, you know – every day of the week in this office. Every day. My job is to look after people – as their trustee, as their adviser, as the executor of their husband's, father's, mother's will – whatever my role may be.' He fixed her with an intense look. 'And I take that really seriously, believe me.'

'I don't doubt that you do.'

'Thank you. And if there's one thing that really gets to me, it's the thought of somebody getting in under the radar and defrauding or stealing – for that's what it is – from one of the people I look after. So if I tell you anything now, it's for that reason. The thought that this man – whoever he might be – is going to take advantage of some other poor woman fills me with . . . well, frankly it fills me with anger.'

Isabel knew that she had made her case and had won. Tam was exactly the person she had judged him to be when she entered his office – a man of principle, a kind man, an old-fashioned lawyer who was not interested in charging high fees and doing elaborate deals, but wanted only to look after those entrusted to his care.

'I take it that you'll need to speak to my client,' he said.

'Yes.'

'I have one stipulation,' he said. 'I go with you. Is that acceptable?'

It was.

'In that case,' he said, 'we can probably get this over and

done with rather quickly. My client is just a couple of blocks away. She lives on Drummond Place. She's likely to be in; she ruptured her Achilles tendon two weeks ago and she's still pretty immobile. Would you be able to go there more or less directly?'

Isabel nodded. 'I'll need to make a telephone call. I have a young child – two, actually – and I'll need to tell the woman who helps me that I'll be a bit late.'

'Please go ahead. And then I'll get my secretary to see if my client's in.'

'Great,' said Isabel.

'Her name is Tricia Ferguson,' Tam added. 'I'll tell you about her before we go over there.'

Tam gave Isabel the background details as they made their way out of the building and began the walk to Drummond Place. Tricia Ferguson, he explained, was the widow of Graeme Ferguson, a man who had owned a large architecture firm. Graeme had been a keen yachtsman who had a classic sailing boat on the Clyde. He was a member of a racing team and competed not only in Scotland but also down on the Solent. In the late summer he sailed mainly in the Western Isles, and often spent weeks going from island to island in the Hebrides. It was on one of these trips, when he was sailing with a couple of friends from Glasgow, that he was caught in a sudden and very violent storm while sailing back to Lewis by night. A reefing line had become stuck, and Graeme had gone forward to deal with it, fastening himself – or so he thought – to a jack line. Something went wrong with the clip – a small thing, but enough to mean that when a rogue wave hit the boat and swept him off the deck he was quickly lost in the darkness.

Graeme left Tricia well provided for. He had established

a trust that would give her an income and deal with all expenses. 'He was very cautious,' said Tam. 'Tricia could make large payments from the disposable income of the trust fund, but the cheques had to be issued by me. I suppose he wanted me to keep an eye on things without spelling it out. Tricia's pretty independent in her outlook and she never really liked that provision.

'Most of the time, of course, there was nothing to worry about. Even so, I very quickly learned that she did not like me to question any payment she requested. Not that she ever asked for anything much; there were a few charitable donations – Scottish Opera, the National Galleries and so on. There were a few gifts of a couple of thousand – mostly to nephews or nieces. I put all these through knowing that she did not like me to question them. It was pride, I think. She didn't like the idea of being looked after, or watched over, perhaps. And I can understand why.

'But then there was this sudden request for a cheque for fifty thousand to a Dr . . . I don't remember the name. It was something very unusual.'

'MacUspaig.'

'Yes, that's it. MacUspaig. And I felt I had to ask her about it. I got a real flea in my ear. She was very upset, and I backed off. But, frankly, I was worried. We put it through – as we had to.' He looked searchingly at Isabel. 'I take it that this MacUspaig is the man you're talking about?'

'It is.'

'Mmm, I don't like the sound of him, I'm afraid.'

'The jury's still out,' said Isabel. 'But I suspect your instinct's right.'

It took them no more than ten minutes to reach Drummond Place. Tricia Ferguson lived in a complete Georgian house with a front door painted in high-gloss black paint, the house number in brass Roman numerals on its central panel. Tam sounded the bell and then turned to Isabel. 'Let me talk to begin with,' he said. 'I think that would be best.'

She agreed. 'I'll leave it up to you. Do you think, though, that you might be able to ask her to speak to the woman whom MacUspaig's currently seeing? She hasn't listened to anybody so far, but a fellow victim, if that's what she is, might just get her to see reason.'

The black door opened and Tricia Ferguson invited them in. Her right foot was in a cast and she was walking with a stick.

'Your secretary phoned,' said Tricia. 'But she didn't say what it was about.' She looked at Isabel with undisguised curiosity.

Tam made the introduction. 'Could we have a word?' he said. 'We won't take up too much of your time.'

The drawing room was on the ground floor – a typical, elegant room with the characteristic Palladian proportions of the Georgian New Town. An Adam fireplace in light pine dominated one side of the room, while the facing wall was shelved from floor to ceiling with books. They sat before the fireplace, a low rectangular upholstered table in front of them, also stacked with books. Isabel noticed a book she had herself – a history of the mapping of Scottish islands. She saw, too, a book on the art of the Scottish Colourists.

'Isabel is somebody who acts on behalf of various people,' began Tam, Isabel having explained to him how she became involved in the matter. 'She acts voluntarily – helps them.'

Tricia looked at Isabel and smiled. 'I see.'

Tam now spoke gingerly. 'She thinks that there is a possibility that there is a man in this city who is seeking out well-off women. She thinks he might be targeting them.'

Tricia said nothing.

'And it occurred to me,' Tam continued, 'that you might have met this man.'

Tricia stiffened. 'Oh? Why do you say that?'

Isabel heard Tam take a deep breath. 'Because you made a direct transfer of money to the very man she's interested in.'

It took a few moments for Tricia to react. Isabel and Tam exchanged glances, ready for a strong reaction.

But Tricia did not appear to be angry. 'You really need to let me get on with my own financial life,' she said quietly. 'It's my money, after all.'

'I know that,' said Tam. 'I wouldn't dream of interfering. I know how you feel.'

'Do you?' asked Tricia. 'Do you really?'

He stuck to his guns. 'Yes, I think I do. And the only reason I'm even raising this with you is because I think that other people might be at risk.'

Tricia examined her fingernails. 'You do, do you?'

'Yes.'

'You're referring to Tony MacUspaig, aren't you?'

Tam nodded.

'Tony is a very nice man,' said Tricia. 'One of the finest men I know.'

Tam looked to Isabel for support.

'You did give money to him?' asked Isabel.

'Yes,' said Tricia. 'Fifty thousand pounds. Tam has probably already told you that – along with goodness knows what other details of my private affairs.'

'None,' said Isabel firmly.

Tricia digested this. Then she turned to Tam. 'You know, Tam, I really resent being treated like an irresponsible adolescent. But I do accept that Graeme set up the system and I respect his wishes.'

'He only wanted to protect you,' said Tam.

'My husband,' said Tricia, now addressing Isabel, 'was one of the finest, kindest men in Scotland.'

'I'm sure he was,' said Isabel.

Now came the surprise. 'And I suspect that what he would have wanted me to do in these circumstances is give you the information you want.'

Tam reacted with relief. 'I think that's right,' he said.

The decision made, Tricia became businesslike. 'Here's what you need to know. Tony MacUspaig is a very fine man. He and I were never lovers. He was a friend and I still see him from time to time. It was a purely platonic friendship; I might have been prepared for more, but it was not to be.

'You may know that he does charitable work in North Africa – in Morocco, to be precise. He runs a clinic there that does operations on kids with hare-lips and so on.'

'I'd heard that,' said Isabel.

'But of course that eats up money. So last year he came to see me and told me that they needed some new piece of equipment and that he was going to sell a painting he owned to fund that. His father was something of a collector and had a few fairly valuable Scottish Colourist paintings. Peploe, Cadell and, of course, Fergusson – no relation. Tony inherited these, and still has most of them.

'Anyway he had a very nice Peploe – quite a small painting, but a lovely one nonetheless. He was going to put that up for auction. He said that he had had it valued by Guy Peploe himself and Guy had said it was worth fifty thousand. The auction house agreed, but of course if it went up for auction then he would have to pay fifteen per cent seller's premium, and so he would get less. If it were sold privately, though, he would get the full amount. So the clinic would get more if he sold it privately.

'Tony then said to me, "That's all very well, but I don't know anybody who wants to buy a Peploe." I said nothing at first, but then I had an idea. I love Peploe's work – so I would buy it directly from Tony. He'd get the full amount, I'd not have to worry about auction prices being upped by other bidders, and I'd have my Peploe. Everybody would win.'

Tricia rose to her feet. 'Come with me. I'll show it to you. It's in the dining room.'

Tam made his relief apparent. 'Well, there you are,' he said. 'That explains it.'

They stood in front of the Peploe.

'It's very lovely,' said Isabel. 'Mull, from across the Sound of Iona?'

'I think so,' said Tricia. 'And yes, it is lovely. Look at the green of the sea – that lovely, almost emerald green. It's like that, you know. I was there earlier this summer. We drove through mist on Mull and then suddenly we were there and could see the abbey and the sea beyond the abbey and the water was that green, that green that stops the heart for its sheer beauty.'

Isabel remembered what Tam had said about Graeme's sailing. 'You must have sailed through there many times.'

Tricia continued to stare at the painting. 'We did,' she said. 'Our last sail together, in fact. We spent the night anchored off Erraid, where Robert Louis Stevenson had David Balfour shipwrecked in *Kidnapped*. Then we went up through the Sound, although you have to be careful to keep well to the east because it's so shallow in the middle. You'd run aground.'

Isabel saw Tam reach out and lay a hand gently on Tricia's forearm. He gave it a squeeze, and she turned to him in appreciation of the gesture. This is what a lawyer should be, thought Isabel.

'Tony loved this painting,' said Tricia. 'It must have been a real wrench for him to part with it, but I think the clinic means more to him than anything else.'

'I think I've done him a great injustice,' muttered Isabel.

'And so have I,' said Tam.

'We all get things wrong,' said Tricia. It seemed to Isabel that Tricia was deriving a certain amount of pleasure from allaying Tam's concerns about the payment. It was, she felt, a 'told you so' moment, and everybody enjoyed those. There's no greater pleasure, she thought, than being shown to be right.

Now in a position to be magnanimous, Tricia proposed a cup of tea; she had made her point. 'Have you got the time, Tam?'

'Always,' he said. 'Priority number one is tea, then clients.'

'That would make a good motto,' said Tricia, smiling. 'You know, I've never liked that "Preserve" thing, Tam. "Tea first, then clients" would be far better.'

'More Brechtian,' said Isabel.

'Yes, that too,' said Tricia.

'I shall speak to the partners,' said Tam. 'But I wouldn't hold your breath.'

When she arrived back at the house, Grace had put Charlie down for his nap. Magnus, though, was wide awake and Isabel picked him up, embraced him tenderly, and then carried him in her arms to look out of the window.

'I don't know how far you can see,' she murmured. 'But that's the world out there.'

'He can't see very far,' said Grace from behind her. 'Babies can't.'

Isabel nodded. 'I know. They see in three dimensions only after about five months.'

'He'll be able to see the trees,' said Grace.

Isabel bit her tongue. She did not need to be lectured on these matters by Grace, but then she thought: *I am the fortunate one here; I am the one who is blessed.* 'You're right,' she said.

They were in the kitchen, and Grace now attended to some dishes that had been stacked in the sink. As she did so, she spoke over her shoulder to Isabel. 'Charlie went on and on about his little brother today. There was no stopping him. My baby brother this; my baby brother that.'

Isabel was surprised. 'Oh?'

'Yes. And he even asked if he could make him some porridge.'

'Well, that's progress.'

Grace laughed. 'And you know what he said? He suddenly announced that he had a list of people he loved. He said he loved Magnus best, and Jamie was second, and then—'

Isabel frowned. Why had Grace broken off? Because it was Grace who came third. Isabel was sure that Charlie had said he preferred Grace to herself.

'And then?'

'And then you,' said Grace.

'I was third?'

'Yes,' said Grace. 'I didn't want to upset you – just in case you didn't want him to love Jamie more than you.'

Isabel laughed. 'Oh, heavens, no – I don't mind. Children say ridiculous things. And they don't know their own minds half the time. Only a few days ago he was very resentful of Magnus. Now that all seems to have changed.'

'They're very fickle, aren't they?'

'Yes,' agreed Isabel. 'But what a privilege to have them in

our lives. You, me . . . we're both so lucky.'

She could tell that Grace was touched by being included, and she was pleased that she had made the remark.

Grace was staring at her. 'You know, I'm not sure if I ever thanked you for sharing your children with me.'

Isabel shook her head. 'You don't have to thank me.'

'I do,' said Grace. 'I have to thank you for lots of things, and that's one of them.'

Isabel smiled. There was nothing more to be said, she felt.

14

Bea answered the telephone breathlessly. 'I can't talk for long, Isabel,' she said. 'I have sixteen people coming to dinner – sixteen! – and I haven't done a thing yet. I've got hardly any of the stuff I need and I'll have to go to Mellis for some cheese and then . . . '

At the other end of the line, Isabel gave a silent sigh. 'And I'm about to add to your list.'

This was greeted with silence.

'I'd like to meet you for coffee,' said Isabel. 'We'd need fifteen minutes – no more.'

Bea struggled. She was, as she had explained, extremely busy, but as a socialite in her inmost being she had very rarely, if ever, turned down an invitation. 'It's not the best of days for that . . . '

'I know,' said Isabel. 'But a break will help you to catch your breath.

'Oh, all right. But where?'

Isabel asked her whether she needed to go to the fishmonger, and Bea replied that she did. 'I'm planning scallops for the first course and I haven't checked up to see whether anybody's got them in. What am I going to do if there aren't any? I'll have to think of something else for the starter and I'm having sixteen people in – did I tell you that? Sixteen.'

'Take a deep breath, Bea,' said Isabel. She remembered how, when they were at school together, there was a gym mistress, Miss Gilchrist, who told them to take a deep breath before they did anything. 'Anything at all, girls – take a deep breath before you attempt it.'

One of the girls in the back, a sultry girl called Frances McMannion, sniggered, as she often did.

'And you, Frances McMannion,' the teacher responded, 'can go and stand in the corridor until the end of gym, and while you are there you may contemplate what a disgrace you are to Edinburgh.'

A disgrace to Edinburgh . . . it was Miss Gilchrist's strongest condemnation, a reproach reserved for a few fitting targets: from the lazy, who put insufficient effort into vaulting, or whose efforts on the ropes and bars were desultory; to the sloppy, who tucked in their blouses without due care; to those who walked rather than ran the cross-country course, hoping not to be noticed; to those who were caught smoking or arranging clandestine meetings with boys. It went without saying that most boys were, in Miss Gilchrist's eyes, a disgrace to Edinburgh unless proven otherwise.

Bea said, 'Take a deep breath . . . Now who said that? Miss Gilchrist, wasn't it?'

'It was,' replied Isabel. 'So, how about eleven o'clock? At the deli? You can go to Hughes the fishmonger beforehand. He'll have scallops, and it's just a few doors down the road. You can kill two birds with one stone.'

'What's it about?' asked Bea.

'Connie,' said Isabel.

'Oh no,' said Bea. 'I'd forgotten all about her.'

'You haven't been worrying? I thought you were worried sick.'

'Oh, I was worried sick, but then you know how it is, you go on to the next thing to worry about.'

Isabel struggled with her feelings of resentment. Bea, it seemed, had simply transferred her anxiety onto Isabel's shoulders. As she rang off, she wondered whether she would say anything to Bea about that. It was tempting, but she decided against it. Reproach or censure were powerful weapons, and should only be used when there was no alternative, as their effect could so easily be to cut the ties of good will that kept people together. A relationship that had taken years to establish, built up through a thousand acts of encouragement and support, could be irretrievably damaged in an instant by an unduly harsh word.

When Isabel arrived at the delicatessen, fifteen minutes before the time arranged for her meeting with Bea, she was greeted by Eddie.

'Cat and her new friend have gone off for coffee elsewhere,' he said. 'Our coffee's obviously not good enough for Miss Pi . . . ' He stopped himself. 'I mean for Peg.'

Isabel ignored this. 'I'm meeting somebody at eleven. I can give you a hand until then if you like.'

'I'll be all right,' said Eddie. 'It's very quiet. I'll make coffee when your friend comes in.'

She sat down at the table with a copy of that day's *Scotsman*. There was an article about research that had rehabilitated eggs: we could eat them again, she read. Not only that, but if we ate several eggs a week our risk of a range of conditions would diminish significantly. She glanced up at Eddie.

'Eggs are good for you, Eddie,' she said.

'You can choke on an egg,' he said. 'I knew somebody who did that. And I knew somebody who swallowed an olive the wrong way. It went into his lung and they said it was too dangerous to remove. He still has it. I'm always very careful with olives.'

'Oh well, everything has its dangers, I suppose.'

'I knew somebody who ate too many green olives,' Eddie continued. 'He really loved them. He ate jars and jars of them. He turned a sort of green colour – I saw him. He was actually green.'

'And what happened to him?'

'He went to live in Glasgow, I think,' said Eddie.

Isabel looked at Eddie. It was a very odd thing, she thought: Eddie inhabited a slightly different universe. It was one populated by people who choked on eggs and turned green through eating too many olives; it was one that was full of strange beliefs, half-truths, and the occasional superstition. It was not dissimilar, in a way, to Grace's world, with its pillars of spiritualism and the belief that just beyond this world there was a dimension – the other side, as she called it – to which we would all in due course cross over and busy ourselves with sending enigmatic messages to people still on this side. What united Grace and Eddie? Was it a lack of formal education? Eddie had not distinguished himself at school and had left at the age of seventeen, as far as Isabel had been able to establish. He was literate and numerate, but he had had very little exposure to history or science, and his geographical knowledge was shaky, to say the least. Isabel had mentioned Malta in the course of a conversation a few weeks ago – it had to do with an order of Maltese olive oil, as it happened – and it had been apparent that Eddie thought Malta was in the Caribbean. But then there were probably many people who thought Malta was in the Caribbean, and indeed many who had never heard of it, who thought it was a hot milky drink or even an illness. *People came down with Malta; they were healthy enough, and then they got Malta – such a pity.*

Not being able to locate Malta, of course, was not Eddie's fault. That was the schools, thought Isabel. It seemed to her that they taught less and less. Children were not taught to recite poetry, or learn capital cities, or commit to memory the names of the principal rivers of the world. How could people sit through years of education and at the end of it know practically nothing? One in five Britons, she had read, were functionally illiterate. This meant that they had difficulty reading the instructions on a medicine bottle – and that could be as dangerous as swallowing an olive the wrong way.

'What are you smiling at?' Eddie asked from across the room.

'I was thinking about olives,' said Isabel.

Eddie rolled his eyes. 'You're very odd, Isabel. You know that? You're very odd.'

She wanted to say: *That's exactly what I think of you*, but did not.

Eddie took off his apron and came to join her at her table. Leaning forward, he whispered, 'I know it's got nothing to do with me – like you said the other day. I know it's none of my business, but I think that Cat's gone off her rocker.'

Isabel glanced in the direction of the closed office door. 'Why do you think that, Eddie?'

His eyes brightened at the prospect of disclosing the secret. 'I'll tell you. The other day I was stacking that shelf over there – the one near her door. I wasn't eavesdropping – I swear I wasn't – but I couldn't help hearing what they were talking about. Cat was reading something to her and every so often she – that's Peg – said, "Oh, that's so true," and things like that.

'Okay, so I thought, Well, they're sitting in there looking into one another's eyes and it's none of my business, like you said. So I didn't do anything, but when they went out at lunchtime I went into the office just to have a look around. I found the book they were reading and it was really weird. It was called *The Prophet* by somebody with a really odd name – Cowhill Gibron, or something like that.'

'Kahlil Gibran,' said Isabel. 'He was a Lebanese mystic. People used to love reading him.'

'Maybe, but why sit around and read it to your friend. Don't you think that's odd?' He tapped the side of his head. 'Don't you think it's mental?'

'No, I don't, Eddie. I think that people have different tastes. There are some people who like reading Lebanese mystics to other people. It's just the way they are.'

He looked at her incredulously. 'She used to read trade catalogues. She used to read those all the time. Articles about cheese and cured meat and so on. Now it's this Kahlil character.'

'Well, perhaps that represents progress.'

'I think she's in love with her. I think Cat's gone nuts over her. That's what I think, Isabel.' He seemed slightly surprised by his own directness, and blushed.

Isabel looked down at the floor. 'Maybe,' she said. 'Maybe they've found one another, and if they have, then I'm pleased.'

'I'm not,' said Eddie.

'You're not pleased that Cat's happy?'

Eddie defended himself. 'I didn't say that.'

'Is it because you don't want her to be happy in that way? Is that it?'

Eddie replied with a sullen look.

'Because if that's the way you feel,' Isabel went on, 'then you're wrong, Eddie. People have to be happy in the way *they* want to be happy. We can't set out the conditions of their happiness.'

Eddie was on the point of answering this when the main door of the shop opened and Bea appeared. She was carrying several large shopping bags, which bulged under their load, and she looked flustered.

'Your friend,' said Eddie. 'I'll make coffee for both of you.'

'We can talk later, Eddie,' said Isabel. 'You and I can talk later.'

'Don't tell me to take a deep breath,' said Bea, as she took her place at the table. 'Just don't. In eight and a half hours sixteen people – sixteen! – are going to turn up for a meal that I haven't even started to prepare.'

'I shan't,' said Isabel. 'All I shall say is that I'm sure you'll be ready in time – as you always are. You were never . . . ' She paused to allow for greater effect for her next pronouncement. 'You were never a disgrace to Edinburgh.'

Bea's mouth dropped open, and then broke into a smile. 'She said that, didn't she? She was always saying that. "You're a disgrace to Edinburgh!"'

'Yes, I hadn't thought about it for years until earlier this morning, when I told you to take a deep breath.'

'Well I did,' said Bea. 'And now I'm here.' She glanced at her watch. 'But I'll have to watch the time. This is about Connie, isn't it? Connie and that MacUspaig man.'

Isabel nodded. 'Connie is not in any danger,' she said. 'You can stop worrying about her.'

Bea frowned. 'Are you sure?'

Isabel explained about her visits to Andrea and Tricia. 'Both of them had nothing but praise for Tony MacUspaig. Only one of them had an affair with him – that was Andrea. Tricia said that she and he were just good friends.'

'And the money? What about the money they gave him?'

'A donation in one case – for his clinic in Morocco. And in the other case, it was a payment for a painting – a Peploe, properly valued and all above board. The money for that was also going to the clinic.'

'I'm going to take another deep breath,' said Bea. 'There. That's it. Are you sure about this?'

'As sure as I can be,' said Isabel. 'I've already made some enquiries to check up on what I heard.'

'How did you do that?'

'I asked a couple of questions – just to make doubly sure that Tony MacUspaig was doing what he claimed to be doing. I checked with the charity regulator. And he does have a registered charity that runs a clinic in Morocco. They file accounts with the charities office – and the accounts are all in order.' She paused. 'And I checked, too, that the Peploe he sold was the real thing. I spoke to Guy Peploe himself, who confirmed it. He gave me the details of when his grandfather had painted it and who had owned it. The painting definitely has its papers.'

'You've been very thorough,' said Bea.

'It's better that way,' said Isabel. 'And so at the end of the day there seems to be no evidence – nothing at all – to suggest that Tony MacUspaig is anything other than a rather kind plastic surgeon who gives his time to helping children with hare-lips in places where that help is needed. Nobody has a bad word for him, it seems, except . . . '

They both uttered the name at the same time: 'Rob McLaren.'

'Why?' asked Bea.

'Why did Rob make the accusation?'

'Yes,' said Bea. 'Why was he so specific? It wasn't as if he was just passing on tittle-tattle – he made it unambiguous. He presented it all as fact.'

'People can do that,' said Isabel. 'They can treat surmise as certainty. They can fail to mention a lack of proof. They can promote speculation to fact.'

Bea was unconvinced. 'I still don't see why he'd be so firm.'

Isabel was thinking. 'Did Rob know Connie before that dinner party of yours? Or did they meet there?'

Eddie delivered coffee, and then returned to the counter. Bea thanked him and reached for her cup. 'Let me think . . . Yes, I think she did. In fact, now that I come to think of it, she said something about him. What was it?'

Isabel waited. Bea took another sip of her coffee. 'I could phone her,' she said. 'I could phone her right now and ask.'

Isabel thought this a good idea. 'Just ask her whether she knows much about him.'

Bea extracted her phone from her bag and dialled a number. Connie did not take long to answer.

'Connie,' said Bea. 'Just a quick question. I've got sixteen people coming for dinner this evening – sixteen! – and I have to get back. But I'm sitting here with Isabel Dalhousie and I was telling her about Rob McLaren. I seem to recollect that you said something about him to me, but I can't remember what it was. Was it about how well you know him? Something like that?'

Isabel could not make out what was being said at the other end of the line. But she did hear what Bea said next, which was, 'That's very interesting, isn't it?'

There was a further tinny indistinguishable sound. Isabel

had always thought that the sound of a distant caller on another person's mobile phone was the sound that ants would make if they talked. Then Bea brought the conversation to an end, rang off, and replaced the phone in her bag.

'That was very revealing,' she said. 'Would you like to hear about it?'

'Of course,' said Isabel.

'Apparently Rob has had a thing for Connie for some time. At first she encouraged him, and then she went off the idea because she thought he was a gold-digger. He kept asking her about her investments. She didn't like it.'

'Ah.'

'Yes, and she feels that he still hasn't given up. She keeps away from him, but she thinks he still feels he has some sort of chance.'

Isabel sat back in her chair. Of course, of course! When we criticise the behaviour of others, we often accuse them of doing the things that we ourselves do *or would like to do.* So if Rob accused Tony MacUspaig of being interested in other people's money, it was because that was exactly what he himself was interested in. And then she remembered her own conversation with Rob over lunch in the Café St Honoré; his interest in her financial affairs had been revealed by his prying into her funding of the *Review.* She had felt at the time that his questions were perhaps a bit personal, but she had not put two and two together. Now she had.

Isabel explained her theory to Bea, who nodded as she spoke. 'It's obvious, isn't it? We should have seen it.'

'Well, we didn't,' said Isabel. 'And now the question is: do we have to do something about it?'

'I'm not sure. What do you think?'

'Is he dangerous?' asked Isabel.

‘I don’t think so. He’s been a bit persistent with Connie, perhaps, and he’s tried to sabotage Tony’s relationship with her. Is that dangerous behaviour?’

‘Yes,’ said Isabel. ‘It could have harmed Tony. It could have been very upsetting for Connie.’

‘So what do we do?’

‘We tell him,’ said Isabel. ‘We tell him that what he said was not only wrong but was actually potentially harmful. My impression is that he’ll slink away. I don’t think he’ll cause any further trouble, especially if he knows that people know what he’s been up to. I get the impression that he’s a rather sensitive, unhappy man underneath. He’ll learn his lesson.’

‘Poor Rob,’ mused Bea. ‘You know, I think he’d make a good husband for somebody – when all is said and done.’

‘Don’t,’ said Isabel.

‘Don’t what?’

‘Don’t matchmake for him.’

Bea laughed. ‘You think not?’

‘Definitely not.’

But Bea had further ideas. ‘What if I matched him up with somebody who had very little money,’ she said. ‘Then, if he fell for her, even in spite of her indigent circumstances, we’d know that it was real love, not cupidity.’

‘Leave that to Cupid,’ said Isabel.

They both laughed.

Eddie watched them from the counter. ‘Laughing over nothing,’ he said to himself. ‘Listen to them.’

It was tempting to put off a further meeting with Rob, or even to leave it to Bea to speak to him, but she did not. Immediately after Bea had left the delicatessen, Isabel telephoned him and announced that she was coming to see him.

He had tried to put her off, saying that he was about to go out, but she brushed his objection aside.

'I'll take no more than ten or fifteen minutes of your time,' she said firmly. 'And this is something that can't wait.'

He did not live far away – in a street behind the Dominion Cinema – and she was there within twenty minutes of making the telephone call. He looked anxious as he let her into his flat, and she imagined that he knew exactly why she was there.

'I have to talk very frankly to you,' she began, as they sat down in his living room.

He was staring down at the floor. 'I'm sorry,' he said. 'I know why you're here, and I'm sorry.'

He did not meet her gaze, and she understood that he was ashamed.

'Why did you do it, Rob?'

He looked up and their eyes met, but only for a moment.

'Desperation,' he said.

'Emotional desperation?' she asked. 'Or financial?'

This stung him into a response. 'Not financial. Definitely not financial.'

'Are you sure?'

He had been slouched in his seat – now he drew himself up. 'Yes, of course I'm sure. Did you think that . . . ' He seemed wounded, and it seemed to Isabel that he was telling the truth.

'It crossed my mind,' she said.

'That I'm a gold-digger?'

She hesitated. 'Frankly, yes.'

'Well, I'm not. I'm comfortably enough off. I don't need anybody else's money.'

She made a gesture of acceptance. 'Then why?'

'Because I fell in love with Connie and that man took her away.'

Isabel was silent for a moment. 'You need to take a more mature view of these things, Rob. And that man, as you call him, Tony MacUspaig, could have been harmed by what you did. In fact, he was harmed – his reputation was called into question.'

Rob shook his head. 'I didn't mean to . . . '

'Well, you did. But it's going to end, isn't it?'

He nodded miserably.

'You'll meet somebody,' said Isabel. 'Look at yourself. You're a very attractive man. You're intelligent. You're a good listener.'

He was staring at her in what seemed like incomprehension. 'Me? Attractive?'

'Of course you are.'

She remembered their lunch. 'Though that doesn't mean anything to me,' she said hurriedly. 'But there are plenty of women who would be very pleased to go out with you.'

Isabel watched him. It was almost unbelievable, but there were people who slipped through the net; people who had never had anything nice said about them, and Rob, she decided, was one of those. It was perfectly possible that nobody had ever said anything to make him feel good about himself, and now this inconsequential remark on her part seemed to be having a profound effect on him.

'I'm not just saying this, Rob,' she told him. 'I mean it.'

His eyes said everything that had to be said, she decided, and so she stood up to leave.

He saw her out wordlessly, and she began to walk back to the house. That had not been too hard, and she was glad that it was done. In fact, she was glad that the whole matter was now safely settled. It crossed her mind that she could have avoided everything by simply not getting involved in the first place – but had that option really been available to her? She had applied her own test to the issue of involvement in this case – the moral proximity test – and it had pointed to a duty to intervene. But perhaps the test itself needed calibration, because whenever she applied it she tended to get the same answer – that she should get involved. She would have to think about this further before she did anything the next time . . . and then she thought, *Why should I assume there's going to be a next time?* She answered her own question: there would be a next time because of something that John Donne had famously said about being an island and she was the way she was and the world was the way it was. That was an end to the matter; it just was.

She and Jamie shared the cooking that evening. With Charlie and Magnus safely in bed, Isabel searched her recipe books for something suitable. She leafed through Delia Smith and her mother's copy of Julia Child. She consulted Jamie Oliver and Elizabeth David, and eventually decided on a cheese soufflé. Jamie would make a starter – a rather complicated terrine involving tomatoes and chopped olives.

They sat at the kitchen table together, two glasses of wine in front of them, the recipe books spread out over the scrubbed pine surface.

'Eddie was going on about olives this morning,' said Isabel.

'Oh yes?'

'He said that he knew of somebody who'd turned green by eating too many olives.'

Jamie laughed. 'Eddie has an imagination. And he believes everything he hears. He really does.' He took a sip of his wine. 'I went to the doctor this morning, by the way.'

Isabel held her breath. 'And?'

'And it's not gout.'

She exhaled. 'Oh, Jamie – that's wonderful.' And then she asked. 'What is it then?'

'He thinks I may have broken a bone in the toe. He says that can happen. The problem was that I told him I hadn't injured it at all. That's why he didn't suggest an X-ray.'

'Good. That's such good news. I never thought it was gout; I just didn't.'

'The blood tests,' Jamie continued, 'showed that my uric acid levels are quite normal. Apparently if you're prone to gout, they'll be higher.'

'So that's it?'

'That's it. Everything is back to normal.' He paused. 'You know, I felt quite euphoric on the way back from the doctor and I did something rather odd.'

She raised an eyebrow. 'Treated yourself to something?'

'Yes, I suppose you could call it that. I went into the Camera Obscura, near the castle. I hadn't been there since I was about seven.'

She imagined the seven-year-old Jamie. 'I wish I'd known you then.'

'And I watched the show. I watched the whole town being projected into the table in the middle. Our city. It gave a wonderful view . . . '

'A distant view of everything?'

'Yes.'

She thought for a moment. 'That's what we need.'

Neither spoke for a few minutes. Then Isabel said, 'I was in the deli this morning. I had two important chats. One with Bea and one with Eddie.'

'Have you sorted out the business of that chap – what's his name – the one with the odd surname?'

'MacUspaig. Yes. All sorted.'

'And he's not after that woman's money?'

'No, he's not. In fact, he's the opposite of what I thought he was. He's a good man.'

'Oh well, that's a relief.'

'But there's something going on with Cat,' said Isabel.

Jamie shrugged. 'There's always something going on with Cat. She's one of these people who attract things.'

Isabel struggled to put her question delicately. Jamie and Cat had been together – years ago – although the relationship had not lasted long. Isabel had never discussed this, and had certainly never quizzed Jamie on what had happened between them. She did not intend to start now. But the new situation could hardly be ignored; sooner or later Jamie would hear something and would be surprised if Isabel had not mentioned it to him.

'Do you think it possible that Cat is not all that interested in men?' she asked.

Jamie looked surprised. 'Cat? Not interested in men? No, the opposite. I think Cat is seriously interested in men. I think men are her hobby.'

'Are you sure?'

'One hundred per cent.'

'You see,' Isabel continued, 'she has a new assistant. She's a girl called Peg.'

'Oh her,' said Jamie. 'I know about her.'

'You've met her?'

'Yes. Once or twice.'

'Cat wouldn't tell me where she met her,' said Isabel. 'And nor would she.'

'Peg wouldn't?'

'No, they both were deliberately vague. So I assumed that it was online. Perhaps on a dating site.'

Jamie gave a start. 'What?'

'On a dating site. You know how it is. Everybody seems to meet these days on a dating site. It's how people find their partners.'

Jamie tossed his head back and let out a peal of laughter. 'No, no, no . . . You've got it all wrong, Isabel. Cat met her in prison. She told me.'

'Cat was in prison?'

'No . . . well, yes, in a sense. Cat's been doing prison visiting. It's her good work. I knew about it because a flautist I know does it too. She met Cat at an induction course for new prison visitors. They help prisoners with their education, with problems of various sorts – it's pretty useful if you're in the jug.'

'Why was Peg in prison?'

'Cat said it was something to do with drugs. She did three months. Often users supply other people and that gets them into trouble. But Peg, apparently, is clean now and is enrolled on all sorts of support schemes. I saw Cat the other day and she told me all this. She's proud of what she's been doing for her. She's really proud. They've been reading things together and Cat has been helping her do some sort of life-review book that will help her to see her life in perspective. Apparently Peg's really talented, but just got mixed up in the wrong, druggy crowd.'

'So they're not lovers?'

Jamie laughed again. 'It would be simpler if they were, I think. Cat's had so much trouble with men that it would somehow simplify matters if she found out that men weren't for her after all. But I'm afraid they are.'

Isabel wondered why Cat had not told her about this, but perhaps she had wanted to keep it to herself. Then Isabel thought of something else. 'Could you go and explain all this to Eddie? You know what he's like. He listens to you. You could explain things to him and get him to be a bit . . . a bit kinder.'

Jamie said he would try.

'And now I'm going to start on the soufflé. How long will your terrine take?'

'Twenty minutes,' said Jamie. 'If I start right now.'

'So I shall sit here while you do that. I shall sit here and think. Then I'll start the soufflé.'

'Timing is all when it comes to soufflés,' said Jamie.

'And to so many other things in life,' observed Isabel.

She watched him as he chopped olives. *There is nobody else in the world I would like to watch chopping olives more than you*, she thought. *My beautiful man. My kind man. My friend. My lover.*

She allowed her gaze to drift – to drift out of the window, to the garden, where the evening sun had touched the wall, the tops of the rhododendrons, the ornamental giant thistles, with gold, with gold. Her other friend, the vulpine one, the cunning one, had appeared on the top of the wall, and he, too, was bathed in the golden light of evening. He raised his nose into the air, as if picking up a scent – and then, quite unexpectedly, he did a somersault off the wall, to land, perfectly, on his feet on the ground below. 'Bravo,' whispered Isabel. 'Bravo.'